THE CLIPPED SAGA

# CLIPPED

DEVON M<sup>c</sup>CORMACK

Copyright © 2013 by Devon McCormack

Cover Photography by Allan Spiers

Cover Design by Shasti O'Leary Soudant

Proofing by Heidi Ryan

This is a work of fiction. Names, characters, places, and incidents either are the product of author imagination or are used fictitiously, and any resemblance to actual persons, living or dead, business establishments, events, or locales is entirely coincidental. All products and brand names mentioned are registered trademarks of their respective holders/companies.

This book is licensed to the original purchaser only. Duplication or distribution via any means is illegal and a violation of international copyright law, subject to criminal prosecution and upon conviction, fines, and/or imprisonment. Any eBook format cannot be legally loaned or given to others. No part of this book may be reproduced or transmitted in any form or by any means, electronic or mechanical, including photocopying, recording, or by any information storage and retrieval system, without the written permission of the Publisher, except where permitted by law.

*To Mom and Dad, who must stop reading now,*

*&*

*To Ashley and Karen, who were allowed to read further and did.*

## CHAPTER ONE

"Fuck."

Kinzer's eyelids flitted open as he came to.

A haze of white and gray came into focus.

White sunlight poured through a rectangular window with chain-link fencing drilled into the frame, scattering the light across bare, cracked, concrete walls.

Kinzer's face felt swollen, like it'd taken a good beating. Blood dripped from a cut in his upper lip, and the taste of iron filled his mouth.

His naked pecs and abs, covered in bruises and welts, stretched across a sheetless mattress.

Kinzer moved to get up. His arms and legs stuck in place, as if he were being pinned down.

He rolled his head back.

A knee in gray slacks pressed into the corner of the mattress. Their owner, a man—his face speckled with liver spots—closed a padlock around two links in a set of charcoal colored chains that wrapped around Kinzer's wrist, binding it to the side of an iron-framed headboard.

Kinzer tugged at his other arm.

It didn't budge.

He tossed his gaze to a matching chain that tied it to the other side of the headboard. A glance at his ankles revealed another chain, locking them together and trailing off the end of the mattress.

*Shit.*

Conscious as he was, Kinzer couldn't make sense of where he was or how he'd ended up there.

"I was a little worried you wouldn't pull through." The liver-spotted man gazed at him through oval-shaped glasses. A patch of sunlight sparkled across his naked scalp, framed in stringy, white hairs. Vertical creases streaked across pale lips. "Glad you did. You cost me a pretty penny, but not too shabby for that cock."

"Who the fuck are you?" Kinzer's biceps pushed streaks of blue and purple veins forward as he struggled with the chains.

"No point in resisting, now. You're not going anywhere." The man stepped off the bed and walked alongside the mattress. "Jerry's the name. Your...*friends*...tell me you go by Kinzer." He sat by Kinzer's hip, his eyes scanning his prisoner's form as if he was taking mental notes. "Doesn't make much difference. You'll go by a lot of different names here. Right now, Jason seems to be popular. But you look like a Brock or a Rocky."

"You just gonna keep me chained?"

"For now." Jerry fondled the mattress, his wrinkled fingers moving over the sewn grooves in the fabric. "Don't want to give you the opportunity to try a first escape. It's a common problem, as you can probably imagine."

"Escape from where?" Kinzer asked.

"That's not important. You could be anywhere, and your duties will still be the same. I'll send one of my guards down. He'll help you get cleaned up, feed you...show you your new living quarters."

"And I'm just supposed to go along with this? Are you fucking kidding?"

Jerry's fingertips moved from the mattress, tickling their way up Kinzer's side, trailing across his abs.

"I'm not a humorous man, Kinzer. Just straightforward. So I want to be clear. As long as you're here, I control your fate. I control how you are used, how you are abused. I control how much fucking you can handle. I control how good of a shape you're in." He pressed his finger against a black bruise.

Kinzer ground his teeth.

"That said, I recommend you be as courteous as possible. Obedience is very important to me. If you don't obey, you will be punished."

Jerry stared into his eyes. Offering a pleasant smile, he rose and left through a door on the other side of the room.

Kinzer tried to contemplate his current predicament. He figured he should be trying to plan an escape or at least thinking about what this Jerry guy had in store for him, but he was preoccupied with a flood of memories that rushed through his mind in an instant.

*"Oh, Kinzer," Veylo said.*

*A lock of his brown hair fell to his nose, obscuring an eye. He stood over Kinzer, a bloody broadsword in hand. "You think you're suffering now?"*

*Kinzer lay on red-stained concrete, naked, covered in blood and black feathers...his own feathers. He cried out in agony.*

*Veylo pressed the end of his sword against Kinzer's bruised cheek. "When I'm done with you, you'll know what it really means to suffer, traitor!"*

*Kinzer imagined that Veylo had thought this would be a great punishment, but he doubted he'd realized that stripping him of everything and torturing him a thousand times over could not have hurt worse than losing his dear Janka.*

At one time, Kinzer had resented Janka—the captain of his task force.

In the golden days of Heaven, before Kinzer and many other higherlings had fallen, Janka was privileged, granted all that he desired from the Almighty. He'd been one of Heaven's most desirable creatures. He was doted on, loved, adored. It left him, like so many of the Almighty's elite, filled with a natural conceit. When Janka gave orders, Kinzer resisted. He fussed and barked. He wasn't going to listen to a higherling, especially not one that had been afforded such luxuries, unlike anything he or his peers had ever experienced under the creator's rule.

Such willful disobedience put the lives of the members of Janka's troop at risk several times before he let his issue with Kinzer be known. They fought it out Kinzer's way—with fists of rage. They weren't just fighting over his disobedience. They were fighting over the inequity of Heaven. Kinzer wasn't known for going down in a brawl, but Janka's superior place in creation made him stronger and a better fighter. Kinzer received serious injuries that left him immobilized for weeks. Janka tended to him, cared for him. Again, Kinzer resisted. He didn't need Janka's help. He didn't need anyone's help. Janka refused to yield to Kinzer's attitude, and gradually Kinzer allowed Janka into his life…into his heart…into his body. They'd spent many nights, lips locked, limbs woven together in a satisfied embrace. Kinzer came to know Janka as his *one*—the only one that could complete him. Their work as soldiers took them away from each other frequently, and as they became spies for the Leader, their proximity to one another became constantly threatened.

A year earlier, they'd taken advantage of a chance to be close. The Leader had tasked them with infiltrating the Raze, a secret organization charged with assisting the Almighty in bringing about the end of the world. Janka and Kinzer were responsible for collecting intel and reporting any progress on the Almighty's planned apocalypse.

All that had gone horribly awry.

*Someone ratted us out*, Kinzer thought.

It was the only explanation. Someone must have told Veylo that he and Janka were spies. Someone on the inside.

Veylo was the leader of the Raze. When he'd discovered their true allegiance, he'd personally executed their punishments.

Kinzer wasn't sure who had exposed him and his lover, but all the Leader's Allies were potentially at risk of being revealed. He had to get out of this shithole and warn them.

How was he going to find them, though? To protect their identities, the Leader's Allies were intentionally kept uninformed as to each other's whereabouts...in case something like this occurred. Each had a contact they could alert if they were outed. Unfortunately, Janka had been Kinzer's contact—the only one who could have warned the others. With Janka dead, Kinzer was without a connection to the other members. He was going to have to find someone who could get news to the others.

*Dedrus.*

That name stirred painful memories. Dedrus hadn't just been a friend and ally. Before Janka, he'd been a lover—someone Kinzer had envisioned himself spending his eternity with. They'd fought in battle together. They'd steadily become each other's greatest confidants. For a time, Kinzer thought Dedrus felt the same, but he had been wrong. The pain of losing Dedrus had been so severe that he was sure he'd never fall in love again.

Until Janka.

Kinzer tried to think of someone else—anyone else. Dedrus was the last immortal he wanted to turn to for help, but he was the only one he knew he could find. He was the only one he knew wouldn't be secretly in league with the Almighty.

But how was he going to get out of this place?

It wasn't going to be easy. Since Veylo had clipped his wings before placing him in whatever trafficking operation this Jerry guy was running, he was weak. He wasn't any more powerful than a mortal.

It didn't matter.

He had to find a way out. If he didn't, the Leader's other allies were dead, and the Almighty would be that much closer to bringing about the destruction of all mankind.

## CHAPTER TWO

"One, two, three, four…"

*Lift, pansy. Lift or you'll be stuck here for the rest of your fucking life.*

Kid pushed the barbell up and lowered it as he took out one hundred sixty pounds of anger on his muscle-bound body.

He was the youngest guy in the workout room, hence his affectionate nickname.

*Lift, you stupid fuck!*

Mirrors lined the walls. Benches, medicine balls, mats, racks, and weights clustered between two rows of support beams. Guarding one of the doors to the workout room, Marzo, a beefy man with a walleye, folded his arms and stared forward (and to the side) blankly, as if trying to dissociate from boredom. He was rumored to have been not so honorably discharged from the army. At the door on the other side of the room, Clive, a twig of a man with stringy arms and a gaunt face, who appeared to be the poster boy for an anti-Meth ad campaign, stared at his feet as he kicked the doorframe.

Jerry stepped between a tray of dumbbells and a column near the wall. A pot-bellied boy nearly half his size, who couldn't have been much older than Kid, walked alongside him. He scribbled frantically in a pocket-sized notebook. Jerry whispered something in his ear. Jerry had a stern, most-serious glare frozen on his spotty face. He and the pot-bellied scribe, who the boys knew as Robb, eyed a few guys doing sit-ups on mats on one side of the room. The Brazilians, as they were called. They were gorgeous, ripped guys who'd been lured to Jerry's under the pretense of working in adult films. Whoever had duped them had made a pretty penny off their asses. They were top of the line, except that they could hardly speak any English. Although, they seemed pretty good with "fuck" and "no" or a combination of the two.

One of the Brazilians did crunches, sweat sliding from his mountainous chest into the sharp hills that swelled across his abdomen. A patch of fat couldn't be found anywhere on his tight body. Of everyone in the workout room, he was by far the prettiest, with flawless caramel skin and blue eyes that glistened under the fluorescent lights.

"Robb, keep our blue-eyed beauty on a high-protein diet. He needs more muscle. And get him on the bench press at least three times a week. I want a chest on him. Those abs are only gonna get him so far."

Jerry and Robb approached Kid, mid-bench-press, breathing heavily as his biceps, shoulders, and pecs contracted with his violent movements.

Jerry's serious glare transformed into a pleasant, even friendly, smile.

"How's it going, Kid?" he asked.

Kid pumped away, sweat rushing like water through a canyon between his pecs.

"Mmmm...That's good. Real good. Just keep right on with what you're doing."

Kid knew he was one of Jerry's favorites. Not because he was particularly attractive or lucrative, but because he was obedient. Obedience meant almost as much to Jerry as money, so Kid's adherence to his rigid, oppressive rules made him one of the few recipients of Jerry's generosity—a decent meal and an occasional used book. Rare as they came, Kid would savor the books. Without access to TV or radio, they were the only opportunities that allowed him a moment of escape—to leave this cruel and unjust world behind.

He kept them stacked under a cot in his room. Over the years, he'd collected novels by Dickens, Shelley, Conrad, Hawthorne, and Golding. Every night before lights out, he'd fish one out and devour it page by page, imagining that he was somewhere else—anywhere else. He didn't care that the protagonists were usually living in the most unpleasant of worlds. Any heinous life was better than his.

At thirteen, Kid had wound up homeless on the streets of Atlanta. "Wanna fuck?" he would say to the pudgy, sad-faced geezers he'd catch leaving the nearest gay bar. He gave blowjobs and took it up the ass, sometimes for as little as twenty bucks. He didn't need much. He just had to have money for meals. He didn't have to worry about shelter, because he squatted at an abandoned church with three other homeless guys. They were older and only one of them ever bothered him with sexual solicitations, which he'd endured on occasion to ensure he'd have a place to sleep.

Kid had been cruising the streets, looking for his next meal ticket, when he'd been knocked unconscious and had woken up in Jerry's place. That was what the other guys called it. None of them really knew where they were—or what kind of building they were in, though several of the guys assumed that it had been an old school.

Though he'd abducted Kid, Jerry was, in many ways, his guardian angel. Within the months that Kid had been on his own, he'd managed to pick up several STDs, which Jerry promptly treated, tending to Kid's health and providing him with reading material while he had recovered. Jerry had made it clear that Kid didn't have a choice but to stay there. In the beginning, Kid was fine with that. Better to have shelter and fuck under those conditions than to have to do it all on his own. However, he discovered there was a price to having so many things provided for him, and he grew to resent Jerry. More important than the security of his body was the security of his freedom, which he desperately longed for. He planned to have it again...one day.

*Lift, you shit.*

He built up his strength. One day, he'd have an opportunity to take on Marzo or Clive, and he'd crawl out of this dump and get the fuck out.

He had plans that didn't involve spending the rest of his life on the streets. He was going to get a job as a waiter or a clerk at a store. He was going to be a normal person, and when he got enough money together, he'd even go to college. He didn't know if he'd ever finish, but he could at least take some classes, make himself a little smarter.

Jerry and Robb continued their stroll through the workout room.

A bead of sweat dripped off Kid's forehead onto the cement floor. His muscles locked and his face turned red, the veins in his neck protruding forward as he pushed his arms to their last possible rep. He forced the bar over his head and set it on the bar rest.

He sat up. Sweat drenched his light-brown hair and dripped onto the smooth flesh that dressed his rift-covered abs. He panted as he tried to catch his breath.

The other guys were far less into their workouts than he ever was. They fulfilled their daily requirements, but that was it. None were eager to make their bodies more pleasing to potential johns.

A man with vampire-white flesh, speckled with black and blue bruises, stepped through the entrance to the workout room.

*Fresh meat.*

Fresh Meat's wavy, jet-black hair, in stark contrast with his skin, looked like a bird's failed attempt at a nest. Sunken cheeks curved up swelling welts that made an already pronounced jawline stick out even farther. A cleft in his chin matched the divot above his upper lip, a groove at the tip of his nose, and even the severe cut dividing his bottom lip.

Kid wondered why Jerry had taken this guy in. Most everyone was like the Brazilians—hot model types who'd been conned into coming to this rat hole by some less than scrupulous street entrepreneur. Some came because this was their way of paying off a debt to a dealer. Others, because some junkie eagerly sold them for quick cash. Regardless of how they ended up there, they were usually in pristine condition, unlike this new guy. At the same time, Kid had to acknowledge that he had been less than pristine when he'd arrived.

Despite Fresh Meat's rough appearance, Kid recognized that he was still a very attractive man. Broad shoulders and thick, curved biceps filled a white T-shirt. His tight ass looked hot in the jeans he wore.

Fresh Meat's eyes, brown and sparkling in the fluorescence, scanned the room until they came to Kid.

Kid avoided his glare.

Fresh Meat stumbled to a tray of dumbbells, picked up two fifty-pounders, and headed to a weight bench by Kid.

Kid lay back on his bench, grabbed the barbell, and started another set.

"Look a little young to be here," Fresh Meat whispered.

Kid gritted his teeth. Didn't respond. Kept working on his reps.

Fresh Meat planted the dumbbells on the floor before him. He picked one up and started doing reps. The veins in his forearm pushed forward. His bicep flexed, inflating and deflating in sync with the muscles in his jaw.

"My name's Kinzer."

Kid's body tensed, more from anger than the tension of the weights.

*This idiot is gonna get us both in trouble.*

Among Jerry's myriad of rigid rules was the "no talking" rule. The boys weren't allowed to fraternize with each another. Kid imagined this was to prevent them from conspiring to overpower Marzo or Clive or from plotting an escape. This rule wasn't something that Jerry took lightly, either. Jerry's guards would usually tase or beat for infractions, depending upon the severity of the transgression. It was easy to slight Jerry, and he wasn't fair with his devised punishments. They were severe. Talking could result in punishments serious enough to prevent a guy from working for two months.

"How long you been in here?" Kinzer asked.

Kid lifted the barbell and set it back on the rest. Sweat rushed down his face. He panted, his bulky chest rapidly rising and falling. His erect, pink nipples shimmered in the light.

"Shut the fuck up," he muttered through his teeth, "or you'll get us both in trouble."

Kinzer set his dumbbell on the floor, picked it back up with his other hand, and started a set.

Kid lay on the bench, gripping his hands against the barbell.

"Listen, I need to—"

Robb stepped between them, squinting and puffing out his already chubby cheeks. "Kid," he fussed. "You know the rules."

He reached into his pocket and pulled out a Taser.

Kinzer's sparkling brown eyes grew twice as big. "What the—"

Kid sat up. He scowled, the look in his eyes full of indignation. "What?! He was the one—"

He didn't know why he was fighting it. Something in him was just so infuriated, so pissed off. He was always so good. Always followed the rules. Surely, Robb knew that it was Kinzer's fault.

Jerry's other boys paused their workouts to watch the confrontation.

"It's the rules," Robb insisted.

Kid resigned himself. There wasn't any way Jerry was going to let his transgression go unpunished, and better a Taser than something worse. He clenched his jaw and pushed his sweat-soaked chest out. Robb pressed the Taser between his pecs.

Zzzz.

Kid convulsed.

He fell off the bench. Robb stepped over it and knelt, continuing his assault.

"Whoa!" Kinzer said. "I'm the one who was talking to him. He didn't do anything!"

"Kinzer!" Jerry shouted from the corner of the room. He stood over a sweat-soaked twink of a boy who had stopped mid-push-up to watch Kid and Kinzer. "Kid knows the rules. This is the way we do things around here, so shut your faggy mouth and let Robb handle it."

Robb sent another fifty thousand volts into Kid's chest. Kid writhed about.

Kinzer dropped his dumbbell. As it bounced off the floor, he tackled Robb.

Robb whined and slapped around as Kinzer pounded into his cushioned stomach.

"What the...fuck! Stop! It's...the...rules!" Robb wailed.

"Marzo!" Jerry exclaimed.

Marzo stomped across the workout room, a stern look frozen on his face.

Kinzer reared back, his fist moving to strike Robb again.

Marzo put a Taser to his neck.

Zzzz.

Kinzer convulsed and twitched about, just as Kid had done moments earlier.

\*\*\*

"What the fuck is wrong with you?!" Jerry shouted.

He sat at a termite-ravaged school desk. Kid and Kinzer sat on a cot before him.

On the concrete wall behind Jerry were two large windows. Like all of the windows in Jerry's place, they were covered in chain-link fencing.

Kid threw Kinzer a foul look.

*Fucking asshat, getting me in trouble.*

"This isn't a fucking Jean-Claude Van Damme movie!" Jerry continued. "No need to act like a fucking animal."

"He didn't do anything," Kinzer said. "I didn't even know that rule."

"I don't care what rules you know and don't know," Jerry said. "If I discipline, I expect you to obey. My rules may not always be fair, but the only way to be any kind of leader is to be consistent. If you discipline consistently, then everybody understands when and why they get punished. Got that?"

Kinzer nodded.

"I'd prefer auditory confirmation."

"Won't happen again."

Kid looked Kinzer over. He doubted that was true.

*A guy doesn't end up with bruises all over him like that and in a place like this for no reason.*

"As for you, Kid, you know better than to be acting up."

"I was—"

"Shh, shh. I don't like this, but I'm gonna have to find a suitable punishment for you. I have to be honest, considering how long you've been with me, it's not going to be generous. You should have known better."

There was no point in arguing. Kid hung his head and nodded.

"And you ever cause a ruckus like that again..." Jerry's gaze shifted to Kinzer. "...I'll make sure you know your place. Now, get to the showers and get cleaned up."

***

A stream of water flowed from an overhanging showerhead.

Kinzer massaged a bar of soap in his palms, building up foamy suds. Black strands of his bangs clung to unhealed wounds on his forehead. At his feet, water slapped against yellow-stained tiles, framed in brown and green grime that fanned out from the grout.

Kid stood under an adjoining showerhead. He wiped a bar of soap across the ripples in his torso and over his naturally-flexed biceps.

They were the only ones in the showers. The others had cleaned up while Jerry had been chastising them.

*Fucking asshole.*

Mad as he was, he couldn't keep his gaze from shifting repeatedly back to Kinzer's cock. Even flaccid, it was hanging mid-thigh. That thing must've been twelve inches. The mushroom head stretched out well beyond the shaft. When he'd first seen Kinzer undress in the shower room, he had a much better understanding of why Jerry had brought him on board. With a dick like that, he was going to be one of Jerry's busiest boys. Even more fortunate, he probably wouldn't have to take it up the ass nearly as much.

"You got me in a lot of fucking trouble," Kid hissed.

"Sorry." Kinzer brushed the suds in his hands across his chest and massaged them against his pecs.

Kid's eyes flashed back to Kinzer's dick. He couldn't help himself. He wondered how that would feel in his hole.

"Your cock's huge."

Kinzer smiled. "I thought we weren't supposed to talk."

His smile was disarming, and Kid found it difficult to maintain his anger, especially as he continued to imagine that chunk of flesh filling him.

"They know we can't get out down here," Kid said, "and they gotta keep an eye on the others."

His eyes remained fixed on Kinzer's member. "But seriously. What the fuck?"

Kinzer eyed Kid's dick. "Not so bad yourself."

Now Kid was really having a hard time keeping his defensive front up against Kinzer. Something about him was charming, fun. Kid's shaft widened and lengthened. Kinzer's twitched and hardened.

Kid threw Kinzer a satisfied glare. "Like what you see?"

Kid's dick was fully erect. He glanced back at the door and lunged at Kinzer, dropping to his knees and placing his lips around the head of his dick.

Kinzer jumped out of the showerhead's path, dropping the bar of soap on the tile. White streams of soap slid down his torso, detouring at the top curves of his abs.

"Come on!" Kid said. "We gotta hurry."

Kinzer's face cringed with confusion. "But, uh—"

"Dude, you clearly want it. And I *need* it. Please. I'm begging you. I'll just blow you. Please."

"You don't get enough sex in a place like this?"

"I don't really consider what goes on here sex."

Kinzer walked back into the hot water.

"This doesn't mean we're cool," Kid said, water webbing between his eyes.

He was pissed at Kinzer for getting him in trouble, but he needed that cock inside him. Pain and pleasure were the greatest distractions from his shitty life. They pulled his thoughts away from his daily tasks and the memories that haunted his thoughts. With a hard girth like that inside him, he wouldn't be able to think about anything other than the unbearable pain that pulsed through him. Not that he was eager to feel *all* forms of pain. He just wanted to feel the pain he chose to feel.

As Kinzer's cock neared Kid's mouth, Kid's lips slid right over Kinzer's mushroom head and down his shaft. Water parted at the bridge of his nose, two paths arcing around his stretching lips and coming together at his chin.

Kid shoved Kinzer's dick as far back as he could take it. Less than half of the shaft fit in his mouth.

*God, he tastes so good. I bet his cum tastes even better.*

Kinzer threw his head back and released a deep, satisfied groan.

Kid slid his lips back, massaging the tip with the end of his tongue. He tightened his hand around Kinzer's girth, stroking back and forth, as he moved his lips to the same rhythm. He closed his eyes, taking in the deliciousness of Kinzer's flesh.

Kid pulled back, giving his mouth a rest.

"You taste so fucking good," Kid whispered. His mouth was back around Kinzer's dick in a heartbeat. He was committed, focused.

He wanted to please Kinzer. Just as he wanted to choose when he felt pain, he wanted to choose whom he satisfied.

Kinzer's skin tasted so good.

Kid filled his mouth with the flesh, sucking gently as he slid his free hand across Kinzer's ass, tucking two fingers between his cheeks, then into his hole.

"Oh, fuck yeah," Kinzer said.

Kid tried to take more of Kinzer's vein-covered goodness, but Kinzer yanked it out of his mouth.

Kinzer grabbed Kid's shoulder, forced him to his feet, and pushed him against the wall.

Kid shoved his ass out, inviting Kinzer inside. He glanced back at the door. "Just please...be quiet. They'll beat the shit out of us if they catch us."

Kinzer pressed his nose against Kid's ear, his hot breath crawling across his neck as he said, "I don't think I'm gonna be the one who has a problem keeping quiet."

He pressed the head of his dick against Kid's hole. Kid's ass, a product of excessive squats, was tight, uninviting.

Kid could tell just by the feeling that it was going to be an incredibly painful experience. He started to rethink following through, but as Kinzer's fingers slid around his side and across his abdomen, he felt a jolt of energy rush through his pelvis like a Taser of satisfaction and arousal. He pushed his ass farther back.

"I'm gonna be slow, okay?" Kinzer said.

"No. I want you to come. We have to do this as fast as we can." He regretted his words, but he was too scared that they wouldn't have time to finish. And right then, all he wanted was for Kinzer to make him bleed.

Kinzer hesitated before he closed his eyes and pushed forward.

Kid gritted his teeth as he felt the inner lining in his ass tear.

Kinzer slid back. He spit in his palm and rubbed the fluid across his shaft. He attempted to enter Kid again, this time successfully forcing his way inside.

Kid thought he was about to rip in two. The pain was so intense, so unbearable. He reared his head back and opened his mouth to scream.

Kinzer slapped a hand over his lips, obscuring the bloodcurdling cry Kid would have otherwise unleashed.

Tears rushed down Kid's cheeks. Kinzer thrust his pelvis back and forth, his cock rough against Kid's dry hole.

Kid thought his insides might explode, and yet, it left him wishing it were even more painful.

All he could think about was the pain, and that was wonderful.

He pressed his ass even closer to Kinzer's pelvis and threw his hand back, pulling Kinzer's face close to his ear. Kinzer breathed heavily against the back of Kid's neck, grunting, groaning, as if taking out all his aggression and anger on Kid's ass.

Kid kept trying to scream out, but as any sound leaked through Kinzer's fingers, Kinzer would tighten his grip even more to block it.

Kid's tears showered over the floor like the still-running streams of water coming from their abandoned showerheads.

"*Fuck me harder*," Kid begged, his words nearly indiscernible under Kinzer's hand. Every muscle in his well-toned body was tense, flexed. His face was red. The veins in his neck popped forward as he struggled with the pain.

Kinzer leaned back, effectively gaining leverage as he slammed into Kid's hole, filling him, hurting him.

Kid pressed his hands against the wall, pushing as hard as he could, hoping to lessen the throbbing pain. As much as he wanted it, his body couldn't handle it.

SLAM!

Kid recognized the sound. On the other side of the door, up a stairwell, there was a door the guards had to come through to get to the showers. It always made that same noise when it closed. Someone would be there in just moments. If Kinzer didn't hurry up, they were going to be fucked…in a bad way.

He flipped his head to the side, slipping free of Kinzer's hand.

"You have to come…now," he grunted. "They're gonna be down here in a second."

Kinzer thrust his pelvis into Kid's ass. The pounding quickened. Sharp slapping sounds echoed through the showers until Kinzer threw both of his arms around Kid's chest and grunted.

Kid could feel Kinzer swell inside him. A warm stream rushed down his leg. His eyes rolled back as he basked in the pleasure and absorbed the pain.

CLICK!

Kinzer pulled out.

He swept down, retrieving the bar of soap he'd dropped on the tile. He hurried back to his shower, acting as if he was finishing up.

Kid limped to his side of the shower and collapsed onto the floor.

"You okay?" Kinzer asked.

"I'll be fine," he whispered, his body trembling.

The door burst open. Robb and Marzo entered.

\*\*\*

*Please let him be asleep, Kid thought.*

*Houses, inches apart, lined either side of the street. Mailboxes planted at forty-five degree angles pointed in various directions. On the side of one of the houses, a jigsaw hole in a brick wall opened into darkness. Before the wall, a line of bricks scattered across foot-tall weeds. Miss Greer sat on the porch of this dilapidated house, cats at her heels. She rocked in her chair as if she hadn't received notice to abandon the condemned property. Kid knew that she had, because he'd heard Mrs. Michaelson and Miss Lanser discussing it just a few houses back.*

*He walked down the street, his thumbs curled under his backpack straps.*

*The streetlamps flickered orange behind him, combating the blue of dusk.*

*Directly across from Miss Greer's house, shattered windows acted as advertising to the occasional squatter that the place was known for. Kid passed the broken-windowed home, walking up a barren yard toward a rusting trailer—white with a once gold streak across the center. It looked like an old faded flag.*

*Please let him be asleep, he thought again.*

*After school, he always snuck off to the woods and spent his time reading. He'd developed decent timing for when Daddy would pass out from his evening binge. Nothing pleased him more than seeing him fast asleep on the couch. It meant he could disappear into his room, read his books, and not have to worry about anything until the next day...when it started all over again.*

*He hopped up a set of peeling periwinkle-painted steps. The screen and the front door creaked open as he slipped inside.*

*Daddy sat on the couch, across from the TV. The familiar Jeopardy soundtrack and the scent of Budweiser and popcorn filled the room. Daddy's belly, stretching a faded blue shirt, rounded over his belt. His eyes looked shut.*

*Thank God, Kid thought.*

*He closed the door and crept through the hall toward the back of the trailer.*

*"Willy," Daddy called out. "Willy-boy. Where you been?"*

*Kid turned around. Daddy's eyes glistened in the TV's blue light.*

*Kid tossed his backpack in his room and started in, hoping Daddy was too drunk to notice.*

*"Willy! You know I'm talking to you, little shit."*

*Kid stepped back out.*

*Daddy undid his belt and unzipped his pants. His thick, semi-erect cock rolled under his belly.*

*"Come over here, Willy."*

*Kid shook his head. He wanted to sneak back in his room and disappear, but he knew what would happen if he didn't comply. He'd resisted too many times only to wind up with a more severe pain than his submission would receive.*

*He slouched, walked over to the man, and dropped to his knees.*

*Daddy's glazed eyes stared into his. "You sneakin' off like your mama? You like gettin' fucked, too? Huh?"*

*Kid gazed at Daddy's now fully erect cock. He couldn't feel pain. He couldn't feel anything as he slid his lips over the head, like he'd done so many times before.*

*"You think you're getting off easy, do ya?"*

*Daddy snatched Kid by the hair, pulled his head up, and yanked him to his face.*

*"You know what Daddy wants."*

*He rolled over, swapping places with Kid. He drove his victim's face into the cushion.*

*"Daddy, no!" Kid cried against the scratchy cotton fabric.*

*Daddy's hand reached around Kid's jeans and undid the button. He exposed Kid's ass, stroking his erect dick in his crack.*

*"That's right. This is what you get for being a whore, you son-of-a-bitch."*

Kid woke, his heart pounding, sweat dripping down his face.

He glanced around his little room, eyeing the concrete floor, the cot beneath him, the thin sheet over his legs. As oppressive as this room was, in some ways, it protected him, reminded him that there was no way Daddy could ever hurt him again...except in his nightmares.

**CHAPTER THREE**

*Mortals are disgusting*, Kinzer thought.

He stood in a lineup with Jerry's boys. Marzo had made them strip naked before entering the room.

A few uneventful days had passed. Since Kinzer's wounds had been healing, Jerry hadn't made him perform any services for his clients. However, as soon as his wounds became less offensive to the eyes, Jerry had decided to go ahead and throw him into their next audition lineup.

Kinzer knew he had to get to Dedrus, but he was going to have to wait until he was in fighting condition before he made an escape attempt. Otherwise, he ran the risk of getting caught and Jerry making future escape attempts even more problematic.

Jerry, Robb, and Marzo stood on the other side of the room, watching as Jerry's client of the day, a white man nearly as big around as he was tall, paced before the line, scanning his options.

The client appeared to be in his late forties. He wore a button-up with the sleeves rolled to his elbows and the top button unfastened, like he'd just gotten off work. He had a double chin that jiggled as he walked across the room. Green eyes sparkled with a look that Kinzer assumed Jerry's boys were familiar with, a sadistic awareness of his power over them, of his control over their next sexual experience.

As the client paced, most of Jerry's boys looked around nervously, avoiding eye contact. Some looked at the floor. Kid fixed his attention on the corner of the room. To Kinzer, he appeared unfazed, uninterested, like he'd done this so many times he didn't care who the client picked.

This boy fascinated him. He wished he knew more about him. At the same time, the sordid horrors he was certain lay in the boy's past troubled him. He assessed Kid's demeanor. So disinterested, so distant, so desirable. Kinzer wondered how many times men like this grotesque creature had abused him.

He didn't want to think about that. He didn't like to consider the plight of mortals.

The client grabbed Kid's bulging biceps.

"This the one you told me about?" he asked, turning to Jerry.

Jerry nodded.

Kinzer figured Kid would have to take this asshat to some sort of fucking room and have the man's most obnoxious feature rubbing across his face as he forced his drug-induced erection into Kid's hole for thirty minutes, maybe an hour.

Jerry tossed Kid a glare, indicating, "You know what to fucking do. Get to work."

Kid grabbed the client's hand and slipped through a doorway beside Jerry. Marzo tagged along behind.

Jerry turned to Robb. "His friends are upstairs. Go ahead and lead them through the back."

"You sure you want to do this?" Robb asked.

"He'll know why," Jerry said.

*Uh-oh.*

He knew this was some twisted punishment Jerry had planned. He was worried about what it might be.

\*\*\*

Kid had not so affectionately nicknamed Jerry's client Double Chin, on account of his most disgusting feature.

Marzo opened a door and ushered Kid and the client into a shithole of a room with a cot shoved in the corner. Chains, handcuffs, and a whip were strewn across the floor.

*This isn't gonna be fun.*

He could take it, though. Under Jerry's control, he'd dealt with plenty of violent clients. He kind of hoped that Double Chin would be just rough enough that he wouldn't have to work for a couple of weeks.

"What are you waiting for?" Double Chin snatched Kid's arm and slammed his chest against the concrete wall. The rough texture scratched at Kid's nipples.

Kid felt something sharp against his neck.

A knife?

"Ah!" Kid whimpered as a blade pierced through his skin.

*Did Jerry put me with a fucking stabber?*

Stabber was the nickname given to Jerry's more sadistic clients. They commonly left guys out of the pool for months at a time. Occasionally, they were the reason boys disappeared.

The blade dug deep into his neck muscles. Kid struggled.

"Oh, you like to fight?" Double Chin pulled the knife back and stabbed it into Kid's triceps.

Kid screamed out. He tried to pull away, but Double Chin had a good grip on his arm.

Kid's assailant twisted the blade.

"Stop! Stop!" Kid cried. He drove his free hand between his chest and the wall and shoved Double Chin's arm back, freeing himself from his grip. He leapt back, the blade tearing through his flesh.

Blood slid down his forearm and dripped onto the floor.

Double Chin held a glistening red blade. Wide, emerald eyes shimmered over a smile that expanded across a drooping, creased face.

*How the fuck am I gonna get out of this?*

The door opened.

Robb entered with two more men.

Kid scrambled through the doorway, slipping past Robb and the new guys.

Marzo, who was just a little farther down the hall, jumped in front of him and grabbed his arms. "Kid, get back in there!"

"Are you fucking shitting me? Let me talk to Jerry!" Kid wiggled, struggling to break Marzo's hold.

"He doesn't want to talk to you." One of Marzo's eyes directed his words at Kid. The other directed them to the wall. "You know what you did. Get back in there."

"This is ridiculous! I don't deserve this! I've been doing this too long to—"

"Chain him down!" Robb shouted.

"No!" one of the two new men exclaimed. Though he wasn't nearly as big as Double Chin, he was heavy enough to crush Kid if he sat on him. He had a full head of brown hair and looked to Kid like he was in his mid-thirties.

The man lifted a hand in gesture. The sleeve of his blue polo revealed flabby arms with splotches of curly hair randomly arranged from his bicep to wrist.

"We want him to be able to fight," Splotchy Hair said.

*These guys could totally kill me.*

Zzzz.

Marzo's Taser was at Kid's chest. He vibrated as he fell to the floor.

Robb and Marzo took him by either arm and dragged him back into the room. They abandoned him, leaving him in the hands of the three clients.

As Kid regained some control over his nerves and appendages, he rose to his feet, the blood from his triceps making a path down his forearm, droplets sliding off his fingertips.

"Listen," he said. "I'm not doing this. Now, please just—"

The last of the clients, nearly a foot taller than Kid—emaciated, the complete opposite of the first client Kid had met—leapt at him, punching him in the face.

Kid fell back. His head slammed against the gray concrete wall. The shock of the blow was so intense it stunned him nearly as much as Marzo's Taser. He slid down the wall, the rough texture grating at his back.

Emaciated knelt beside him, and like a boxer practicing on a punching bag, laid one punch after another into his torso.

Kid tried to block the attacks, but it was useless.

"You like that? You like that, you fuckin' pussy?" Emaciated halted his assault. He whirled around, snatched a chain off the floor, and twisted it around Kid's neck.

Kid struggled against him, but even with his impressive muscles, he felt far too disoriented to put up a good fight.

Emaciated tightened the chain. Kid gagged and desperately tried to loosen it.

Double Chin and Splotchy Hair snatched him by his wrists. They hoisted him in the air and flipped him, pressing his abs against the freezing concrete wall.

"Let me go!" Kid cried through the chokehold.

"We're gonna tear you the fuck up, ya little bitch!" Double Chin pressed his knife against the edge of Kid's hole.

"No! No!" Kid's face turned scarlet as his body demanded a chain-embargoed supply of oxygen.

Double Chin allowed the tip of the knife to navigate inside Kid's ass.

*Please just let me pass out, so I don't have to feel it.*

Kid wished that some deity that he didn't even believe in would hear his cry and come to his aid. A tear formed at the corner of his eye and slid down his cheek.

"Hey! What the fuck?" Marzo's voice called from outside.

"You can't—" Robb added.

Zzzz.

Sounds of punches and shouting muffled together as Kid started to lose consciousness.

He was the only one who seemed to notice the noise. Emaciated and Splotchy Hair were too busy fondling him while Double Chin slipped the tip of the knife inside him.

The door burst open.

Kinzer rushed in, still butt-naked, the veins in his neck purple and blue, his face bright red. He nearly had the same tense, desperate expression on his face as Kid.

"A twofer!" Double Chin's eyes lit up, his face expanding into a grin like the one he'd had after stabbing Kid.

"Oh, fuck yeah!" Emaciated added.

"You get the fuck off him..." Kinzer's cheeks trembled like a dog before a bark. "...before I rip your sick dicks off your scrawny balls."

"Oh, yeah? Make me!" Double Chin pulled his knife slightly out of Kid's hole and started to shove it back in.

Kinzer lunged at him like an animal—ferocious, violent, and untamed. He slugged Double Chin in the face. Double Chin shook it off. Sliding the blade out of Kid's ass, he jabbed at Kinzer.

Kinzer jumped back to avoid the knife.

Emaciated smiled broadly, as if he was thrilled that Kinzer had come to play with them. He released the chain around Kid's neck and ran at Kinzer, throwing a series of punches in his already battered face.

Kinzer bobbed a bit. The hits hardly affected him.

Kinzer threw a punch that knocked Emaciated against the wall so hard that he collapsed to the floor.

Kid uncoiled the chain around his neck. He took a deep, refreshing breath. As his senses returned, he looked to Kinzer.

Across Kinzer's back, black marks appeared, stretching in vertical parallel lines between his shoulder blades.

*What the fuck?* Kid thought.

Splotchy Hair came up from behind Kinzer and wrapped another chain around his neck. Kinzer grabbed at it.

Double Chin came up beside him. He slapped a cuff around Kinzer's wrist and affixed the other to a pipe in the wall.

*Oh, shit. This guy's in way over his head.*

"Hold him!" Emaciated said, crawling toward Kinzer.

Kinzer kicked at him.

Grabbing him by the ankles, Emaciated forced Kinzer's legs apart.

Double Chin slid Emaciated's pants and boxers to his knees.

Emaciated's erect head tapped against Kinzer's hole.

"Fuck, this is hot!" Emaciated exclaimed.

Everyone was distracted, too busy to notice Kid, who lunged at Emaciated, grabbed him by his full head of hair, and rammed his skull against the pipe that Kinzer's hand was cuffed to.

He rammed his head into the pipe again...and again.

The pipe split open.

Double Chin seized Kid by his ankle and dragged him across the floor. Kid's shoulder blades burnt against the cement as the now-unconscious Emaciated collapsed.

"Get over here, you rat!" Double Chin flipped the knife so the blade was facing Kid.

Kid did the fastest sit-up of his life and bashed his fist into Double Chin's balls.

"Fuck!" Double Chin dropped the knife and curled into a fetal position.

Kinzer slipped his cuff through the break Kid had made in the pipe with Emaciated's head. He pointed his fingers out and threw them behind his head, jabbing them into Splotchy Hair's eyes.

Splotchy Hair screamed out and dropped the end of the chain.

Kinzer loosened the chain tied around his neck and gasped for air.

Kid was impressed with his and Kinzer's handiwork. Watching the wounded johns writhe in pain was satisfying.

"What the fuck are you doing?"

Marzo stood at the door, his face red and covered in welts Kid presumed he'd received when Kinzer'd beaten his way into the room.

Marzo zapped a Taser in his hand.

Kid's excitement diminished.

"Kid," Marzo said, shaking his head. "You've been a bad boy." He stomped toward him.

Kinzer kicked Marzo's ankle.

Marzo fell forward, the Taser flying from his hand.

His elbow hit the bare concrete floor.

Kid caught the Taser mid-air.

"Fuck," Marzo said, nursing his elbow.

Kid knelt down and pressed the Taser against the back of Marzo's neck.

"This is called karma, asshole," he said.

Zzzz.

For a moment, Marzo's pupils appeared perfectly symmetrical as his body tremored, just as Kid and so many of Jerry's other boys had done before.

Kid smirked.

Revenge felt good. Very good.

Robb ran into the room, his Taser out.

Kid ceased his attack on Marzo, who was now a spasm of muscles and nerves. He held his Taser out in front of him.

"Want a turn?"

Robb looked around at the battered victims. A bead of sweat rushed down his forehead. He raced out the door, down the hall.

Kid sprang forward, ready to chase after Robb and give him exactly what he deserved.

From his side, Double Chin tackled him.

"Kinzer, catch!" Kid tossed the Taser across the room.

Kinzer caught it as Double Chin slammed Kid's shoulder against the wall.

Double Chin wrapped his sausage fingers around Kid's throat. "I'm gonna kill you, you motherfucker!"

Zzzz.

Kinzer stood beside him, the Taser flashing blue sparks just a few inches from his face. He held the bloody knife in his other hand. "Any of you fuckers try something and I will fry your fucking brain."

\*\*\*

"You fucking dicks!" Jerry shouted.

He lay in the bed Kinzer had woken up in, his wrists cuffed, his ankles chained. Kinzer and Kid stood over him.

It'd been an hour since their encounter with Jerry's perverse clients. In that time, they'd managed to apprehend all of Jerry's guards and unlock all the doors in the house, allowing his imprisoned boys to come and go as they pleased. They'd also found some nice clothes, most likely from boys that Jerry had abducted. Kinzer wore a form-fitting polo and jeans that fit perfectly around his sculpted ass. Kid's hard nipples poked out of a too small brown-and-white striped T-shirt that he'd picked out to show off his impressive muscles.

"Kid, you don't know how good you had it!" Jerry exclaimed.

Kid slipped a Taser out of his pocket, then pressed it against Jerry's neck.

Zzzz.

"Fuck!" Jerry cried.

"That's how good I had it, you asshat."

"We'll be leaving now," Kinzer said. "I just wanted you to know who was responsible for ruining your little operation."

"Go to fucking Hell!"

"Already done it," Kinzer said. He and Kid headed for the door.

"I'll get you bastards for this!"

They stopped in the doorframe. Kid turned back around.

"By the way." He smiled. Kinzer wondered how long it'd been since he'd smiled that big. "You have a few guys that wanted to schedule some time with you, so I just went ahead and booked everyone at the same time. Have fun."

He winked and skipped out behind Kinzer.

They passed a line of Jerry's boys, their faces stern, some with Tasers in their hands. They filed into the room.

Kinzer heard Jerry groan, "Fuck."

\*\*\*

"Order whatever you want."

Kinzer dropped onto a bench in a booth. Across from him, Kid fidgeted with a laminated menu.

They sat at a table in a nearly empty diner. A cook and a waitress chatted behind the front counter.

After leaving Jerry to suffer with the consequences of his disgusting actions, Kinzer had stolen a car. They'd driven for a few hours before stopping so they could grab something to eat.

*Gotta warn the others*, Kinzer thought.

It was the only thing that mattered right then.

"That thing on your back." Kid cocked his head to the side. "What is it?"

Kinzer picked up his menu, studying it as if it were an instruction manual. "A scar." He shrugged dismissively.

"You think I'm an idiot? Scars don't just magically appear out of nowhere. And even if they did, they wouldn't look like that. So what's it really?"

Kinzer set his menu back on the table.

"Y'all know what you want to drink?" The waitress approached their booth. Her black-as-night hair was in pigtails. A purple streak, matching her apron, ran from her bangs through one of the pigtails.

Kid eyed the menu uncertainly. "Um," he stammered. "I uh..."

"What you got?" Kinzer asked, trying to help Kid out.

The waitress set her hand on her hip and cocked her head to the side. Her purple-streaked bangs covered her eyebrow. "We got orange juice, milk, coffee—"

"Coffee!" Kid exclaimed.

"Cream and sugar?"

Kid stared at her blankly.

"Yeah," Kinzer replied by proxy, "I'll take a coffee, too."

"'Kay." She slipped back behind the counter.

"How long were you in that place?" Kinzer asked.

"Few years."

"How'd you end up there?"

Kid shot him a look that let Kinzer know he didn't want to talk about it.

"You gonna tell me about that *scar*?" Kid asked, mockingly emphasizing the word scar.

Kinzer hesitated. There were rules against talking to mortals about immortal affairs, but at this point, Kinzer didn't care. His world had been ripped out from under him, and right then, with his thoughts jumbled and disoriented, he desperately wanted someone to talk to. And given Kid's circumstances, he didn't imagine there was much that could shock him. He took a breath, recognizing the consequences of what he was about to do. That wasn't going to stop him.

"You believe in God?" Kinzer asked.

Kid snorted. "You serious? Listen, I don't need you or anyone else shoving their religion down—"

"You want me to answer your question or not?"

Kid eyed him skeptically. "Okay, okay. Go ahead."

"God's a bad word. It means too many different things to too many different people. What I'm trying to say is, there is a creator of this world. A very powerful being that we call the Almighty. Before he created this planet, he created another set of creatures. People here usually refer to them as angels. We call them higherlings. These immortal creatures were his pet project, designed to imitate his most self-appreciated attributes."

"You trying to tell me you're some sort of angel? I was actually curious. You don't have to be a douche."

"Not an angel."

The waitress approached their booth. From a tray she carried, she set two white mugs with brown-stained rims before them. Black fluid waved against the white sides of the insides of the mugs. She placed a plate of sugar and creamer packets in the middle of the table.

"You fellas know what you want to order?"

"Fuck," Kid said.

"Can we have another minute?" Kinzer asked.

"Whatever." She went back to the counter.

"If you're not an angel, what are you? A demon?" His arched eyebrow assured Kinzer that he wasn't buying it.

"We prefer to be called fallens. Will you look at your menu before she comes back and gets bitchy with us?"

Kid scanned it again.

"Ooo! They have waffles! I haven't had waffles in forever." He sipped his coffee. "Mmm. That's really good."

Kinzer tasted his. It was burnt. He scowled. Grabbing five packets of sugar off the plate, he ripped them open and emptied them into his mug.

"Sorry," Kid said. "You were saying? You're a demon?"

"A fallen." Kinzer stacked a few of the creamer packets by his mug.

"You trying to steal my soul? 'Cause I think you're a little late."

Kid was so much giddier than he'd been at Jerry's. Kinzer imagined it was his excitement over his new freedom.

"You mortals have a pretty fucked up sense of what's really going on. That's not even close to how this works." Kinzer peeled a packet lid back and poured the creamer into his mug. "After the Almighty created the higherlings, He fell in love with the one you guys call Satan, Lucifer, Prince of Darkness. We fallens know Him as the Leader. They had a fling. According to legend, they had some pretty great sex."

"God's gay?" Kid asked. "Top or bottom?"

"Eh. The Almighty's kinda a hermaphrodite, so I don't know if He'd be considered *gay*, but I think you can rest assured that He's a top. Anyway, they were lovers for eons. During this time, the Almighty created a present for the Leader: the world. However, the Almighty was so disgusted by it that He tried to hide it. Eventually, Satan found the world, and when the Almighty explained that it had been intended as His gift, the Leader...Satan...thought it was pretty sweet. Not long after that, they split up."

"Why?" Kid's eyes widened, as if he was surprised that he'd asked that.

Kinzer figured he must've sounded like the nuttiest guy in the world. Maybe it was better that way.

"The Leader and the Almighty always fought over the hierarchy of Heaven, which divided higherlings into different classes. The Almighty's most beautiful and intelligent of creations made up the ruling class. His more usual creations, like me, belonged to the lowest class."

"Oh, you're not usual." Kid's gaze lowered, clearly indicating Kinzer's dick.

"You'd be surprised. Anyway, the division and inequity enraged the Leader. He inspired a lot of us with speeches and writings about equality. After eons of social strife and protest, the Almighty cast the lowest class out of Heaven with the Leader, allowing us to form our own society in Hell. This was called the Fall. Part of the agreement between the Almighty and the Leader was that anyone who went with the Leader was banished from Heaven forever, and they had to char their wings as a symbol of their transgression against Him. He was very overdramatic about the whole thing."

The waitress re-approached. "You guys figured out what you want?"

"Um...yeah," Kid said. "Can I get three pecan waffles, two chicken parmesana omelets, and a chocolate pie? Oh, and hash browns covered in chili?"

Kinzer and the waitress eyed each other.

She turned back to Kid and smirked. "Hungry?"

"Yup."

"And you?"

"Just two eggs," Kinzer said, "over easy."

"Be right out." She dashed behind the counter.

Kid pressed his thumb to his cheek. "So, God and Satan fuck. Breakup. And Satan and his peeps go party in Hell?"

"Pretty much."

"That has nothing to do with your scar."

"I'm getting there. After the Fall, the Almighty and the Leader agreed to leave the world alone—to let it run its natural course. However, the Almighty went behind the Leader's back and tried to destroy it. This started a war between Heaven and Hell, a very brief war that ended in far too much bloodshed. The Leader created powerful weapons, Morarkes, creatures with one purpose: to kill higherlings. To prevent them from attacking fallens, the Leader gave Morarkes a keen sense of smell to distinguish between higherlings and fallens. But the Leader discovered that he couldn't control them. They turned against the fallens and wreaked havoc in Heaven and Hell.

"For a brief period, the realms united and fought against the Morarkes. And fearing that another war would wipe out not only the world but Heaven and Hell, the Almighty and the Leader created a special assembly, the Council, to moderate any immortal activity that happened in the world. Like the United Nations for immortal realms. The Leader hoped that the Council would prevent God from trying to destroy the world again. The Almighty hoped it would prevent the Leader from creating another devastating weapon.

"As you can probably imagine, if the Almighty doesn't destroy the world, then He looks like the Leader's bitch and like any immortal can walk all over him. So the Almighty is still trying to annihilate the world, but in a very sneaky way. The Leader has figured this out, and it's turned into a massive chess game."

"So...when you say this kind of shit, do you know you sound crazy? Or do you think, 'This is going to make total sense to someone else'?"

Kinzer was relieved that Kid wasn't taking him seriously. It meant he could ramble on without having to worry about him freaking out about the horrors of mortals' vain plight in the Leader and the Almighty's petty feud.

"In Hell, there are a lot of fallens who, for whatever reason, are trying to get in good with the Almighty again, to restore their place in Heaven. These fallens will do just about anything to get back, including helping to bring about the end of the world. One group is called the Raze. I'm with a special operative for the Leader, the Leader's Allies. They sent me to investigate this group, to see what their plans were. But someone ratted me out. They clipped my wings, and I'm guessing their leader, Veylo, sold me to Jerry just to piss me the fuck off."

He wasn't going to tell Kid about Janka. That would be too much for him. He'd lose control of his emotions.

"Bullshit," Kid said. "You're telling me that shit on your back used to be wings? Like bird wings?"

"No. Like fallen wings."

Kid shook his head. "Whatever. If you're really some immortal demon, prove it."

"How?"

"I don't know. Don't you have powers or shit? Don't you do things different from people? Isn't there some way you can show me?"

"When they clip you," Kinzer explained, "you lose your powers. And other than having unusually large genitalia, we're pretty similar to humans. We're actually the original model. But maybe if you get a closer look, you'll get it."

\*\*\*

"Where are they?" Kid whispered.

Kinzer, his eyes closed, sat on the toilet, shirtless. He looked like he was meditating.

Kid, crammed between Kinzer and the stall door, stared at his naked back.

"We could totally fuck in here," Kid said.

"Shh!"

The foul restroom stench filled Kid's nostrils. He cringed.

Oily marks—the marks he'd seen back in Jerry's place—started to reappear, until they were black with tiny points protruding from them.

Kid leaned down to get a good look. They were sharp, barb-like. He moved his fingers close, but just as he was about to touch one, several shifted together.

"Holy fuck. What is it? A mutation?"

"That's where the wings used to be."

The marks were weird, but it was too big of a leap for him to believe Kinzer's story. Kinzer was either lying out of his ass or bat-shit crazy. Either way, he didn't care. Kinzer had rescued him from Jerry's, so he would swear his loyalty to him regardless...even if that meant going along with all this nonsense about angels and demons and wars between Heaven and Hell.

"Okay," he said. "What do we gotta do?"

"I gotta warn some higherlings."

## CHAPTER FOUR

"Dillon and Aaron on standby."

Pop music blared so loud that Kid could barely hear the intercom voice as he and Kinzer made their way through a smoke-filled bar.

Kid was still chuckling at the sign outside. "This place really called Dick Dongs?"

A dim, orange light illuminated a box of a stage where two late twenty-something guys rubbed their steroid-induced muscled bodies against black poles, posing with the music.

The place was pretty empty, except for a few balding men—well into or beyond their fifties—who were tended to by shirtless gym-rats that looked barely legal.

Kinzer had driven for nearly twenty-four hours without rest until they'd reached Atlanta, where he claimed his friends would be to help him. Kid still thought it was a bunch of nonsense, and now that they were in a strip bar, he was even surer of it.

Kinzer approached the bar. An older guy—his broad chest covered in curly black hair, his love handles nearly nonexistent—set a crate on the floor and stocked beers in a chrome tub of ice. His shirt dangled from his back belt loop.

Kid looked around uneasily. His eyes drifted to the stage. The less-than-enthusiastic steroid-ripped dancers bobbed around and dipped fairly low for wide-eyed frumpies that were slipping bills into their underwear. Kid saw the same look in the dancers' eyes that he was used to seeing at Jerry's. Sad, empty, defeated. He imagined that was what he looked like.

Kinzer set his arm on the bar and glanced around.

Kid finally asked the question that had been burning on his mind since they'd arrived.

"I'm sorry. You said these were angels, right?"

As much as Kid didn't buy Kinzer's story, he was still curious about how this all worked in his head.

Kinzer nodded. "AKA higherlings."

"Um...what are they doing here?"

Kinzer smirked. "Seems like God has a pretty fucked-up sense of humor, right?"

The bartender popped up from the beer tub and approached the counter. "Hey, man."

"Jack on the rocks," Kinzer said. "And can I change out for some ones?"

He reached into his pocket, pulled out a wallet he'd lifted from one of Jerry's clients, and handed some cash over to the bartender.

Kinzer turned back to Kid. "Better to keep higherlings in places you wouldn't expect them. These guys are liaisons for the Almighty's secret organizations on Earth."

The bartender slid a glass of Jack across the counter and handed Kinzer a wad of ones. Kinzer curled the cash up and slipped it in his back pocket.

Kid rocked his head to the pop beat. He smiled. "This is kinda fun."

He scanned the pack of trim bodies that pranced around the room in just jeans.

A pretty-faced brunet, his chest pushed forward, his abs sucked in, approached Kinzer.

"Hey, man. Wanna lap dance?" He winked.

Kinzer shook his head. The brunet frowned. His chest sank in. His abs pushed out. He moved along.

"So," Kid began, "how will I know when I see one of these guys?"

"Don't sweat it. I got this."

The song faded out. An awkward silence filled the room, followed by the sound of a toilet flushing. The dancers hopped off the stage.

"Dillon and Aaron on deck."

The orange stage lights shut off. Two black lights flipped on, illuminating both poles.

At the back of the bar, a door opened. Two glow-in-the-dark thongs, one green and one pink, floated out and approached the stage. As the black light illuminated the physiques they were affixed to, Kid's mouth dropped.

The guy in the pink thong had a flawless body. Two veins crawled like vines up a deep rift that outlined either side of his belly button, which was so shallow it was nearly flush with his washboard stomach. Kid wondered if the guy'd ever had a carb in his life. Two locks of his blond, spiked hair curled inward like devil horns.

The music started back up.

The pink-thonged stripper grabbed the pole and swayed his torso—embedded with a deep vee, a seeming invitation to savor his package, which was so enormous that it was dangling out of the far-too-small thong. Kid was sure it had to have been nearly a foot and half long.

Narrowed eyes and crinkled temples made the stripper appear to be perpetually wincing, lost in some deep thought, even while he was shaking his ass and wrapping his leg around the pole. Indented around his mouth were two sickle-shaped dimples that were so defined, they were visible even as he stood there, expressionless.

His knees gyrated. His juicy, round ass jiggled. He was hotter than the other two dancers Kid had seen on the stage. More than that, there was something different about him. He appeared to actually be feeling the rhythm, caring about the beat, enjoying what he was doing.

The dancer closed his eyes, massaged one hand down the pole as his ass dipped to the floor. He stroked his other hand across his thick pecs, which protruded so far from his chest that the dip between them had to be several inches deep.

"You like what you see?" Kinzer asked.

"Mmm hmmm."

Kinzer grinned. "You and every other higherling. Follow me." Kinzer stepped toward the stage. As he approached the stripper in the green thong, Kid found himself inching toward the other.

"Kid, take a seat. I think it'll be easier if I talk to him one on one."

*Okay, crazy.*

He appreciated Kinzer's suggestion. It gave him an opportunity to be closer to the other stripper. He made his way to a table between the two poles, so he could keep an eye on both his favorite dancer and favorite hero. Kinzer approached the green-thonged stripper, who was shaking his cheeks in the face of a bone-thin corpse of a man. The corpse eagerly stuffed a dollar bill in a glow-in-the-dark strap around the stripper's thigh.

Shorter than the other stripper, his muscles were less bulky, less defined. However, it was still a hell of a body. Dark-brown hair waved down either side of his cheeks, fanning out over his shoulders. Tiny hairs speckled across his plump face, indicating a fresh beard. Where the other stripper seemed confident in his place on the stage, this one seemed awkward, out of his element.

The green-thonged stripper finished entertaining the older man and returned to his pole. He climbed and wrapped his legs around it, gripping on with his calves. He threw his body back, arching his torso so his abs pushed forward, tense, rigid.

\*\*\*

*Not gonna make any fucking money tonight*, Dedrus thought.

He arched his back.

He'd just finished entertaining one of his regulars, a nasty old man who was very generous with ones but never paid for VIP.

While he'd been working the regular, Dedrus had noticed a young guy in his peripheral vision. Maybe he had some cash.

He'd made his way over to the pole and performed his moneymaker move, hoping it would pay off.

He tossed his head back and threw the guy a seductive glare.

"What the—"

His calves lost their grip. He plummeted to the floor.

"Shit!"

The stripper at the other pole, Treycore, threw him a concerned look.

Dedrus couldn't believe it.

*Kinzer?*

Was this a dream? He had plenty of dreams about Kinzer—dreams where his ex-lover returned to him and confessed his love. They'd make up and run off together. Was that why he was there? Dedrus knew better. He remembered the cruel day when he'd expressed his true feelings for Kinzer and he'd been shot down.

Dedrus had endured war and torture. Neither compared to the pain he had felt the day that Kinzer left him. Since their split, Kinzer had made every effort possible to keep his distance from Dedrus. Even when Dedrus tracked him down and sent him letters, he never responded. Maybe Kinzer was just following protocol. They weren't supposed to fraternize with the other members of the Leader's Allies, but he couldn't help himself. He couldn't shake Kinzer from his thoughts, his life. Kinzer's image haunted him. He couldn't feel the stroke of a customer without immediately comparing the dead, empty interaction with the passionate, sensual one he'd had with Kinzer. He couldn't wake in the morning without wishing that as he rolled over, there would be his beautiful friend and lover, resting peacefully, wanting just another hour of rest. He couldn't eat a delicious meal without thinking on all the shit that he and Kinzer had eaten together during the war. If only he could have been with Kinzer, he would have eaten that shit for all eternity.

His heart fluttered with excitement. His mind cluttered with confusion. As much as he wanted to believe otherwise, he knew Kinzer wasn't there to confess his love. Something was wrong. Very wrong.

"Dedrus, you okay?" Kinzer rested his palms on the stage.

Dedrus shook out of his confusion.

The fall had hurt his back, but he'd be fine. He'd suffered falls from greater heights.

*Don't be obvious.* He couldn't make a scene at the bar. He and Treycore had worked too hard crafting these covers for him to blow them in one night. He pushed his ass in the air and crawled toward Kinzer. As he reached the edge of the stage, he groped his hands along his fuck-me lines, raising his torso until he was face to face with Kinzer. He didn't say anything. Just stared at him.

"That looked like a pretty serious fall," Kinzer said.

"Had worse." He flicked his nipple with his thumb, doing his best to be inconspicuous, although he could only imagine what Treycore was thinking.

Kinzer tucked a dollar in his thigh strap.

"You know why I'm here."

Dedrus looked around uneasily. He rose on his knees until he was crouching. He twisted his ass toward Kinzer, groping and shaking to the beat.

"Hey," the regular called from the other side of the stage. "Come back here, Aaron!"

*Now is not the fucking time. What is he doing here? What's happened?*

Kinzer's gaze drifted for a moment. As they returned attention to the dancer, he slid another dollar into Dedrus's strap. "Janka's dead."

Dedrus froze, stopping midstroke.

Janka.

The sound of that name evoked a sting in his chest. It was the name of the higherling that had stolen Kinzer from him so many years earlier. Had it not been for Janka, he would have had Kinzer. They would have been together for all eternity. As much resentment as he still held for Janka, he couldn't help but be overwhelmed by sadness. Janka had been with him since the dawn of creation. They had been friends since before the split between Heaven and Hell. They were childhood friends that had eons of memories together.

"Someone has names," Kinzer continued.

Dedrus nodded. "I don't want to be the one to tell Treycore."

Kinzer threw Treycore a look. Dedrus checked to see how he was reacting.

Treycore would be pissed that Kinzer was violating protocol. Also, being Dedrus's friend and confidant, he knew how damaged Dedrus had become since Kinzer had left him. He'd tried to force Dedrus to move on, to find new lovers to replace his ache for the fallen, but it never helped.

Treycore stared Kinzer down, but he continued dancing, just like Dedrus. He wrapped a leg around the pole and whirled around.

***

Kid had been eavesdropping on Kinzer's conversation with the stripper he was calling Dedrus. Who was Janka? And what kind of names were Dedrus and Treycore?

He didn't question it too much. He was too focused on trying to keep Treycore in sight.

Treycore turned his pink-covered ass toward Kid. He bent backward until he was facing him, his skin tight against his abs, stretching out his shallow belly button. The head of his penis rolled across the bottom ripple in his six-pack.

"Hey, you!" Treycore called out.

Kid looked around to see who the stripper was talking to. Surely, not him.

"You. Come here."

Kid rose from the chair and approached the stage.

"You got any money?"

Kid shook his head.

"Then scram! I don't do this shit for free."

He nodded and snuck over to Kinzer.

By now, Dedrus had pulled down his thong and was twirling his foot-long dick in Kinzer's face.

*Where the fuck do they make all these ginormous cocks?*

"Dedrus," Kinzer said, slipping another bill in the strap. "You're the only one I can trust right now."

"Hey!"

A tall man with fat, hanging cheeks, but a fit form, came up beside Kinzer.

Dedrus slid his thong over his dick.

"You gonna just keep putting out ones, or you wanna get a deal for the VIP?"

Dedrus mouthed, "VIP."

"How much is it?"

"For Aaron here? Two hundred for thirty minutes."

"For thirty minutes? That's not a fucking deal!"

The man glanced Kinzer over. "You gonna be stingy, or you want a good show? You've seen this one's dick. Pretty impressive. Now sit on the pot or get off the can."

Kinzer turned to Dedrus with a shocked glare. "You worth it?"

"Am I ever."

Kinzer slipped the wallet out of his back pocket and sifted through the billfold. "What can I get for twenty?"

"I'll give you directions to the nearest McDonald's."

"Whatever." Kinzer slipped the wallet back in his pocket.

"Tell you what. Fifty for fifteen minutes."

"What if I want the other one, too?"

The boss thought for a minute. He glared at Treycore. "That one's our little show stud. I'll throw him in for another seventy-five."

"I'll take them both for a hundred or walk." He motioned to Kid. "And my friend comes, too."

The man held out his hand.

\*\*\*

The boss pulled a white sheet across a metal rod, exposing a room illuminated by a dim, blue-bulbed lamp on a box. A couch with foam pushing out of its edges was pressed against the chipped and cracked wall—littered with carelessly taped event posters with pictures of well-endowed go-go dancers.

The boss ushered Kid, Kinzer, and Dedrus in. As Treycore approached the doorway, the boss grabbed his bicep and pulled him aside. "Remember, no BJs. I'm not looking to get shut down."

"Fuck off," Treycore said, slipping back inside. He grabbed the edge of the sheet and pulled it closed.

Air rushed through the foamy cracks in the cushions as Kid made himself comfortable on the couch.

Dedrus peered out the side of the sheet over the doorway.

Treycore stared at Kinzer, his narrow eyes disapproving, stern.

"This ain't—" Treycore began.

Dedrus tapped him on the shoulder. "Quiet...wait...and...okay. Go ahead."

"This ain't fucking happening!"

"Quieter," Dedrus insisted.

"Fallen," Treycore hissed, "you better have a good fucking reason for being here. And what the fuck are you doing with this mortal? He smells like shit!"

*Do I smell really bad?*

Kid was glad the light was dim, so no one could see him blush.

"Janka's dead," Kinzer said. "Someone ratted us out. That means they have names."

"And you came to us?" Treycore asked, his expression tense. "Why the fuck do you think you're still alive? They probably have a Tracker keeping an eye on you. For all we know, they didn't even know about us. Fuck!"

"I didn't have anyone else to go to. Janka's my only contact. They clipped me, so I can't cross realms without an elixir. Dedrus is the only one I knew I could find...or trust."

"And why the fuck does he know where you are?" Treycore asked, a serious gaze locked on Dedrus.

"I...just—" Dedrus began.

"Huh?" Treycore's gaze flashed between Dedrus and Kinzer.

"He wrote to me, okay?" Kinzer explained. "He mentioned this place."

"What the fuck are you? Pen pals? You couldn't have just called?"

"Totally. Let me just run and grab my cell from Hell! Treycore, I don't give a shit how pissed you are. I just need you guys to warn the others. We all need to get our asses into hiding."

"Treycore," Dedrus said, nudging him. They exchanged knowing glares.

"I know what you're thinking." Treycore said. "You want to bring this bullshit in, and I'm telling you that's a really bad idea. You don't think it's a little odd that the Raze would just let him go? Why just kill Janka? It doesn't make any sense unless they're using him to get to the rest of us. The Raze thinks that if the wounded, clipped Kinzer comes running for help, dumbasses like you will take him in, and then they'll hunt the rest of us down." He shook his head and tossed Kinzer a foul glare. "As far as we know, you're the rat, and you're responsible for Janka's death."

*Who the fuck is Janka?* Kid wondered. *And are these guys actually drinking the angel/demon Kool-Aid?*

Kinzer rushed at Treycore, getting in his face.

Treycore stood firm. They stared each other down. "Be careful," Kinzer said.

A thick vein curled up Treycore's bicep as he balled his hand into a fist.

"This is not the time." Dedrus pushed between them, his biceps swelling as he pushed them apart. "Treycore, do you really think Kinzer would've ratted out Janka?"

"I think," Treycore said, "you need to stop making decisions with your dick."

Dedrus glanced at Kinzer meekly and looked back to Treycore.

"Please," Dedrus said.

Treycore folded his arms. His knuckles pressed into his bulbous pecs. The head of his dick dropped from his thong and slid down his thigh.

An erection stirred in Kid's pants.

"We can't risk this," Treycore said. "Not right now."

"What do you mean?" Kinzer asked. "What is it?"

"He could help," Dedrus said. "And you know we'll need any help we can get."

"What are you talking about?" Kinzer asked.

Kid was asking the same question, but about so many more things.

"If this blows up in our face," Treycore said to Dedrus, ignoring Kinzer, "it's on your head."

"Deal."

"Okay," Kinzer said. "Now, someone want to tell me what the fuck is going on?"

## CHAPTER FIVE

"Are you guys psychotic?" Kinzer asked.

A woman, her wrists and ankles bound in rope, duct tape around her mouth, slept curled between a bed and a nightstand. Her skin was even whiter than Kinzer's. Her cheeks sunk to a narrow jawbone, in extreme contrast to her swollen, round belly. A ponytail of thin, dirty-blonde hair fell across her chest.

"You kidnapped a pregnant woman?"

"We did what we had to do," Treycore said.

They stood in a bedroom that wasn't much bigger than the backroom at Dick Dongs.

After Treycore and Dedrus's shift, they'd driven Kinzer and Kid back to their place. Treycore now wore a short-sleeve button-up. The sleeves were so tight that, as his muscles flexed, the seams tore ever so slightly.

Dedrus was in a polo and khakis, far more conservative, as if he was trying to hide the good body he had.

Kinzer knelt by the woman, gazing at her belly.

*To think, this child could end all the pain...all the hurt...all the torture that the Almighty has used to oppress this world.*

"Janka told us about her," Dedrus said. "I guess, before..."

"He knew where the Antichrist was?" Kinzer asked. "And he never said anything to me?"

"He told me he didn't want you to have to handle that burden. He would rather you not know than be implicated by the Almighty."

*If only he'd known.*

"Why is she tied up?" he asked. "Does she know what's going on?"

"You think we were gonna tell her," Treycore said, "that she was having the devil's kid?"

Kinzer glanced at several dirty bowls, spoons, and bottles of water that were scattered at the woman's feet.

"Do either of you do dishes?"

"We both work," Dedrus said defensively.

"At night! You can't leave her like this."

Kinzer assumed her horrible treatment stemmed from Treycore and Dedrus's inability to see mortals as equals.

Kinzer grabbed the edge of the duct tape around her mouth and pulled.

*RIP* went the tape as it exfoliated her lips.

"Fuck!" she moaned, stirring to consciousness. "What did I tell you about the tape? Who the fuck are you?"

Eyes that seemed too large for her tiny, frail face locked in a bitter stare. She pursed her lips and cocked an eyebrow.

Her irritation made sense. Kinzer didn't imagine there were many who wouldn't have been equally enraged had they found themselves in her situation.

"It's okay," Kinzer said. "I'll explain!"

"If you bunch of faggots want to rape me or get BJs, let's just do it and get it over with."

"No, no. It's not like that."

"I don't have time for this shit. I'm gonna have a baby. Or can't you tell? And you know, it wouldn't kill me to have a cigarette. Anyone got a beer?"

Her words scrambled Kinzer's thoughts. He tossed a glare over his shoulder. "Dedrus," he whispered. "Where did you find her?"

"Well..."

"She did tricks," Treycore explained, "over at Cheshire Bridge."

"Oh." Kinzer's eyes returned to the woman. "Um...I'm not going to let you smoke or drink while you're carrying the Leader's baby."

"What? Who? You know who the father is?"

"Yes. That's actually what I want to tell you. Now, I'm gonna untie you and explain—"

"Don't fucking untie her!" Treycore exclaimed.

"Yeah," Dedrus said. "Don't do that. She's a biter."

"Just let me handle this. I think you guys have done a shitty enough job with this as it is."

He fiddled with the ropes around her wrists, loosening them with care.

The foul look on the woman's face softened.

"What's your name?" he asked.

"Maggie."

"Maggie, you're carrying a very important baby."

As he finished untying the rope, he set it beside him and worked on her ankles.

"Are you a religious person?"

She hesitated but shook her head.

"Good. That'll make this easier."

He started his tale of God and Satan, just as he had told it to Kid. He explained the war between Heaven and Hell, allowing her thoughts to reel through the mind-fuck that accompanied the reversal of thousands of years of the Almighty's religious propaganda.

Kid stood in the doorframe, glancing around uncomfortably.

Kinzer was fairly certain that Kid thought he was insane. He knew he shouldn't have told him as much as he had, but after all that had happened, he didn't feel like there were any immortals he could trust, and it was nice to have someone to talk to. However, considering Kid's clear disbelief, he couldn't figure out why he was still hanging around.

"For a long time," he said, still attempting to soothe her concern, "the Almighty has planned to have a child—a ruthless, sinister, malicious monster that will bring plague and death to the world, wiping it into oblivion. This child is referred to as the Christ. The Council has restrictions against him creating a Christ. It would be like China deciding to use a nuke. Through our team's infiltration into the Raze, we learned that God is already in the process of bringing a Christ into the world. The Leader, as we call him, knowing this, has launched his own Antichrist, a child that will take on the Christ. This child will bring peace and love to your world."

Maggie's eyes were wide. "Which one am I having?"

"The Antichrist."

She stared at him blankly.

"That's the good one," Dedrus said.

"So...I'm having the devil's baby. But the devil's good? And you guys are demons?"

"We prefer the term fallen," Kinzer corrected.

"Okay. You are fallens, and you're going to protect my baby so that it can save the world? Am I hearing this right?"

Kinzer sighed, relieved. It was wonderful that she'd been able to absorb all that so fast.

"See?" he said, turning to Dedrus and Treycore. "It doesn't hurt to communicate with mortals."

"Um—" Treycore muttered.

Something hit the back of Kinzer's head. His face smacked into the floor. Ceramic shards scattered across the carpet around him.

It was the lamp from the nightstand. Evidently, when Kinzer'd turned to his higherling friends, Maggie had made haste with finding a weapon.

In a flash, she was at the window, unfastening the lock.

"Oh, fuck!" Dedrus hopped over the bed.

Treycore ran around and wrapped his arms just above her belly.

"Let go of me, you crazy fucks!" she shouted. "Help! Rape! Rape!" She scratched at his arms. Exposing her teeth, she bit into his hand.

"Fucking bitch!" he shouted.

Dedrus struggled to restrain her.

A few bite and scratch marks later, they had her stabilized on the bed.

"Please don't kill me!" she wailed. "God, save me from these crazies!"

"Guys," Kid said. "Why don't you show her something?"

Kinzer, Treycore, and Dedrus exchanged uncertain looks.

Treycore threw him a condescending glare. "What?"

"She's scared 'cause she thinks you guys are insane. Don't any of you have wings or something you can show her, so she'll believe?"

Treycore's glare transformed from condescending to curious. He undid the buttons on his shirt, pulled it off, and tossed it aside.

The dip in his back ran down to a peek at his ass crack.

"Finally!" Maggie exclaimed. "Just rape me and get it over with! Fuck, it's not rape with those abs. Jesus!"

Treycore closed his eyes and took a deep breath. Feathers shot out from between his shoulder blades and expanded until they filled just over half the room.

"No fucking way!" Kid exclaimed.

Maggie's mouth dropped open. "Shit. What am I on?"

\*\*\*

"Anything?" Treycore asked Dedrus. He held his cell to his ear. He leaned against a doorframe, his blond hair in a swirled pattern created by Maggie's frenzy. His shirt, only buttoned halfway, exposed the grooves down his chest. As he looked at Kinzer with disdain, his wince intensified.

*You're such an asshole*, Kinzer thought.

Kinzer hated that wince, which made Treycore appear as if he was disapproving of everything his gaze beheld. Did Treycore make this face because he found himself constantly disapproving of creations lower than himself? Or, had the Almighty crafted the expression to compliment his beautiful features?

Before the Fall, Treycore had been one of the Almighty's most prized creations. He'd been free to delight in whatever he desired. After the Fall, he'd sided with the Leader. Still, Kinzer couldn't help but despise the span of time when Treycore had basked in the fruits of Kinzer and other inferior immortals' labor.

"No," Dedrus replied, his cell also against his ear. With his free hand, he pushed a brown lock of hair out of his eyes, curling it behind his ear. He knelt between a couch and a coffee table. He weeded a plate and bag of Oreos from between the couch cushions and added them to a pile of TV dinner trays and magazines on a side table.

"Sorry about the mess," he said, his eyes scanning the room for more debris.

Dedrus's panic about his and Treycore's wreck of a place reminded Kinzer of how adorable he could be. He'd always been messy and wildly ashamed of it. During the war, he'd dig through piles of hoarded garbage, searching for his shit. His cot had always been covered with so much crap that it looked like he was trying to make a nest. It was a habit that, even after all this time, Dedrus hadn't been able to overcome. He was clearly ashamed of that, but Kinzer found the hoarding—coupled with Dedrus's embarrassment about it—charming. It was part of what Kinzer had fallen in love with.

Kid stood before a wooden rail to the stairwell that led to the second floor, where Maggie's room was. His gaze flashed to Treycore.

Kinzer figured Kid was smitten. Treycore's physique was impressive, even to immortals. He could only imagine how it affected a mortal.

"This is bullshit." Treycore shoved his cell in his pocket. "Where the fuck is everyone?"

Dedrus ducked beneath the coffee table. He rose, his hands filled with white cracker bags. He set them on the table.

"Dedrus, seriously? Are you gonna keep cleaning, or are we gonna figure out what the fuck we're gonna do?"

"Voicemail," he said. "Maybe someone already warned them." He pressed his thumb against his phone screen and set it beside the cracker bags.

They'd been attempting to reach their contacts, Donna and Krimson, for the past half an hour. Anxiety rushed through Kinzer. Something was up.

"Yeah. They'd warn them and not us?" Treycore said. "Doubtful."

"We need to get her out of here," Kinzer said. "If the Raze is on to the Leader's Allies, they could come here."

"No way." Dedrus, still kneeling, picked up wrappers and Styrofoam coffee cups off the floor and added them to his collection on the table. "All our work is tied to another location. We don't use this house for any transactions. Not with the Council. Not with the Leader's Allies. There's no way they can find us."

"You're sure?"

"Yes, we're sure." Treycore stepped toward Kinzer, broadening his shoulders like he was trying to intimidate Kinzer. "You think we're morons?"

"Not both of you," Kinzer said.

Treycore's face flashed red. A ripping sound filled the air as his biceps flexed against his sleeves. He balled his fists and marched at Kinzer.

Dedrus leapt up from the floor and wedged between them, as he'd done back at Dick Dongs. "Are we seriously gonna do this all night? Treycore, Janka's dead. Give him a break."

Those words pained Kinzer. They made him want to tear into Treycore, not because of anything Treycore had done, but because he wanted to beat the shit out of something—anything.

"Whatever," Treycore said. "We're done with this shit. I'm gonna go to bed."

"Good," Kinzer said. "Let the grown-ups handle the planning."

"Kinzer," Dedrus hissed.

Treycore shoved Dedrus's shoulder to the side as he headed across the room. He slipped by Kid and started up the stairwell.

"Will you get Kid settled?" Dedrus asked.

Treycore stopped halfway up the stairs. He rolled his eyes and turned his wince to Kid.

"What am I? A babysitter?"

Dedrus didn't respond. He just eyed him until Treycore finally said, "Get your ass up here, smelly."

Kinzer thought it was harsh to call a mortal *smelly*. It was true, but it wasn't their fault that the Almighty had been so sloppy with their creation.

Kid turned to Kinzer, his eyes filled with concern, as if he was psychically saying, *"This guy's not gonna kill me, right?"* Kinzer tossed his head to the side, indicating that he should follow Treycore.

Treycore was an ass, but he wasn't going to hurt him.

Kid's jeans flashed behind the wooden rail posts as he made his way up the stairs.

\*\*\*

"Again, sorry about the mess," Dedrus repeated.

A lamp from a nearby desk illuminated a bookshelf before him.

Stacks of books covered rows of shelves that lined every wall. Crinkled wads of wide-ruled paper surrounded the base of a desk covered with a mix of potato chip bags, Hershey's wrappers, files, and books.

Had Dedrus known he was going to have immortal company, he would have tidied up—especially if he'd known it'd be Kinzer.

"It's fine." Kinzer stared off, apparently not noticing the mess. The cleft in his chin and the divot in his nose hid in shadows created by the lamplight.

A wave of Dedrus's dark bangs obscured his view. He tossed his head back, jerking the clump behind his ear. Standing on his toes, he pulled a book toward him. The bookshelf swung open, revealing a secret compartment.

Dry, glistening tissue that had grown over the cut on Kinzer's lip expanded with a smile. "Glad you're still putting that brilliant mind to use."

Dedrus blushed. No one appreciated his handiwork anymore. No one ever saw it. During the golden days of Heaven, his inventions had been adored. His craftsmanship had been praised by the most ingenious of his higherling peers. They'd held ceremonies in his honor, praising him for his innovation. Those days were so long ago that memories of them seemed more distant than the blurred images of a nearly forgotten dream.

Not his memories of Kinzer, though.

Those were vivid. Being an engineer for the Almighty, Dedrus was a member of an elite higherling class. Kinzer had been a laborer, a builder. He pieced together, with millions of other builders, the magnificent visions that the elite conjured up to satisfy their vain tastes.

Had the realms divided based on loyalty rather than hierarchy, Dedrus would have fallen as well, for he had actively worked against the oppressive institution that exclusively served the Almighty's most beautiful of creations, leaving those perceived as less remarkable at the bottom of the order. Though an insignificant creation to the Almighty, Kinzer wasn't unremarkable. Not to Dedrus. When the war came and he and Dedrus had joined the Leader's fight, they worked together, defending the Leader during the Siege of Hell and fighting the Morarkes when they turned against their creator.

Kinzer wasn't a leader. Just a soldier. A hardworking, passionate soldier. Dedrus had fallen in love with his passion, not just for the rights of all higherlings, but for life—a better life than the Almighty had ever promised his lowliest of creations. Kinzer and Dedrus shared a tent. They'd lain in cots as Kinzer read the Leader's philosophies on equality to Dedrus. They'd spent nights discussing the troubles of Heaven and the promises of Hell. Kinzer wasn't a great philosopher. His arguments were weak, emotion-based, and devoid of logic, but they were passionate. It was that passion Dedrus had fallen in love with—the same passion that stirred the fire in those sparkling brown eyes.

"I can't have you walking around without any protection." Dedrus pulled the bookshelf open like a door, revealing racks stocked with swords, daggers, and knives. He reached in, pulled out a sword, and handed it to Kinzer. "Recognize it?"

Kinzer smirked, his eyes on the hilt—on an emblem of a dove in flight. It was Dedrus's emblem. "You took out a lot of Morarkes with this guy."

"*We* did."

The Morarkes had been designed to defend Hell and attack Heaven. When they turned against the fallen, the immortals formed a task force known as Feint to destroy the beasts. Morarkes, having been created with an incredibly narrow focus that forced them to isolate their assaults to higherlings, were incapable of multi-tasking. Their attention fixated on their victim higherlings until their mission was accomplished. Members of Feint used this weakness against the monster. Working in teams of two, one immortal drew the attacking creature's attention. The other attacked its weakest point. Dedrus's swordplay was vastly superior to Kinzer's, so Kinzer always acted as the distraction while Dedrus acted as the attacker.

With Kinzer's assistance, Dedrus had slain hundreds of the menaces.

"I'm not gonna take this," Kinzer said. "It's yours."

"You pissed off the Raze. You need a sword."

Kinzer had to have an immortal weapon, one created from the minerals of heavenly realms. The weapons of Earth were insignificant against immortals.

"Not gonna do me much good," Kinzer said, "now that I don't even have my strength. Or my gift."

His gaze drifted across the blade. He sighed.

Dedrus knew he was reminiscing about more than the loss of his strength or gift. He was reminiscing about the war. About his days with Janka. As supportive as he wanted to be, he couldn't stifle the spark of jealousy that stirred within him. He hated himself for feeling it. Janka had been a good friend. They'd worked together on the Almighty's heavenly empire at the dawn of creation, combining the skill of Dedrus's engineering with the craft of Janka's architecture. They'd built a kingdom worthy of the Almighty's precious creations.

As much love and reverence as Dedrus had for Janka, he had never been able to shake the sting that surged in his chest, reminding him that Kinzer could never be his. His resentment stemmed from his initial courting of Kinzer, interrupted when Janka became a captain with Feint.

At the time, an affair between Janka and Kinzer seemed impossible. Despite Janka's siding with the Leader, he had never been one to care for the plight of the lower class. He'd only ever expressed disgust for them. However, a change of heart left him caring, not only for the lower class, but mortals as well. It was a dark day when a fellow soldier whispered rumors of Janka and Kinzer's relationship to Dedrus. The sting he'd felt became a surge of rage that overwhelmed him. He'd been livid. He'd had to isolate himself for days as he abused desks, chairs, and even books, leaving them ripped and tear-stained. What could someone as compassionate as Kinzer see have ever seen in the vain whims of Janka? Dedrus spent many nights in fits of anger, consumed by jealousy. What was he to do now that he'd found the one creature in the uncountable span of time that was the only one he could ever love?

"I appreciate it." Kinzer gripped the shaft of the sword. "So how have you and Treycore been holding up in this mortal rat hole?"

"What? You don't love the place?"

Kinzer smiled. "Not exactly the flash of your castle in Heaven."

Dedrus had been spoiled with one of the greatest castles in the Almighty's kingdom. He and Treycore had once lived the most luxurious of lives, basking in the great pleasures of the elite. Now, they opted to live in squalor among the mortals in their work as liaisons.

"It's easy for Treycore. Attention is attention, and most creations have always been beneath him, so he adores it regardless of where it's from."

"And you?"

"Hard to choose where I'd rather live out my lonely existence."

*Stop being pathetic.* Dedrus chastised himself. He was just trying to get Kinzer to pity him.

Kinzer's gaze shifted around the room, as Dedrus recalled him doing when he'd attempted to convey his affections for him long ago.

"But this place is so wonderful," Dedrus said, in an effort to lift Kinzer's discomfort, "sometimes I forget I'm not in Heaven."

Kinzer chuckled. His eyes lit up.

*There's that gleam*, Dedrus thought. *Stop thinking like that!*

This wasn't the time to be swooning over Kinzer. There were serious matters to tend to, and most importantly, Kinzer needed time to mourn the loss of his Janka...the immortal that had ripped Dedrus's love right out from under him.

"I'd kill myself if I had to be around Treycore every day," Kinzer said.

"He isn't the easiest immortal to live with." Dedrus gestured, presenting the room to Kinzer. "As you can see, I'm not either."

"I guess when you've spent eons with servants waiting on you hand and foot, it's hard to adjust to cleaning up after yourselves. How is his verse these days?"

"Time hasn't improved his talent, but that's what happens when the Almighty prioritizes aesthetics over intellect."

"Well, I gotta hand it to him. He's given up a lot. Of all the elite that have joined the cause, he had the most privilege."

"When you're on a pole in a thong, feeding the shallowest of mortal impulses, it's easy to forget you ever had privilege."

"Not such a big fall for an immortal like me. But Janka probably felt the same way."

There was that name again. Dedrus hated himself for cringing at it. He'd loved Janka. He considered him a brother—a brother he loathed for taking the only thing in all the Almighty's realms that made eternal life worth it.

"You never should have both been sent into the Raze," Dedrus said.

"I insisted." Kinzer gazed off.

He was clearly thinking about all that had happened. He needed to talk about it. Get it off his chest.

"Here," Dedrus said. "Come on. Let's sit down."

He passed Kinzer, heading into the adjoining room.

Frozen dinner trays, water bottles, and unopened bills covered the table by the couch.

*This is so embarrassing. At least it's better than before.*

He approached the couch and motioned for Kinzer to sit.

Kinzer did. Dedrus made himself comfortable in the corner, relaxing his triceps on the arm of the couch and angling his legs over the side. His distance from Kinzer was calculated. Though he wanted to wrap his arm around him, to hold him close and ask him to tell him everything, he knew that wouldn't be appropriate. Even worse, he wouldn't be able to resist the urge to take things further—to a place that would take advantage of Kinzer in his moment of weakness.

"You want to talk about it?" Dedrus wanted to be there for his friend in whatever way he could, but he questioned his motives. Did he want to help out of the goodness of his heart? Did he secretly want Kinzer to notice his kindness and come to appreciate him as he'd come to appreciate Janka? Surely, both elements were present within his intentions, but he hated himself for the part that selfishly wanted to use this opportunity to get closer to Kinzer—to pick up where Janka had interrupted.

Kinzer leaned back on the couch, his fingers massaging the edges of the sword. He stared forward, as if he was looking through the wall on the other side of the room. His eyes no longer reflected the gleam that usually enchanted Dedrus.

"Veylo's mad with power," Kinzer said.

Dedrus shook his head. "He was always that way. His mind is too close to the Almighty's—in a way that breeds corruption. He can create powerful, mystical technology. He can give life to inventions that no other immortal could conceive of. That power breeds arrogance. When I worked with Janka, Veylo trivialized our work. He saw us as limited, narrow-minded. Whereas we would work to use the tools that surrounded us, Veylo worked to create new tools that took creation to another level. I'm not saying he's not a genius. He is. Veylo could do more with the elements of the heavenly realms than any other creation I've ever known. But that power...there's something dark within it. Something twisted. It lacks ethics. Morality."

"That's him in a nutshell."

"The only reason Veylo ever fell was because he thought he'd have more power in Hell. Fortunately, the Leader was too smart to give him any. The Leader knows he'd use it to usurp him. I remember how upset Veylo was when he wasn't allowed in the weapons division. I think Veylo wanted to work on the Antichrist Project. What great mind didn't? Kamin, Erisar, Vegir...there was something alluring about the idea of working against the creator. But even those immortals knew that creation without hesitance would bring about annihilation. Hesitance has never been Veylo's strength. I take it you don't know what he was working on?"

"Whatever it was, it was big. Veylo said it would have the power to end all the realms. Sounded like the next Morarke. I just don't get how someone can work to create something so destructive and be proud of it, especially after all we went through during the war."

"You're sure he wasn't talking about the Christ?"

"I'm sure. Janka said it was more powerful than that."

"More powerful?" Dedrus knew Veylo was irrational, but it seemed absurd of him to believe that Veylo could challenge the greatest minds the Almighty had ever created—the ones responsible for developing the Christ.

Kinzer nodded. "It's like he's trying to outdo the Almighty."

"That sounds like Veylo. Mad with irrational, wild, impatient ambition. You have any idea how close he is to finishing it?"

"Close. Very close. I didn't have a lot of pull with the Raze. I just supplied them with bogus intel from the Leader about our underground operations. Veylo never let me in on his secrets. He'd tell Janka things here and there, but kept him at arm's length, so I'm sure that he was never going to tell me shit. Janka was in charge of properties. Veylo needed a lot of space, a lot of land for whatever he was working on. He also helped set up a lot of operations that worked to transport materials between realms."

"You think he's transporting heavenly minerals to Earth?"

"Definitely."

"Why didn't we just take that to the Council? Veylo would have been executed immediately."

"The Leader wanted us to find out *what* Veylo was working on. If we exposed him too early, someone else could have just picked up where he left off, and we'd never have a chance to stop them."

"What do you think it is?"

"No clue. Janka was having a hard time figuring it out. I think Veylo tried to confuse him about it. He went on all these wild goose chases. Initially, he thought the Almighty had charged Veylo with the Christ."

"No. No way," Dedrus said. "The Almighty wanted him back in Heaven, but He'd be insane to give him that much power."

"Later, Janka suspected that Veylo was trying to rework the Morarkes. Evidently, some of the materials he was transporting were Morarke corpses."

"And?"

"Another dead end. Veylo was dismantling them entirely. Janka never figured out what he was up to. Janka would think he was onto something one day, and the next, he'd reach a dead end. He'd tell me about them, though. That's what surprised me when you guys mentioned that he'd told you about the Antichrist. Janka told me all the pieces he was working on with Veylo, but never anything about that."

"He probably just wanted to make sure Veylo wouldn't be able to torture it out of you."

"You're right. If he'd said anything to me about it, and they'd...done what they did, I would've told. I'm not proud of that. But when it came down to it, Janka's life mattered more to me than all of creation. I would've told. Janka knew that."

That was what Dedrus loved. That passion. It wasn't intelligent. It wasn't reasonable. It was what it was, and it was beautiful.

"What about the guy who outed you?" Dedrus asked. "You have any idea who it is?"

"I don't, but when I find him, I swear to our fucking Leader, I'll—" Choking on his words, Kinzer rested the sword on his lap and pressed his hands against his now-trembling face.

Dedrus scooted across the couch, wrapped his arm around him, as he'd wanted to do all along.

*You're horrible*, he chastised himself. *You know why you're doing this. Don't.*

Another part of him wanted to be there for Kinzer. He wanted to ease his pain, to provide him with some relief from the horror he'd experienced at the hands of the Raze.

Kinzer threw his arms around Dedrus, squeezing tight. His body quivered.

Dedrus wanted to feel Kinzer's lips on his, to taste his delicious immortal flavor. He wanted to feel Kinzer's cock inside him, filling him, as he had on so many of the nights they'd spent together.

*It isn't right.*

Kinzer pulled away, freeing Dedrus of his guilt. He sniffled and wiped the back of his hand across his nose.

"Sorry," Kinzer said. "It's just…"

"Don't. You have every right to be upset."

*Upset. That's a trivial word for what he's been through, you idiot.*

Dedrus scanned Kinzer's body, admiring his massive biceps, his brown eyes, and his black waves of hair. Even with the wounds and tears that still tainted his face, he was beautiful. Dedrus wanted to press him back against the cushions, rip off his clothes, and provide him with the ease he deserved. But no! He was just wanting it for himself, and he was pretending that it was to serve Kinzer's pain.

"I loved him so much." The words cracked through Kinzer's lips. His cheeks and forehead shivered. Tears filled his eyes. "I know we had so much time, but it wasn't enough."

The sting in Dedrus's chest intensified. His cheeks flashed red as anger washed over him—anger that he loathed because it made him feel like a terrible, selfish creature.

He set his hand on Kinzer's back, his palm stroking softly across the blue fabric of his polo. He wanted to say, "You'll find love again." He couldn't, because he knew he'd really be saying, "Please find love in me." He thought of saying, "Everything will be alright." No. He couldn't make that kind of promise. "It'll take time," felt appropriate, and yet, as an immortal, Dedrus never perceived time as a generous gift as much as a twisted, agonizing punishment.

"I wish I could think of something right to say about this," Dedrus said, "but I can't. I know how much you loved him, and I know how much he loved you, and I can't imagine how hard this is going to be for you. But I'm here. As your friend. I don't know if that means much, but I know the feeling of having something so perfect and wonderful torn away from you."

Kinzer's gaze met his. His eyes were sad.

*Does he know what I'm talking about?*

"Tell me you've found someone," Kinzer said.

"Of course," he lied. "I'm just being overdramatic."

"I figured as much. Considering where you work, I'm sure you get a lot of offers."

It was true, but not the way Kinzer was suggesting. There were nights when Treycore dragged some pathetic mortal back to ease Dedrus's pain. Those nights were the loneliest. Though he could bring himself to climax, it was an empty relief that just stirred the cruel memories of those moments filled with so much more.

Dedrus hugged him again. "Let's get to bed," he said. "You need some sleep."

Kinzer nodded.

"We have plenty to sort through tomorrow. You can have my room. I'll just sleep here."

Dedrus released him.

Kinzer picked the sword up off his lap and stood. He reached his hand out. "Come on. It won't be the first time we've shared a bed."

The upward curl of his lip let Dedrus know that Kinzer was more than interested.

Dedrus's dick swelled. "I don't think I can." He wanted Kinzer so bad, and if he put himself in that position, he was sure he wouldn't be able to resist making a move—especially if Kinzer initiated something.

"I'd rather not disrespect you like that," Dedrus said.

Kinzer's hand fell, bouncing against his jeans. His head drooped.

"Then I guess I'll see you tomorrow."

Dedrus smiled. "'Night, Kinzer."

Kinzer knelt, offering a light peck on Dedrus's lips.

*Don't tease me with a taste!*

"Up the stairs, first room on the right."

Kinzer walked up the stairs, headed down the hall, and slipped into Dedrus's bedroom.

Dedrus had hoped that Kinzer's exit would provide some relief.

It didn't.

He ached for him. His thoughts dwelled on Kinzer's lips tickling his nipples, his gaze appreciating his body, his tongue delighting in his body's grooves. He wanted to run upstairs and throw his arms around him, to hold him for the night, and tell him that no matter what happened, he'd be there for him. He wanted more than that, but he wouldn't press his friend. He wouldn't dare cross that line...even if Kinzer insisted.

Spreading his limbs across the couch, he rested his head on a lace pillow at the end and rolled so he was facing the cushions.

He closed his eyes.

A few moments passed before something pressed against his ass.

He flipped over and hopped to his feet, ready for a fight.

Kinzer stood before him, holding his hands out, as if showing a cop that he was unarmed. "Whoa, cowboy. Chill the fuck out."

"Sorry." Every hair on Dedrus's immortal body stood on end. "You freaked the shit out of me. Did you need something? Another cover? Pillows?"

Kinzer wiggled his thumb behind the waistband in Dedrus's khakis.

"Yeah. I need something." He pulled their pelvises together.

His hot breath rushed across Dedrus's lips, settling in the bristles across his cheeks. The warmth combined with a rush of blood that surged to his face made him feel like his cheeks were about to catch on fire.

Kinzer pressed his lips against Dedrus's.

Amidst the creases in Kinzer's lips, Dedrus felt the smooth, subtle dip where Kinzer's cut was healing.

He trailed his palm over the rough fabric of Kinzer's polo. As he reached the smooth flesh of his neck, curly black hairs pricked his fingertips.

Kinzer opened his mouth wide. Dedrus eagerly reciprocated, tilting his head and allowing their lips to seal together. A swirling sensation gathered at the base of his spine and rushed to the crown of his skull.

Guilt nagged at his thoughts. He couldn't do this. Kinzer didn't really want him. He was just vulnerable and ached for a physical distraction from his grief. It would be wrong to take advantage while he was still recovering from Janka's death.

Kinzer's tongue flicked his.

He wanted Kinzer so bad, but not like that. Pressing his hand against the dip between the bulbous, jagged pecs before him, he broke their sealed kiss.

"What?" Kinzer rested his hands on Dedrus's hips.

"This wouldn't be right. I don't want to disrespect you."

"I know. But I want you to."

Kinzer wrapped both arms around Dedrus. Spinning them around, he pushed Dedrus back against a painting that hung on the wall.

Kinzer's eyes glistened with that gleam—the one that was so familiar to Dedrus.

Dedrus couldn't control himself. His lips returned to their passionate embrace. His fingers found their way under Kinzer's shirt, feeling about fervently, savoring the dips in his torso.

The wooden frame of the painting dug into Dedrus's back, scraping along the wall before dislodging from a nail and breaking free of its frame as it hit the floor.

Kinzer gripped the hem of Dedrus's shirt. Dedrus threw his arms over his head, allowing his friend to pull it off and toss it behind him. Kinzer's fingers went right for Dedrus's khakis, unbuttoning and unzipping at lightning speed before they were at his ankles. Dedrus kicked off his shoes, letting them roll across the wood-paneled floor. He stepped out of his pants. Kinzer tossed them beside his shirt.

"Ooo. Lookie, lookie," Kinzer teased.

Dedrus glanced down at the white bikini briefs he wore. Deep arches in his torso dipped down either side of his hips, disappearing under a waistband. He blushed. "Shut up. I didn't think anyone was going to be looking."

Dedrus tucked his thumbs into the waistband and slid them down his thighs. Kinzer grabbed his wrists.

"No, no," Kinzer said, sliding them back up. "I like them." He knelt so he was eye level with a monster bulge in the briefs.

Dedrus giggled like a schoolboy, but being that he'd been alive since before Earth's creation, he wasn't fooling either of them. This was fun, frisky—like the good old days. Dedrus couldn't enjoy the moment without immediately remembering that this encounter was finite. Unlike the old days, when he knew he could return to his lover at any time, he had to soak up every drop of goodness from this experience.

Kinzer pulled the front of Dedrus's briefs down. His cock and sack sprang forward as if they were reaching out to attack.

"Been a long time since I've seen this guy," Kinzer said.

*Been a long time since I've gotten any.*

It hadn't been *that* long. He and Treycore fooled around on and off, whenever they needed to de-stress. But Treycore was so big that Dedrus never let him go inside him. He'd fucked a few mortals that he'd met at the bar or that Treycore brought back to the house, but he'd never let them penetrate him. After all, most mortals' cocks couldn't even reach an immortal's prostate. For a long time, Dedrus had desperately wanted someone who could just slide into his ass and fuck the shit out of him. He knew that Kinzer would do just that. Kinzer knew how rough he liked it. Kinzer knew exactly how much teasing and pain he required.

Kinzer tucked the waistband behind Dedrus's balls. It pushed his sack forward as if presenting his nuts to Kinzer.

*Stop it! Stop this!*

He couldn't. The promise of this intimate encounter with someone he cared so much about was too much for him to fight. He didn't want Kinzer like this. He wanted Kinzer to love him...to want to be with him. However, he was willing to take whatever Kinzer was willing to give.

Kinzer's tongue swept up the middle of his scrotum, stirring about, massaging between his balls.

The cool air conditioning rushed through Dedrus's curly, brown pubes, freezing Kinzer's saliva. His balls shrank. His sack wrinkled.

The cool air amplified the intensity of the heat of Kinzer's breath, making his length swell even more.

Kinzer's tongue tickled the base of his shaft, barely licking, just teasing. He wrapped his hand around his friend's girth and squeezed, his lips rushing just barely halfway down the head of Dedrus's cock.

"Please!" Dedrus enjoyed the excitement. He wasn't even as aroused by Kinzer's actions as he was by the anticipation of what was to come.

Kinzer slid his lips back, freeing them from Dedrus's flesh. He gripped Dedrus's hips, twisted him around, and pushed him forward.

Dedrus spread his arms out. His hands pressed into the wall like he was about to do a pushup.

Kinzer slid the briefs down Dedrus's thighs, exposing two tight, c-shaped cheeks. He removed them, adding them to the abandoned clothes behind him. He massaged Dedrus's ass-flesh, his thumbs sliding through the crack between them, pulling them apart.

Kinzer's hands were so warm, so smooth.

Dedrus wanted Kinzer's pelvis to use his cheeks like a hacky sack.

Dedrus shifted his pelvis so his ass pushed closer to Kinzer's face, inviting him to savor it in whatever way he desired.

Thoughts of Janka itched at Dedrus's conscience, but a twisted part of him didn't care. He wished that Janka could see him now—to feel that same pain he'd felt when he'd lost his chance with Kinzer. It was a terrible thought. He scolded himself for having it, but it didn't make it any less true.

With his tongue, just as he had done with the base of Dedrus's cock, Kinzer tickled his way around Dedrus's hole. Dedrus wrapped his fingers around his dick and jerked back and forth. Kinzer released one of his cheeks and snatched his wrist.

"No!" he ordered.

Dedrus glanced over his shoulder. Had he done something wrong?

"I want you to get off without touching yourself."

Excitement stirred in Dedrus. He'd forgotten how playful Kinzer could be. As Kinzer released his wrist, Dedrus placed the hand back on the wall. Kinzer's thumbs pulled Dedrus's cheeks back apart. He pressed his lips against his hole. He kissed softly at first. Like he was warming it up. His tongue stroked up and down and whirled about in a frenzy.

An intense rush of energy, like hands caressing up his back to his neck, swept through Dedrus.

Kinzer's lips retreated. He kneaded his thumbs against either side of Dedrus's hole. He was slow, deliberate.

*Why is he teasing me?*

"I want you in me so bad," Dedrus said.

With both hands, Kinzer pressed his index and middle fingers together and pushed them into Dedrus's hole. Leaning so that his face was millimeters from Dedrus's crack, he spit a thick, juicy web of saliva inside and massaged it against the walls of his ass.

Dedrus contracted the inside of his hole, as if he was thirsty and this was the only way he could hydrate.

Kinzer's fingers pulled out.

A clinking sound hit Dedrus's ears as Kinzer unfastened his belt and slid his pants down to the white socks that covered his feet.

A stiff, vein-covered erection poked forward.

Kinzer sprang to his feet and stuck the hard-on between Dedrus's cheeks.

With one hand, he gripped Dedrus's waist. With the other, he stuck the head of his dick against his saliva-lube and forced his way into Dedrus's hole.

Stinging. Burning.

It felt as if someone was jamming a knife inside him.

It was painful, but erotic. The more it hurt, the harder he became.

Unlike humans, who Dedrus found tended to favor pleasure, immortals found greater satisfaction in the dance between ectascy and pain...in exploring the complexity of their creaturehood through blissful—yet at times—excrutiating sex.

White feathers ripped from the flesh between Dedrus's shoulder blades, stretching out, just as Treycore's had done earlier. He lifted his leg off the ground, struggling to position himself so Kinzer would have an easier time assaulting him.

It was like a butcher knife reaching for his intestines.

If Kinzer hurt this bad, he couldn't even imagine how painful it would have been to have Treycore in there.

Kinzer's arms crossed as he pulled his polo over his head and tossed it with Dedrus's clothes. He wrapped his arms around Dedrus, beneath the inner edges of his wings. Trailing his fingers around Dedrus's torso, he caressed them across his abs.

His nose tucked behind Dedrus's ear as his lips offered soft kisses against his neck.

He thrust back and forth, seemingly without regard.

"Fuck!" Dedrus cried, his feathers shaking feverishly.

It was so painful, and yet, he wanted more. Kinzer sure did know how to fuck him.

"Fuck me, Kinzer," he pleaded. "Harder!"

He didn't know if his body could actually handle harder, but he needed it.

He lifted his leg higher and twisted it around Kinzer's hip, resting it on his farthest ass cheek—a position he credited to his current occupation. He'd hoped that it would impress Kinzer. Make him want him more.

Kinzer pulled his shaft out and thrust back in.

It was deep. So deep that it forced Dedrus into convulsions. His rigid back muscles tensed. His wings fluttered.

Kinzer pushed in and out. With each thrust he offered, Dedrus eagerly pushed back, encouraging Kinzer to destroy his hole.

Kinzer flicked his finger over Dedrus's erect nipple and pinched it with his thumb. He tugged at it and pressed down, as if it was a button.

*Fuck*! *Yes*!

Dedrus unleashed another cry of pain, as he had when Kinzer had first forced that big dick in him.

"Hurt me!" Dedrus exclaimed. "Please, hurt me!"

Kinzer released Dedrus's nipple and grabbed his hips, continuing to pound him. As his pelvis smacked into Dedrus's ass-cheeks, a sound, like someone being slapped repeatedly, filled the room.

Dedrus could feel Kinzer's cock hardening, elongating even more. As it reached Dedrus's prostate, a wave of tickles rippled through his brain. He rolled his head back as what felt like jolts of pleasure rushed across his face. All the while, his ass felt like it was going to split in two.

Kinzer moaned. His pelvis thrust so hard, so fast, the slapping started to sound more like punching.

For Dedrus, it was as if he'd pressed a button that had released painkillers in his spine. It was so relaxing, so delicious. He wanted so much more.

"I'm gonna come," Kinzer said.

"No!" Dedrus cried. He crawled up the wall, but he couldn't lift high enough to get Kinzer's cock out of his hole. "Please don't!"

As much as he wanted Kinzer to come inside him and for Kinzer to make him come, he wanted to savor this delicious experience. He didn't want it to end. He wanted to fuck Kinzer for hours. He wanted it to last all night. It wasn't fair for it to be this short when he wanted an eternity of this wonderful immortal.

"I can't stop it!"

Dedrus flapped his wings, flying high enough that he was able to dislodge Kinzer.

His ass throbbed. Tremors overtook his legs. He collapsed to the floor and lay beside the fallen, painting.

"No, I need it," Kinzer said. He reached down, grabbed Dedrus by his hair, yanked him to his feet, and slammed his face into the wall.

Dedrus's foot scraped across a jagged edge of the painting's broken frame. It tore through his sock, slicing into his skin. It hurt like fuck, but it was nothing compared to the sensation of Kinzer forcing himself back in.

"Oh, fuck! No!"

But all he could think was, *Yes! More! Hurt me!*

Still, he couldn't let Kinzer come. If he did, that was the end.

He tried to turn to his side, but Kinzer wrapped his arm around the base of his wing, holding him in place.

"Ah!" Dedrus shouted.

Kinzer's insistence on being inside him was even more arousing. Pre-come gushed from the head of Dedrus's cock like a spider shooting its web.

"Stop, you're gonna make me come, too!"

*This isn't right. It shouldn't feel this good. I hate myself.*

Despite his guilt, he was greedy, determined to steal as much time with Kinzer as he could.

He wrapped his arm around Kinzer's leg and yanked on it as hard as he could.

Kinzer tumbled backward. He released Dedrus's wing and grabbed him by the waist.

He landed on his ass. He'd carried Dedrus with him so that Dedrus was sitting in his lap, Kinzer's cock still inside him.

Dedrus continued his desperate struggle, but Kinzer grabbed his hips and clung on as if it was his most important mission.

Dedrus reared back and punched over his shoulder, hitting Kinzer on his cleft chin.

Kinzer rocked forward and wrapped his arm around Dedrus's neck, pulling him so that his back was flush against his chest.

"You like that? Huh?" Kinzer teased.

Dedrus screamed out. This position enabled Kinzer to get so much deeper, to cause him so much more pain and simultaneously press that intoxicating button deep within him so much harder.

Dedrus glanced down. Through the slits in his wavy bangs, he saw his pre-come pouring in strings from his swollen cock, pooling into his belly button. His balls burned, as if all they wanted to do was empty their load. It was nearly unbearable. He imagined this was what Kinzer was going through, too. But he wasn't going to give up. Besides, this tug-of-war was partly responsible for how aroused he was.

Dedrus grabbed at the arm around his neck, fighting, struggling to get free. He lifted his ass into the air, trying to get Kinzer's cock out enough so he'd be free, but Kinzer was so big that he would've had to get his hips higher than physically possible for that to happen.

Between Dedrus's attempt at freeing his hole and Kinzer's insistence on penetrating it as deep as he could, Dedrus's ass was like a basketball, bouncing up and down in fury and excitement.

Dedrus twisted his pelvis, managing to pull over half of Kinzer's cock out of him.

Kinzer grabbed Dedrus's firm love handles to pull him back on.

It was too late. Dedrus rolled just enough that head of Kinzer's cock fell out, bouncing on his own abs.

Kinzer rolled with him until Dedrus's stomach was flush against the wood floor panels, which chilled his flesh.

Kinzer reached for Dedrus's wrists.

"No!" Dedrus cried. He thrust his elbow back, smacking Kinzer in the face. He crawled out from under his attacker. As he managed to achieve his freedom, he darted to the doorway to the study.

Kinzer started after him but stumbled over his jeans, which were still at his ankles. He knelt down to remove them.

Dedrus tucked his wings back as he stepped into the study. He started to turn when a blow from behind knocked him forward, forcing him on top of the desk amidst the stray papers and files.

He hardly had time to react as an arm reached under his armpit and flipped him on his back so his wings lay stretched out beneath him, flapping amongst the stacks of papers, some of which were slicing into his back.

Kinzer propped Dedrus's legs up until Dedrus's hole was lined up with his erection. He drove it right back in.

It stuck cattycorner, tearing into the wall of Dedrus's ass, sending a sting rushing through him. As Kinzer's dick tore across his flesh, it pierced into the depths of Dedrus.

It smashed into Dedrus's prostate. A thousand swirling vortexes of relief spiraled across Dedrus's chest. It was a sensation he could've only hoped for, and here it was, delighting him beyond anything he'd believed possible.

*No, no! I shouldn't be enjoying this!*

Kinzer wiped his hand across Dedrus's abdomen, collecting some of the pre-come that was still stuck in his belly button. He pulled his fingers to his mouth and licked it off.

"Oh, that's good."

Dedrus could hardly hear him. He was too busy savoring Kinzer's cock while feeling it against the walls of his ass. Feeling it tear and rip. Feeling it throb. He wanted it to hurt more. He wanted the pain to be so intense that it made him forget about Janka and his selfishness altogether. But it only aroused him even more, amplifying his awareness of his sins.

Kinzer leaned forward, gaining leverage and making broad strides as his dick's head nearly left Dedrus's hole, but then swiftly reentered, striking its farthest distance and sending Dedrus into a fit of spasms as his body was ravaged with hypersensitivity.

As Dedrus returned to his senses, he remembered the battle that he was having with Kinzer. He had to keep Kinzer from coming—from ending this experience. Pressing his shoulder blades against the desk, he bounced up, his fists clenched, and punched Kinzer in the cheek.

Unfazed, Kinzer snatched Dedrus by his wrist, and as the other fist came at him, he snatched it, too.

Dedrus wasn't about to give up that easily. He wiggled, struggling against Kinzer's hold.

He yanked his pelvis back, his ass sliding across the papers, escaping from Kinzer's cock. As he freed himself, he jerked to the side and rolled off the desk. Kinzer lost his grip and dropped him.

SMACK!

Dedrus hit the floor. He scrambled to his knees.

Kinzer pounced on him from behind, forcing him back onto the floor. He grabbed his wrists and pinned them to the carpet.

Dedrus tried to use his elbows to fight, but his wings obscured his attack.

"Godfuckingdammit!" Dedrus cried.

He had wrestled with Kinzer while fucking in the past, but he'd never lost this badly.

He swayed his hips violently side to side, hoping to make it a challenge for Kinzer to get back inside him. His dick burned against the carpet bristles.

Kinzer's erect cock stabbed against his cheeks a few times, missing its target.

The failed attempts delighted Dedrus. He giggled with excitement. He felt victorious. It really did feel as if he'd taken a time machine back to the best years of his life.

"You fucking asshole!" Kinzer exclaimed.

Dedrus continued to sway, but as he reached one side, Kinzer's dick rushed in.

Dedrus reared his head back. It was the most painful and the most delightful sensation he'd ever experienced. His head tossed back and forth as he writhed in the delicious sensation that poured through his back, as if his nerves had been shot full of morphine—everywhere except his ass. Pre-come projected out of his cock, onto the carpet.

It was too much for him to handle. He caressed his hard cock against the floor, forcing it against the red bristles. His cock needed relief. It needed to come.

"Harder, harder!" he begged. "Please, harder!"

Kinzer released Dedrus's wrists and pressed his hands against the back of his wings, arching his back, pushing his abs forward, as he thrust with all his might in and out of Dedrus's ass.

Dedrus knew he should be quiet, considering how many people were probably sleeping, but he couldn't. He screamed.

Dedrus struggled against his cock's desperate attempt at climaxing. He moved his ass in circles, another move that he'd acquired through his profession.

It must've been more than Kinzer could handle, because Dedrus felt him swell. He loved knowing that Kinzer was filling his hole, his come spewing deep inside him. A quick thrust as Kinzer's dick slipped across his own come sent him even deeper inside Dedrus than he'd been before.

Dedrus's cock was like a gun. A runny, translucent pre-come preceded a flurry of thick, white rockets that soared through the air and scattered across the red floor.

Dedrus's legs quaked. His back trembled.

*Oh, I fucking needed that.* Chills followed the thought as an awareness stirred within him. *Why did I do that?*

He'd reveled in the idea of the deceased Janka watching him fuck his lover. He'd injured himself by revitalizing the sensuality that had solidified his love for Kinzer so long ago.

He'd made a huge mistake. A mistake that, given the opportunity, he'd make again.

***

Kid stood by the door.

The small room reminded Kid of some of the fucking rooms at Jerry's, except it was far less empty. On the far end, by a window, a comforter and pillows were piled together in the middle of a twin bed. Across from the bed was a desk with an old computer and printer. Mounds of paper surrounded it. Books and CDs scattered across the floor.

*Books*? Treycore didn't seem like the kind of guy that read much.

"My only rule is," Treycore said, "don't fucking hog the covers." He unbuttoned his shirt.

Kid eyed the twin bed. "Um," Kid began, "maybe I should just sleep on the couch downstairs."

"You saying you're a cover hog?"

"What? No. I just don't want—"

"Then don't be stupid. No reason to sleep on the couch. We're all adults. We can share a fucking bed, right? What? You worried I'm queer?"

Kid shook his head. Although, he'd hoped.

Treycore undid the last button on his shirt and slipped it off. It took a bit of effort, considering how tight the shirt was against his flesh.

Kid's eyes fixated on the curves at the edges of his abs, the sculpting just under his plump chest. Treycore had tiny, perky nipples. Kid's mouth salivated as he imagined licking, titillating them.

Treycore tossed Kid a suspicious glare.

Kid's eyes raced around. Had he been caught?

"You gonna get ready for bed?"

"Oh, yeah," Kid said. He walked over to the bed, sat, and untied his shoes.

"You younger mortals smell worse than the old ones," Treycore said, unzipping his jeans. He pulled them down with his underwear, revealing his massive cock.

It was even bigger than Kid had realized at the bar. He wasn't sure if that was a good thing. It seemed too big for any human to take.

Treycore's ass muscles shifted about as he walked by a door, then opened it, revealing a closet, the bottom piled with clothes. He threw the jeans and underwear on top of the others and forced the door shut.

Kid slid his jeans and shirt off. He slipped under the covers, trying to keep Treycore from seeing his rock-hard erection.

Treycore opened another side door and stepped into a bathroom.

"You need to wash off?" he called out.

Kid heard a creak, followed by the sound of running water.

"No. I'm good."

What he really wanted to say was, "Yes, and will you fuck the shit out of me while we're in there?"

"Suit yourself."

Kid could hear the water slapping against Treycore's skin. He wished he could have been in there, tasting that enormous cock, trying to see how far he could get it inside him. He might not have been able to get it in far, but he figured he could surprise Treycore with how much he could take. Even if he couldn't take it, he would do whatever he needed to so Treycore could get off. He would lick and suck until his gums bled. He would let Treycore slap him around, spit on him, abuse him. It was a small price to pay for the pleasure he would experience just by feeling that body against his.

A part of him was just glad that he was going to get to be so close to Treycore's hot body. He just hoped that he wouldn't try to hump this gorgeous creature in his sleep. That would be embarrassing.

Kid fixed the pillows and the covers around him. When he'd positioned everything just right, he rested his head on the pillow. It felt so much better than the cots at Jerry's.

A few minutes passed before Treycore stepped out of the bathroom. He shifted his hands side to side as he rubbed a towel across his back, leaving his nude muscles on display. Kid couldn't help but look.

Treycore ran the towel through his hair and tossed it in the bathroom.

Making his way back to the bed, he switched off the light and scooted under the covers, leaving just a few inches between him and Kid.

A streetlamp shone through the window, covering the room in an orange glow.

Treycore closed his eyes and rolled his head back. A bulge in the covers moved up and down.

Waves of heat rushed through Kid. His own cock couldn't get much harder.

"You mind?" Treycore asked.

"No."

Treycore's eyes shifted to Kid's concealed cock.

"You wanna get off, too?"

"Um...yeah."

Was Treycore serious? Had he heard him right?

Treycore pulled the covers down, revealing his rigid muscles, tense, swelling as he massaged his impressively massive dick.

Kid slid his boxers down and wrapped his fingers around the shaft of his penis.

"That's a pretty good size," Treycore said. "For a mortal, that is."

"Thanks," Kid said, not sure whether Treycore was offering an insult or a compliment.

Treycore licked his fingers, dipped his hand down, and rubbed the liquid over his thick flesh.

"Sorry," he said, "I don't have any lube. Here."

He licked his fingers again and wiped them across the head of Kid's dick. Kid's shaft tightened as it grew even bigger. A ripple, like an electric shock, rushed from the head of his dick to the back of his pelvis.

*Is this really happening?* He hoped it was.

Treycore went back to stroking his own girth, rubbing his thumb over its head, massaging the base of his shaft with his pinky. He closed his eyes and tossed his head back. Even his thick, veiny neck muscles aroused Kid.

"Oh, fuck yeah," Treycore moaned.

Kid just wanted to sit on his cock. He wanted to feel Treycore's arms around him, his fingers kneading his flesh, his thumbs torturing his nipples. He wanted Treycore to roll over, trap him beneath him, force his hot breath across his face and curse into his ear.

Unfortunately, Treycore just lay beside him, jerking himself off.

Kid scooted ever-so-slightly closer, attempting to feel Treycore's body heat. Just a little. That was all he needed. He hoped he wouldn't notice the movement, but Treycore's eyes squinted open. He looked to Kid, his blue eyes sparkling, his damp, curling, blond bangs falling over his eyebrows.

"You mind giving me a little help?"

Kid's thoughts scrambled. Did he just ask that? Or was that in his head?

He stared into those blue eyes, waiting to see if something would happen to prove he wasn't serious.

Nothing.

Kid couldn't restrain himself anymore. His mouth dropped onto Treycore's chest, engulfing his pec.

"Oh, fuck yeah!"

Kid's tongue swirled around his tit. His hand slid across Treycore's abs. They felt as hard and solid as he'd imagined they would. He let his fingers delight in every crevice, every sinew. His mind whirled with excitement.

"Ah! Oh!"

A huge load, like whipped cream spraying through the air, spilled across Treycore's abs and chest.

Several drops landed on Kid's abs. They were warm, and they were Treycore's. He continued rubbing his own cock, feeling himself nearing climax.

Treycore smirked. He rolled on his side and positioned his lips beside Kid's ear. "Thanks for the help," he whispered.

As his hot breath hit Kid's earlobe, Kid exploded, shooting like a geyser in an arc that landed in the outlines of his abs.

"Oh, fuck. Fuck, yeah!"

Treycore hopped up, grabbed the bathroom towel, and wiped himself off. He threw it to Kid, who did the same. After returning the towel to the bathroom, he hopped back in bed, turning away from Kid without another word.

*What just happened?*

## CHAPTER SIX

Kinzer kissed his way down Dedrus's stomach.

After their first delicious, frenzied encounter, they'd fucked their way into Dedrus's room. They savored each other for a third time. It was just what Kinzer needed: a good revenge fuck.

Kinzer knew that look in Dedrus's eyes. Dedrus wanted him, and Kinzer took advantage of it. He wanted Dedrus to know what he was missing—to remember the days when they'd fucked like this so often. Even with revenge on his brain, Kinzer hadn't been able to distance himself from the pleasure—those erotic sensations that Dedrus stirred within him. Those sensations had awakened his past with Dedrus, reminding him of the pain of rejection when he'd lost Dedrus forever.

When Dedrus had been sent to work with another troop in Feint, Dedrus had fallen for another higherling, Ryson. Ryson, like Dedrus, had been part of an elite class of the Almighty's higherlings, and so it made sense that they'd wound up together. After all, Kinzer was, and always would be, a laborer. Kinzer wasn't sure how he'd ever convinced himself that Dedrus could love him. Perhaps he'd just wanted to believe that.

Painful as it was for Kinzer, Dedrus's affair with Ryson convinced Kinzer that Dedrus could never love him...not as much as he loved Dedrus.

Kinzer descended onto Dedrus's swelling cock, his tongue swirling, his lips dripping with saliva.

"Oh!" Dedrus cried.

*That's right. This is all you can ever have.*

As much as he still cared for Dedrus, a part of Kinzer wanted him to experience the same pain he'd felt the day he'd found out about Ryson. But Kinzer doubted he could ever cause Dedrus that much pain, because Dedrus could never care for him as much as he'd cared for Dedrus.

BANG!

Kinzer's mouth withdrew. He sat up, alert. "What the—"

Dedrus hopped to his feet and scrambled to a closet. "The front door," he whispered, digging through hanging button-up shirts.

The sword Dedrus had given Kinzer was propped beside the bed. Snatching it by the hilt, Kinzer slid out of bed.

"Go out the window." Kinzer tiptoed to the door. "Get to Maggie's room. See if you can sneak her out."

"What about you?"

"At the least, I'll be a good distraction."

Dedrus unfastened the window.

CREAK!

He slid it open. As he slipped out, he turned back to Kinzer.

"Be careful."

Stepping beside the door, Kinzer nodded. He cracked it open, peering into the hall. Holding his sword in front of him, he stepped into the hall. He glanced over the rail, looking down into Dedrus's living room. Light from a streetlamp out front outlined everything with a soft, orange glow.

Nothing out of the ordinary, and no sign of an intruder.

His cock swung like a pendulum as he made his way down the hall, his focus shifting about, ready for someone to pop out at him.

He came to the door to Maggie's room and pushed it open.

A deep, heavy breathing spilled into the hall. It was the most obnoxious snoring Kinzer thought he'd ever heard come from a mortal. It sounded like a dog growling.

Maggie lay in bed, fast asleep. Dedrus ducked as he slipped through the open window beside her bed.

Kinzer took a moment to appreciate the view of his ass. Dorky as he was, he really did have a nice little body.

Dedrus gave him a thumbs-up.

Kinzer turned the knob and pulled the door shut ever so quietly, starting back down the hall.

As he came to Treycore's room, he noticed the door was already cracked open.

*Fuck.*

He pushed against it. A sword rushed through the crack. Kinzer threw his before him and...

CRASH!

He blocked the oncoming attack.

The door flew open, revealing an equally naked Treycore. His vein-ridden flesh bobbed between his knees.

"Fuck," Kinzer said.

"Did you hear that?" Treycore asked.

"Yeah. Dedrus is taking care of Maggie. I'm about to head downstairs to check it out. Keep outta sight in case I need backup."

"All over it."

"And promise me, if anything happens, you'll protect Kid."

Treycore sighed.

"Just fucking promise me, okay?"

"Okay. I promise. Now get down there and see what's up."

Treycore shut the door, keeping it cracked open, just as it had been when Kinzer had noticed it. Kinzer started down the stairwell, his eyes scanning the shadow-filled living room.

It was quiet.

As he reached the bottom of the stairs, he scanned the bookshelves, the couch, and the table—trying to see if anything had moved or shifted. Everything appeared to be just as messy as it'd been before they'd gone to bed. He peered down the hall to the front door.

A cool breeze rushed against him. The door swayed back and forth.

*Fuck.*

"What is this?" a voice came from behind him.

He spun around, slashing his sword through the air to let the intruder know that he meant business.

"Careful where you point that thing," a dark shadow said as it stepped out from Dedrus's study into the light from the streetlamp. Kinzer recognized the fallen, and he was less than thrilled to see him.

"Hello, Mika."

"Kinzer," Mika said through perfectly arched, m-shaped lips. As he stepped into the living room, his feathers fanned out behind him, moving slightly in the breeze from the front door.

"I'm assuming you didn't come alone," Kinzer said.

A shadow, far more massive than Mika, stepped out from behind his wings.

The seven-foot-tall fallen's flat face and narrow, snake-like eyes were a familiar and unpleasant sight. His name was Craetis, and his existence reminded Kinzer of how sloppy even the best of the Almighty's creations could be.

"Last I saw you," Craetis said, "you were begging us to spare your dearest Janka's life."

His words tossed Kinzer's thoughts to a few days earlier.

*Blood trickled off Janka's square jaw and streaked through the bushy eyebrows that hung above wide, blue eyes. His pupils roamed back and forth, seemingly without direction. His lips, long and full, trembled.*

*Craetis smashed his fist into Janka's face.*

*They were in a warehouse. Overhanging halogen bulbs illuminated boxes and pylons.*

*Cuffs fastened at Kinzer's wrists, connected to chains that wrapped around support beams on either side of him. He was stark naked.*

*"No!" he called out. As he struggled with the chains, the muscles in his back shifted and jiggled.*

*It was clear that the chains weren't going to give.*

*Black feathers rushed from his back. His wings fanned out instinctively, ready to attack.*

*Mika and Deter had grabbed either wing.*

Kinzer struggled to dam the flood of memories. He didn't have time to think on that. He had to be strong, ready for the fight that was certainly about to ensue.

"Where's Veylo?" Kinzer asked.

"He had other errands to run." Craetis stomped up to his sword, seemingly without fear. He stopped just before the tip. "We came for Dedrus and Treycore, but looks like we'll have the added bonus of finishing you off, too."

*Finishing them off?* Kinzer wondered if they knew about Maggie or if they were just here for Treycore and Dedrus.

Mika and Kinzer stared each other down. Mika slipped his hands to his sides and pulled two daggers from holsters strapped at the waist of the black suit pants he wore. The daggers sparkled in the orange glow from the streetlamp. Mika twirled them about. He charged Kinzer.

Kinzer drew his sword back, preparing to strike.

"Now, now, boys," a voice came from behind Kinzer.

Mika stopped and gripped his daggers by their hilts.

Kinzer didn't turn around. He didn't need to. "Vera," he said. "Glad you could make it."

"Me, too. Someone gonna turn on a light?" She must've flipped a light switch, because the lamps around the room illuminated. "Much better. Oh, this place looks like crap."

She stepped around him and joined Craetis and Mika.

Next to the seven-foot Craetis, she was a midget. She had a scrawny frame with long, skinny arms that were concealed beneath a thin layer of black sheer that ran from the wrist-cuffs to the bust-level of the black dress she wore. A chrome belt glistened around her nothing of a waist, matching a diamond-studded collar around her neck. Kinzer knew that every part of her outfit had been meticulously planned, down to the nine-inch heels that, given the chance, she would no doubt use to gouge a higherling's eyes out with.

She stroked her fingers through coal-black hair that fell to her chest, indicating where breasts should have been.

"Are Treycore and Dedrus here?" While Craetis had snake-like eyes, Vera's were like those of a lizard. Her forehead was wide, and her jaw narrow, giving her eyes and features a sort of fun-house mirror effect. Her lizard eyes stared Kinzer down. "Yes. I see they are. You know, Kinzer, we've made quite a few rounds tonight, and we're very tired, so we'd appreciate it if you'd just direct us to their rooms, so we can slit all your throats and move on to our next targets."

*Targets?*

He'd been right. Someone had revealed the whereabouts of all the Leader's Allies.

"Fucking bitch."

Vera smirked.

Kinzer scoffed. "Don't even pretend like you're going to kill your precious Treycore."

Vera and Treycore had been lovers, as all the immortals knew. Kinzer didn't know all the details, but from what he'd heard, it was with great strain that Treycore managed to pull himself from her twisted grip.

Vera's smile transformed into a twitching line. She turned away. "Go ahead and kill him. He's not going to tell us. We'll find them ourselves."

Craetis chuckled. "Can I play with him first?"

"You've done good tonight. Have fun."

Craetis winked at Kinzer and licked the air before him.

Kinzer pulled his sword back and stabbed forward, aiming for Craetis's chest.

Craetis grabbed the blade. The edges slit into his flesh, drawing a rush of blood, before coming to a stop.

Craetis chuckled. "Come on, Kinzer. You don't have your wings, your powers, or your immortal strength. You'd better just lay back and take it. It'll hurt less."

Mika's eyes lit up. Vera started up the stairs.

"Mika!" she snapped.

"I want to watch," he pleaded.

She tossed him a fierce glare.

Sighing, he hopped over the rail and tailed behind her.

Craetis tugged on Kinzer's sword, reeling him in. He wrapped his massive, muscle-bound biceps around Kinzer's chest and pulled him close, pressing his lips against his cheek.

"You know how long I've wanted to fuck you?" Craetis nuzzled his nose against Kinzer's neck.

Kinzer struggled against his grip, but he knew it wasn't going to do him much good. Craetis not only had his immortal strength, but a superior strength to most immortals, as his gift.

With his free hand, Craetis unzipped his jeans, unleashing a veiny, deadly two-foot spear. Kinzer knew that one fuck from Craetis would easily kill, or severely damage, his clipped body. The very thought made his ass cheeks twitch.

Craetis leaned into Kinzer, pressed his mouth next to his ear, and whispered, "Bet Janka never fucked you with one this big. This is gonna be like fucking a mortal, but better."

He pinched Kinzer's nipple.

"Ah!" Kinzer cried.

Craetis chomped at his other nipple, pulling and tugging with his teeth.

Kinzer screamed even louder. It felt like Craetis was going to bite it off.

Craetis's mouth released it. "Fuck yeah," he said. "I like hearing you scream."

He grabbed Kinzer's balls and squeezed.

"Goddammit!" Kinzer pushed Craetis's arm in vain.

"Fuck yeah. Say you like it."

"Go to Heaven!"

Craetis grabbed Kinzer's neck and tightened his grip. "Say you fucking like it!"

"Never!"

"Oh, you dumb bitch." He whirled around and hurled Kinzer by his neck across the room.

Kinzer's back slammed into a bookshelf. He dropped to the floor, a few books and tchotchkes capsizing on top of him. He crawled to a nearby chair at a table and climbed it.

Craetis stomped across the room. He knelt down, grabbed Kinzer by his ankles, and flipped him over his head onto the couch, ass up. He straddled Kinzer. His hard cock rubbed between his cheeks.

"Say it!" Craetis exclaimed.

"No!"

"Then get ready to be ripped apart!"

"No," a voice came from beside him. "You get ready!"

The tip of a sword slashed across Craetis's neck. "Fuck!"

***

Treycore stood beside Kinzer, blood rushing across the end of his sword. He'd changed back into his jeans and button-up—the ones he'd been wearing earlier.

He glared at Craetis, whose sight disguted him.

It reminded of him of his time with Vera—a time he wasn't all that proud of.

When he'd seen Vera and Veylo's goons corner Kinzer, he'd slipped out the window and crept around to the front door. Kinzer, being clipped, wasn't in any shape to take on a single immortal...let alone three.

Craetis's hand rushed to his neck. "You fucking bastard!"

"Long time no see," Treycore said. "Now, get the fuck off Kinzer before I cut that little dick off your nuts."

As much as he was annoyed with Kinzer for how much pain he'd put Dedrus through, he wasn't going to let him get raped and murdered by the fucking Raze.

Growling, Craetis jumped up. He stumbled to the other side of the couch. "You're dead, Treycore," he said, his voice laced with rage.

"Not quite yet. Kinzer, you okay?"

Kinzer nodded. He turned over and massaged his nipple.

"How many others are there?" Treycore asked.

"Fuck off!"

"Hello, my love," Vera said.

She leaned on her elbows against the rail upstairs. A sweet smile spread across her face as she gaped at him.

*Fucking bitch.* Flashes of his time with her, the love, the hope, the betrayal, all raced through his mind. As he looked at the treacherous bitch that he'd been with for so long, he wondered what he'd ever seen in her.

"Come here to kill us, did you?" he asked.

"When else do I get to see you?"

"How'd you find us, cunt?"

"I knew something smelled!" Mika called from upstairs.

Kid, in his striped shirt and jeans, tumbled out of Treycore's room into the upstairs hall. Mika stepped out behind him.

"Who's got the mortal fetish?"

Kinzer looked to Treycore, as if psychically projecting to him, "What did I tell you?!"

*I'm not his fucking babysitter.*

"I've got this," Treycore assured.

"Clearly," Kinzer said.

*When I get you out of this, I'm gonna beat the shit out of you.*

"Vera," Treycore said. "What do you say you and your goons get the fuck out of here before I lose my shit?"

Vera smiled. "That's what I always loved about you, my Treycore. Gumption. You really think you can take on three members of the Raze?"

It was ambitious, but Treycore was confident. He'd taken on more than that during the war, but few were as skilled and trained as the Raze.

"Bring it." He recognized the boldness of his statement. It was three immortals against an immortal, the foulest smelling mortal he'd ever encountered, and the fucking clipped. Not very promising.

Mika headed down the stairs, twirling his daggers at his side. Craetis, still nursing his bleeding neck, stomped around the couch.

Treycore held his sword out in front of him.

"Treycore!" Kinzer called out. "Look out!"

He knew what was up. Because he knew his Vera—a Teleporter who'd sneak up on an immortal like a snake in the grass.

He didn't have time to react. She was at his side in a flash. Clasping her hands together, she rammed them across his face.

He tripped over a side table and fell back.

Before he hit the floor, Vera drove her heel at his face. He maneuvered his sword so her heel ricocheted off it. The momentum threw her at a nearby chair. Grabbing its back, she flipped over it. Treycore bounded at her, sword-first.

She landed on her heels and lifted the chair. Treycore's sword drove through the seat, slicing it in two. One half collapsed to the floor. Vera tossed the other at his face.

\*\*\*

Kinzer had forgotten what impressive fighters Treycore and Vera were. He could only imagine how they used to fuck.

Mika threw himself into their fight, juggling his daggers about. Treycore's swordplay was fast...fast enough that it kept both of Mika's daggers occupied.

Craetis was on his way to join in.

There was no way Treycore would be able to handle all three. Kinzer grabbed a lamp off a side table by the couch and smashed it into Craetis's head. Maybe he couldn't do any serious damage, but he could piss him off enough to distract him.

Craetis shook it off, grabbed Kinzer's wrist, and hurled him across the room.

Kinzer slammed into the edge of a shelf.

*Fuck!*

It felt like his ribcage was about to burst open and spill his immortal intestines across the floor. Craetis continued on toward Treycore.

*Didn't fucking work like I planned*, Kinzer thought, paralyzed on the floor.

Kid popped out of nowhere. He leapt on Craetis's back and wrapped a belt around his neck.

"The fuck?" Craetis asked.

Craetis reached over his shoulder to get a grip on him, but Kid shifted about, evading his stubby fingers while tightening the belt around his neck.

*Kid, what the fuck are you doing?*

Craetis could easily rip him in two. Kid still didn't understand how powerful immortals were, especially one like Craetis.

Vera appeared by the couch. She swooped down, her fingers slipping around the hilt of the sword Dedrus had given Kinzer.

She disappeared. Treycore was going to have to take care of himself. Right then, Kinzer's only concern was Kid.

\*\*\*

Treycore kept up with Mika's daggers. A sword rushed him from the side. He caught a glimpse of Vera.

Another sword came crashing down on hers, effectively deflecting it from its course.

*Fuck, that was close*, Treycore thought.

"Dedrus," Vera said. "So good to see you again."

\*\*\*

Dedrus eyed Vera with contempt. "Not a very fair fight, is it?"

He'd snuck through the front door, having instructed Maggie to slip through the woods behind the house and hide out at the nearby gas station until they were finished handling their current predicament. He had no intention of letting Treycore and Kinzer fight this battle on their own.

"Now it is," Vera said.

She disappeared.

*Oh, here we go*, Dedrus thought, acknowledging how fast his attacks were going to have to be to keep up with Vera's advantageous gift.

As Vera appeared on the opposite side of him, Dedrus whirled around and struck at her.

"So predictable," he mocked. Their swords clashed again.

\*\*\*

Maggie crept through the woods. A chill bit at her exposed arms and cheeks. The dim moonlight sparkled off branches and trunks as she navigated her way through the foliage.

*What am I doing?*

Everything that Kinzer had told her had been insane—the ravings of lunatics.

They had to be. There was no other reasonable explanation. She didn't believe in God. Even if she did, she wouldn't have believed that He was evil.

That was not the God her mom had told her about.

"God doesn't like a girl that throws her legs up," her mom used to say. When Maggie was little, she believed that her mom was talking about cartwheels.

*A hallucination*, Maggie thought. That must've been how she'd seen the wings. She'd hallucinated plenty of times, writhing in the intoxicating sensations of pleasure and dissatisfaction of her most familiar drug of choice. They must've given her some earlier. It was just a big, long, terrible haze that she was going to wake up from. Although, she felt more lucid than ever before. This wasn't like the days where she met Kirk so he could slip her some dick and G. Then things were blurry. Days and nights would pass like moments, like days when, as a child, she'd woken and fallen asleep repeatedly in a night, surprised by the rapid intervals in which time seemed to pass. Despite their brevity, the most vivid of the moments she experienced were those of enchantment, of delight, of magic—those moments that she so desperately reached for. A night in the back of Kirk's car, her body trembling in the cold, could be better than any night she imagined that she could have had anywhere else in the world.

Maggie was very familiar with the hallucinations associated with usage. Sometimes, they contained meaning that linked to her past. Giant snakes, like the ones her mom used to cradle to demonstrate faith, would slither through nearby halls. They'd watch her through mirrors and windows. Sometimes, she could hear the chanting of her mom's tongues in the background. She expected her mom to fall out of a closet, trembling and rambling as she collapsed to the floor.

"Don't give in to the serpent," her mom had said.

Maggie hadn't understood that statement until she let Tommy Rager drive her home from school. He'd shown her the serpent on the side of the road, a few miles from her house. The moment was brief and filled with tears, but she wanted Tommy, so she let him give her rides every day from then on. She knew something was wrong when the bleeding didn't come, and when her mom discovered the reason, she took her to the city to get the abomination removed. Maggie didn't want to get rid of it, though. That wasn't right. She ran off and decided to care for it on her own, but life wasn't so kind to the unwed mother, and she quickly stumbled into obstacles, having to barter with her body in exchange for shelter. A pool of blood among white sheets announced the failure of the pregnancy and birthed a darkness within Maggie that led her down a painful, unrelenting path—desperate to find ease from the sadness she felt about the loss of the baby, her mother, and Tommy.

Some days, when she was being fucked, she'd wished that her mom could see her legs high in the air. Sometimes, she'd work to force them higher. She'd look into her john's eyes, hating him, hating herself. She wondered about their lives, about their families. She wondered what diseases they had, just waiting to spew through a broken condom. Wasn't that what she deserved? That was what mom always said happened to girls who threw their legs up in the air.

When she'd discovered her new pregnancy, she'd wanted to kick the shit. She'd wanted to do the morally responsible thing, as society would have preferred. She just couldn't bring herself to release the habit, and her life was hardly appropriate for nurturing a child. Based on her calculations, which could have been flawed considering her stunted stint with public education, it could have been one of any number of the boys Kirk had lined up for her. And if it was going to grow up as disgusting as any of its potential fathers, what was the point of existing? Rather than quitting the habit, she had hoped that it would expedite her ultimate goal. Her belly continued to grow, bloating to the point where Maggie was of little use to Kirk, who by way of fist, had tried to assist her in releasing the parasite on several occasions. To their disappointment, it hadn't helped. With her first pregnancy, she had seen murder as a disgusting cruelty. Now, she saw that in life.

*Who the fuck are these guys?* she thought as she stumbled through the darkness.

She remembered Kirk introducing her to the two men who'd gone by different names than they called themselves after they'd abducted her. They gave her something they said would elicit an incredible experience—a new drug that would send her into a rapture beyond anything she'd ever experienced before. After attempting this allegedly mystical drug, she'd woken tied to that bed. It wouldn't have been the first time. She'd had a similar experience with two of Kirk's clients who'd gagged her and killed cigarette butts on her breasts for three days before abandoning her in a motel near Taco Cabana. Unlike those clients, these men hadn't fucked her, which led her to assume that their motives were far more sinister. Surely, they got their thrills from watching the eyes of their prey deaden, not from rushes from their own cocks (unless the former resulted in the latter).

The men tied her to that bed and gave her such miniscule doses of her luxury that she thought even with it rushing through her veins, she was going to die. She needed more.

She always needed more. But Kirk never came. Just these two surely sadistic men. What kind of bastards would abduct a pregnant woman and force her to get clean? Regardless of her attempts at understanding their motives, she couldn't. They didn't hurt her, and they supplied her with plenty of food. Had it not been for depriving her of something she felt she needed as much as water, the stay in that dirty little room would have been like cruising through exotic locations. However, considering the torment of her deprivation, it felt far from something so delightful.

*Where the fuck am I supposed to go?*

Cracks harmonized with the crickets and frogs as Maggie stepped on branches and twigs.

She didn't know where she was going or what she was going to do when she got somewhere else. Would this Dedrus guy find her? Did she want him to find her? He had to be insane. All those guys had to be. Didn't they? There was no such thing as God or Satan. There was no such thing as any of this!

A series of white lights glistened through slits in the trees.

Was it the gas station Dedrus had mentioned?

CRACK!

She started to turn.

Something snatched her arm.

\*\*\*

Kid's biceps burned. His face wrinkled with the stress of his efforts. Red hands clasped the black belt around the juggernaut's neck.

*How fucking strong can this guy be?*

The mammoth man threw himself back.

Dry wall exploded around Kid. His arm rammed into a two-by-four.

He screamed out, but he maintained his fierce grip on the belt. It hurt like fuck, but he knew if he let go, he was dead.

"You're a little rodent, aren't ya?" the juggernaut said. Leaning forward, he reared back and slammed Kid's back into the two-by-four again.

"Fuck!"

"Get ready to die, mortal." He leaned forward again.

*I really am going to die*, Kid thought.

As the man started to rear back, a baseball bat rammed into his balls.

He groaned and collapsed onto his chest.

\*\*\*

Kinzer stood before Craetis, a baseball bat in hand. While searching for a weapon to help Kid, he'd managed to find it in a nearby closet.

"Say you like it," Kinzer sneered.

Kid was still on Craetis's back, tightening the belt around his neck.

*Damn*, Kinzer thought, *Kid's a feisty little guy*.

\*\*\*

Dedrus felt like they were back in the war.

Vera disappeared and reappeared all around him, coming and going like camera flashes.

She breathed heavily. Moisture beaded around her lizard eyes. A glistening drop of sweat slid from under black locks of hair that ran down the side of her face.

Dedrus knew that the more she teleported, the less energy she'd have, and the better chance he had at surviving her vicious swordplay.

Treycore and Mika fought just a few feet away, trapped in an endless tit for tat.

"Look at the sweetlips I found trying to get away," a voice said.

A fallen stepped in from the front hall. He was nearly as tall as Craetis, with broad shoulders and eyes that sparkled in the lamplight even more than the other immortal's eyes.

It was Deter, another of the Raze's emissaries.

*Fuck*, Dedrus thought. *Do they know it's the Antichrist?*

"It's a mortal," Deter said. "She was sneaking through the woods out back."

"Let me go, asshole!" Maggie slammed her fist into his chest. She tugged at her arm.

Vera's eyes fixed on Maggie's bloated belly.

*She must know something's up*, Dedrus thought.

Maintaining her duel with him, her eyes shifted from Maggie to Treycore.

Dedrus knew Treycore couldn't bluff. She knew him too well. Any little twitch—any slight shake in his pupils would tell her all she needed to know.

Treycore stared back at her, still exchanging blows with Mika.

Vera's pasty flesh grew a shade whiter. Her eyes returned to Dedrus.

"Well, well," she said as she blocked a slash from his sword. "You boys have been busy, haven't you?"

Deter looked around, confused.

"It's...the Antichrist," Vera hissed, "you dumb shit."

"Holy fuck," he said.

"She's gonna go for her!" Dedrus warned.

\*\*\*

*Gotta get to Maggie before Vera does*, Treycore thought, his sword still in swift battle with Mika's oncoming daggers.

If she got to her first, she'd teleport her to who-knew-where and that would be the end of the Antichrist.

Vera disappeared from before Dedrus and reappeared next to Maggie. She reached out to snatch her.

*Fuck!*

SMACK!

Kinzer had come up beside her and rammed a baseball bat into her face, sending her falling backward.

"Fucking dick!" Deter yelled. He released Maggie and pulled a sword from a sheath affixed to his belt. He rushed Kinzer.

Dedrus leapt over the couch and blocked Deter's sword as they started up their own duel.

*Of course, he'd be there for Kinzer*, Treycore thought. *Fucking doormat.*

Maggie fled across the room, toward the study.

Treycore sliced at Mika's hip. As Mika used both daggers to block the attack, Treycore reared his fist back and decked him. Mika toppled over the couch, rolling across the floor.

Treycore hurried after Maggie.

Vera appeared behind her.

Treycore sliced between Vera and Maggie, but Vera disappeared again, reappearing on the other side of his sword. Treycore snatched her by her scrawny arm, hurled her over his shoulder, and slammed her into the floor.

The sword in her hand broke free and slid across the living room floor.

\*\*\*

Dedrus's peripheral vision worked overtime as he maintained his battle with Deter and kept an eye on the action around the room.

Craetis finally managed to get a grip on Kid's arm. He twisted until Kid caved and released him. Standing back up, he grabbed Kid by his throat and tossed him across the room.

Kid plowed into a table so hard that it snapped in two.

Craetis loosened the belt around his neck and gasped for air.

"Fucking shit," he said. He fondled his balls and turned to Kinzer. "You!"

Dedrus dropped to the floor, scooped up Kinzer's sword, which had slid near him just moments earlier. Keeping up with Deter's attacks, he sliced through Craetis's shin.

Craetis's face flashed red. Veins swelled across his temples. He unleashed a howl that echoed across the walls. As his leg was sliced off, he toppled like Goliath.

Blood oozed across the wood-paneled floor.

Dedrus spotted Mika, who'd been lying listlessly on the floor for some time after Treycore had decked him. Mika stumbled to his feet and headed for Dedrus.

*Just what I need.*

He used Kinzer's sword to defend himself against Mika and continued using his own to defend against Deter.

Craetis cried like a baby as he nursed his bloody stump.

\*\*\*

Kinzer raced into the study.

He was right behind Treycore. Maggie headed toward a window behind the desk.

Vera appeared, midair, her wings outstretched, soaring at her.

"Come here, sweetlips!" she exclaimed.

"Behind you!" Kinzer called. "Don't let her touch you, Maggie!"

Maggie squealed. She ducked and crawled under the desk. Vera landed on top of it as Treycore bounded into the air, swinging his sword violently before him. As the tip of his blade grazed her feathers, she disappeared. Kinzer landed on the desk, his feet dancing about as he struggled to maintain his balance on the stacks of papers and files scattered across it.

As Maggie crawled out the other side of the desk, Vera appeared behind her, covered in sweat, breathing heavily, her eyes savage as she reached for Maggie's leg. Treycore swiped his sword toward the floor, slicing her hand off.

"Ahhhh!" she wailed and vanished.

Hopping off the desk, Treycore knelt to cover Maggie.

\*\*\*

Dedrus's chest vibrated rapidly as he tried to catch his breath. He didn't know how much longer he'd be able to take on Mika and Deter. They continued swapping attacks when he heard, "Boys!"

Vera stood on the stairwell, cradling a bleeding stump. Her hair was drenched with sweat. Her chest trembled as she breathed. She looked like she was about to shake to the floor.

"We've gotta go," she said.

Craetis limped to the stairs.

"Vera, we can do this!" Mika shouted, not taking his eyes of Dedrus.

Red flashed in her eyes. "Now!"

Mika and Deter pulled back. Dedrus halted his attack as they exchanged knowing looks, agreeing to have a peaceful retreat.

"We'll be back," Vera said. A river of blood rushed down her dress, sparkling in the glow of the lamplights. Her wings fanned around Deter, Mika, and Craetis.

They disappeared.

"Godfuckingdammit," Dedrus said.

He ran into the study to join the others. Kid, rising from the two halves of the table, followed after him.

"They know we have the Antichrist!" Dedrus exclaimed.

Treycore wiped sweat from his brow. Kinzer fell back against a bookshelf, his penis sliding across his thigh.

Kid hurried to Maggie and helped her to her feet.

"We need to leave...now." Kinzer approached Dedrus at the door. "Vera could pop in at any second and nab her."

"Naw," Treycore said. "Bitch needs to find herself another hand. And she was already getting too weak. Her moves were slowing down. Probably only has a few teleports left in her."

"And I saved them just for you, sweetlips."

Vera stood between Kid and Maggie, sweat dripping off her arms and chin. She panted, desperately struggling for air. Stretching her arms out, blood spewed from her stump, across Kinzer and Dedrus's faces as she lunged at Maggie.

"Stop her!" Dedrus cried.

Kid pounced on her back and wrapped his arm around her neck. Treycore slipped between Vera and Maggie. Vera's arms wrapped around him, blood spraying across the room. Vera snarled as she, Treycore, and Kid disappeared.

"Fucking cunt!" Dedrus shouted.

"Get her!" Kinzer said, motioning to Maggie. "We're getting the fuck out of here."

\*\*\*

*What the fuck?* Kid thought.

Blue moonlight illuminated a forest with trees nearly twenty times the size any Kid had ever seen. Foliage surrounded him on all sides. The hum of tree frogs came from every direction.

Kid sprang to his feet. The back of his jeans were soaked from the damp ground.

He glanced around worriedly. Was he alone?

"Fuck." Treycore popped up from behind a cluster of ferns.

"Where the fuck are we?"

Treycore studied their surroundings. "A jungle," he said. "Judging by the plant life, I'd say somewhere in South America."

"Who the fuck was that bitch?"

"My ex-girlfriend."

*Ex-girlfriend?* Kid thought. *He totally just jerked off with me.*

"That doesn't explain why the fuck we're in the middle of a fucking jungle."

"That's not what you asked. If you had, I would have told you that her gift is teleportation. She can take us anywhere on earth or between the heavens. It's a rare power. She's one of the few immortals to possess it. While she was teleporting, I managed to sneak us away. That's why we're here."

"You couldn't have gotten us out somewhere closer?"

"It doesn't work like that."

"Well, what are we gonna do now?"

"Listen, Kid," Treycore snapped, "I promised Kinzer I'd protect you, but I'm not your babysitter and—"

"I don't need a fucking babysitter!"

Treycore rolled his eyes. "Whatever. I'm going to look for some wood to make a fire."

He rushed through the foliage, disappearing into the night.

*What have I gotten myself into?* Kid wondered.

## CHAPTER SEVEN

SCREECH!

The car sped around a corner.

*This is insane*, Maggie thought.

She sat in the backseat, her eyes vacillating between Dedrus and Kinzer.

The nauseating scent of pine from a tree air freshener hanging around the rearview mirror filled her nostrils.

She couldn't believe all that she'd just experienced. The wings. The flying. The woman chasing her. It was more disorienting than waking mid-tweak to hot breath, sweaty palms, and an ever-expanding pain deep inside her.

She'd had some bad tweaks, but this was unlike anything she'd ever experienced. Perhaps this was withdrawal. Yes, that was it. Those assholes had kept her from her shit for too long, and now she had to deal with the negative side effects. *Those fucking bastards!*

Her mind was too scattered to process all that had happened. Surely, she didn't need to...since none of it was real.

Who were these guys who were driving her off to who-knew-the-fuck-where?

She eyed a sword that lay beside her, across the seat.

***

Dedrus pressed his foot against the brake.

The car jolted back as it stopped before the two dangling, red-dotted stoplights.

Dedrus and Kinzer bobbed forward with the momentum of the car.

"Can you be a little more careful?" Kinzer barked as he tossed on his blue polo, which he'd grabbed with his other clothes when they'd hurriedly scrambled from the house.

"I'm doing my best!"

CLICK.

*What the fuck?* Kinzer thought. He turned to look behind him. The back door was open.

Maggie was gone.

"Shit!" He unfastened his seat belt.

"What are you doing?" Dedrus asked.

"She's out. I've got to get her."

He lunged out of the car.

The orange glow from the streetlamps lit up the back of Maggie's flower-print dress as she ran for a kudzu-draped wood on the other side of the curb, one hand flailing at her side, the other tucking Dedrus's sword close to her.

"What the fuck are you doing?" Kinzer rapidly approached her. She spun around, holding the sword out before her.

Kinzer stopped and stepped back.

"Get the fuck away from me!" she shouted.

The sword trembled in her frail grip.

"Maggie, what's wrong?"

"What the fuck do you think's wrong? I'm seriously tweaking here!"

"Maggie, we're gonna take care of you. Now, please, just get back in the car."

"No!"

"Maggie, please..."

"Quit saying my fucking name! I don't know you. I don't want to know you. I want you and your friends to take me back to Kirk right fucking now!"

"I can't do that."

His gaze sank to her belly.

She pulled the sword back and pressed it against her stomach.

"Is this what you fucking want? Huh?"

"Maggie!"

"I didn't ask for this! I didn't fucking want this! I can make it all go away."

"Maggie, right now—"

"I said stop saying my name! What are you, a fucking shrink?"

"What's in your belly is the only hope your world has right now."

"This isn't real." She lowered the sword. "It isn't real."

Kinzer stayed back, his arms at his side, signifying that he wasn't going to attack.

"I know you weren't asked to do this. I know it's not fair. But Maggie, if you don't come with us, those guys back there are going to find you and then you're really going to have shit to deal with."

Dedrus stepped behind Kinzer. "Do I need to get some rope?"

"Leave me the fuck alone!" Maggie barked.

"Can you *not* help?" Kinzer shot Dedrus a severe glare.

Tears rushed down her face. She glanced between Kinzer and Dedrus, her eyes wild, frantic.

"This isn't happening," she said. "It can't be."

"Yes, it is," Kinzer said in as calm a voice as he could manage under the circumstances. "It's happening, and we have to get you somewhere safe."

She shook. Dropping the sword, she fell to her knees in a patch of grass and weeds.

Kinzer approached her.

"Why me?" Her face sank. She cringed as if she was in pain.

Kinzer knelt beside her, set his hand on her shoulder.

"I just need to get back to Kirk. He's gonna be so mad. He gets mad when I'm gone too long. He gets real mad. Am I being punished? Why is this happening?"

"I know this might not seem very helpful right now, but what's happening inside you is the most important event in all of creation. We have the power to save your world from the most painful, agonizing apocalypse you can conceive of. We can't do this without you."

She wrapped her arms around him, pulling him close, trembling.

"I didn't want it. I didn't ask for it."

As much as Kinzer wanted to console her, he knew there was little he could do. She was right. She hadn't asked for this burden, and she was a mortal, now caught up in a world that was far beyond her ability to comprehend. It wasn't fair, but it was her lot, and Kinzer could only hope that she was willing to go along with their mission, if only to simplify the heinous ordeal that surely lay ahead.

\*\*\*

*Has he really never found someone else?*

Kinzer sat on a twin bed. Cream floral designs scattered in patches across his beige comforter. He watched Dedrus's ass shake in his khakis as he paced before a painting of engorged purple petals.

Dedrus pressed his cell to his ear, his eyes scanning the room, not noticing the tacky décor.

*Of course, he's found someone. Doesn't even matter if he hasn't. He sure as Hell didn't want me.*

Kinzer assumed he was dramatizing his loneliness, just as he had dramatized his love for him so long ago. He dismissed these thoughts. Now wasn't the time to dwell on the past. They had far more serious problems.

Maggie had showered off and lay in another twin bed on the other side of a nightstand. Her dirty-blonde locks, stringy and splitting, draped over her neck and crept across the pillow. She stared blankly at the TV as muffled voices spewed from the speaker.

"Shit," Dedrus said. He pulled his phone from his ear, eyeing it.

"Nothing?" Kinzer asked.

Dedrus shook his head and put the phone back against his ear. "Hey, Fie. This is Dedrus again. Call me back if you get a chance."

Since they'd arrived at the motel, Dedrus had been trying to get ahold of some of the Leader's Allies.

He wasn't having any luck.

"Hopefully, someone's warned them." Dedrus pushed the phone into his pocket. He brushed his fingers through his tousled locks.

"That sounds optimistic." Especially considering Vera had mentioned that they'd been hunting the Leader's Allies earlier that night.

"I'm gonna take a shower." Dedrus stepped into the white light of the adjoining bathroom, shutting the door most of the way, but leaving it cracked open slightly.

Dedrus was stressed, and Kinzer wanted nothing more than to bring him some ease. Dedrus had been there for him, now was his chance to return the favor. Or was he still trying to punish him?

No. Not that. Even as he'd revenge-fucked him, he was still enjoying himself, and as much as he didn't want to admit it, he still had strong feelings for the higherling. Maybe there was something more there. They had always had fun together. He loved talking to him, playing with him, fucking him.

*No!* Dedrus didn't want him. They'd already established that. He had to shake that from his thoughts.

He chastised himself for his stupidity and for even considering anything with Dedrus when he was still mourning the loss of Janka. He shouldn't have been thinking like that. If anything, he should have just been having fun. But was it dangerous to enjoy his time with Dedrus? Did he run the risk of falling in love with him all over again?

That couldn't happen. If there had been a time where Dedrus could have loved him, it had passed. Now, they were just friends—fuck buddies. Kinzer just had to make sure that he always remembered that.

*I can do this. I can handle it.*

He stripped to his boxers and slipped into the bathroom. A hiss came from behind a white shower curtain, framed by gray walls. He closed the door, slipped next to the curtain, and wiggled out of his boxers. As he pulled the curtain open, its metal hooks rattled together.

Dedrus's hair lay flat against his scalp—wet, milk-chocolate locks curling into his neck. He scrubbed a white washcloth in circles over his nipples. His brown eyes met Kinzer's. They were the same eyes that he had come to love, to adore. His hairy face, damp and sparkling under the room's fluorescent light, shifted with a smile, like he was so happy that Kinzer had decided to join him.

Kinzer stepped into the tub and closed the curtain behind him.

"It's a little cold," Dedrus warned as he stepped back under the showerhead, facing away from Kinzer. He ducked his head, letting the water splatter across his scalp and shoulders.

He stroked the washcloth up and down his arm, building a creamy layer of suds.

Kinzer felt drops of the cool water prick at his flesh.

"Will you get my back?" Dedrus tossed a glance back.

"Yeah." Kinzer reached around, taking the washcloth from him. He rubbed it against his palm, letting the suds stir before rubbing circles between his friend's shoulder blades.

*A friend. That's all he is. A friend. Why does that make me sad?*

He pushed the thought away, pressing the washcloth tighter against Dedrus's flesh—that smooth, soft flesh.

He couldn't bear it anymore. Kinzer dropped the washcloth, threw his arms around Dedrus, and buried his face behind his ear. The chilled water raced down his torso, flowing over his fresh erection that tapped against Dedrus's ass cheeks.

The water didn't faze him. He kissed Dedrus's neck.

Dedrus threw his head back, resting it on Kinzer's shoulder. Kinzer glanced at a shelf that hung in the middle of the wall. A bar of soap lay across it. He grabbed it, lathering it in his palm to create moisture for lube.

He stopped. Dedrus didn't deserve that consideration. Not after what he'd done to him.

He dropped the bar. It slid across the bottom of the tub, ending up beside the chrome-lined drain.

He spit in his palm and massaged the fluid across his shaft.

Grabbing Dedrus by his hair, he shoved his face forward and pressed it against the plastic lining of the shower-tub combo. Dedrus's ass lifted. His pelvis dipped. Kinzer knew he wanted it bad. Like he always did. He pressed his shaft's head into his hole. He figured Dedrus would be a little loose from their earlier encounter.

It was still a rough entry and burned the edges of his shaft.

*Fuck.*

Dedrus groaned. It took a few thrusts before Kinzer was comfortably inside him, reeling in the pleasure from Dedrus's tight hole. Dedrus's groans amplified.

Kinzer pulled out. He grabbed Dedrus's hips and flipped him so his shoulders hit the adjoining walls in the corner of the tub. Wrapping his arms around Dedrus's hips, he cupped his hands under his ass cheeks and hoisted him into the air.

The weight threw Kinzer off balance for a moment. He worked to stabilize, kicking his foot to the side. It came down on the bar of soap by the drain, which slipped out from under his heel, sending his foot flying forward.

"Oh, shit!"

Thinking quickly, he shifted on his other heel so his shoulder blade rammed into the wall beside him. His body shook and jerked as he adjusted his feet so he wouldn't fall.

Dedrus gasped. He glanced around like he was waiting for Kinzer to drop him. "Holy shit!"

Kinzer regained his balance. He giggled. "Whoops," he said. "Close call."

Dedrus chuckled, his hand quickly covering his mouth, as if he was embarrassed to be so amused by the situation.

*He's so cute, so precious.*

Kinzer wanted him so badly. He shifted and leaned Dedrus's back against the corner of the tub, finagling his dick back inside him. Dedrus let out another chuckle before grinding his teeth. His head rolled back. His eyes shut.

"Oh fuck! Kinzer, yes! Fuck yes!"

Kinzer rocked his hips, pleasuring his cock in the tight passage of Dedrus's hole.

"You feel so fucking good!" Dedrus's eyelids sealed shut. He cried out. His arms pressed against the walls like he was using them to brace himself.

Water splashed about as Kinzer continued driving in. Dedrus moaned with pleasure as his hair stuck against the walls behind him.

The water, rushing across Kinzer's side, warmed against his flesh.

Dedrus's eyes opened. He looked right at Kinzer.

*Why is he looking at me like that?*

The look in his eyes was like the one Kinzer had once mistaken for love. He fought against the painful memories.

*He didn't really want you*, he reminded himself as he forced another deep penetration into Dedrus.

Dedrus screamed out, but didn't shift his gaze.

*Stop looking at me like that!*

Kinzer plowed him a few more times, hoping to force him to look elsewhere.

Dedrus cried out louder, but his eyes stayed fixed on him. That was it. He couldn't handle it. Kinzer pulled his cock out and lowered Dedrus to the floor.

"What is it?" Dedrus's eyebrows shot up on his forehead.

"Nothing. I just can't do this." Kinzer stumbled through the curtain. He grabbed a towel off a metal rack and dashed through the door.

"Kinzer, I—"

"Where'd she go?"

A black Bible, surely the motel's, poked out from the folds of Maggie's sheets.

"Holy shit," Dedrus said.

Kinzer's jeans lay on the other bed, but he knew he had left them on the floor.

He snatched them off the comforter and rifled through the pockets. "Bitch took my wallet." He pressed his fingers against his water-glazed hip and tossed Dedrus an exhausted glare. "Better start looking."

It didn't take long to find her.

Shops were clustered together on the other side of the street. The only one open was a bar. Through the glass windows, Kinzer could see the back of Maggie's flower print dress as he and Dedrus walked side by side through the parking lot.

"Let's just hog-tie the bitch," Dedrus grumbled. Strands of wet hair stuck to his face. Patches of water were scattered across his shirt.

Kinzer put his hand out, halting him. "Hey, just head back to the room. I got this."

"You sure?"

"Yeah."

He kissed Dedrus. Dedrus's fingertips caressed his shoulder, then he turned around and headed back to the motel. Kinzer approached the glass door to the bar and stepped inside.

A haze of smoke filled the air. Three men in denim and flannel lounged in a corner booth. In front of a bar on the opposite wall, Maggie twisted back and forth, the flower print across her ass stroking against a black stool. She sipped from a glass and gazed longingly at the Miller Light bottle a guy in a baseball cap tossed back a few stools to her side.

*Seriously?*

Kinzer approached Maggie's stool. "Where the fuck did you think you were going?"

"Give me a break. I wasn't running."

Ice clinked against the glass of clear fluid that trembled in her grip.

Kinzer snatched it.

"Hey, hey!"

He ran his nose across the rim.

"It's Sprite, dumbass."

"This guy bothering you?" A bartender in a tank top set his palms on the counter. Freckles dotted his face. A red beard fell to just below his shirt collar. He leaned forward, pressing down to demonstrate his muscular physique.

This was Maggie's chance to get away, to get help. Was she going to take it?

Her lips curled upward, and then fell into a frown. "I'm fine."

She took another sip from her rattling glass.

The bartender's green eyes watched Kinzer suspiciously. He withdrew to the other side of the bar.

"Where the fuck's my wallet?" Kinzer asked.

Maggie reached into her cleavage, pulled it out, and set it next to a jagged crack in the top of the gray-and-black-speckled granite bar.

"Why didn't you just stay in the room?" he asked.

He sat in the stool beside her as she set her glass next to the wallet.

"Wasn't really interested in sticking around to hear you fucking in the shower."

"Sorry."

"I'm not one to keep anybody from having a good time. Just didn't want to hear it. So what's with you and that guy? Boyfriends?"

Kinzer rested his elbow on the bar. "I don't want to talk about it."

"Yeah. 'Cause I'm sure that's a bigger deal than all the other shit we've been talking about."

The guy with the Miller Light took another sip from his bottle. Maggie's tongue massaged her bottom lip. She leaned close to Kinzer. "You mind ordering me a beer?" she whispered.

"What?"

"A pregnant girl can have like three glasses of wine a day, so I think I can have a beer."

"You're full of shit."

"Something like that. Jesus was all about the wine, right? Just get me a damn beer. No one else will."

He looked to the curve of her belly. "I can't imagine why."

"Shut the fuck up. What right does anyone have to decide what I shouldn't do? I'm sorry that I need something to take the edge off. You don't think I deserve that with the night I've had? The shit I saw? The shit you told me?"

It was a lot for any mortal to take in, especially one that was tasked with something so important, but Kinzer still wasn't going to let her poison Earth's future salvation.

"I get it," he said. "It's rough, but I'm not getting you a drink."

"A cigarette?"

He shook his head.

Maggie's plush lips pursed. "I hate you." She scratched her fingernail into the crack in the bar. "Shitty fucking night."

"Amen."

She snickered. "You guys have really done a number on me. You know, you need to find a better way of telling people about that God and Satan shit. Some of us got a lot of baggage about that."

She and Kid were the only ones he planned on ever explaining the details to, so he didn't really need to get better at it.

"Know anything about Pentecostals?"

*What?*

"Pentecostal? Religion? Churches? Yes? No? Did you stop understanding English?"

"You expect me to remember one religion? Maggie, I've been around since the dawn of creation."

"What, are you bragging? Chill the fuck out. I'm Pentecostal. Well, no. I'm not Pentecostal. I was raised one. We do this thing. Speak in tongues. Know what that is? It's where the Holy Spirit…or God…speaks through you. People shake, shout out inarticulate nonsense. Mom was always good at it. She'd drop faster than any of them."

She pressed the glass to her lips and took a drink.

"When you're little, that kind of shit makes sense. I guess it makes sense to adults, too. Everyone loved it. Loved her. She would do it all the time, and she was convincing. I mean, some people do it, and it looks like an act. Like they just want attention. Others, you're like, something's going on there. My mom was one of those where it really looked like something was going on. When it happened, she wasn't my mom. She was speaking for something else—something bigger, more powerful. I'm not saying I bought it. I'm just saying how it looked, okay?"

Something about the way she said that last part made Kinzer think that she had bought it.

"I used to fall down, too. I'd work up a fit. Copy her. I wasn't very believable. At least, I didn't think so. I never felt the Holy Spirit. But I prayed. I prayed, and I prayed, and I prayed, because she told me that's all I needed to do. Never felt anything, but I just kept praying anyway. I thought, He'll come. He'll let me know He's there. Bible was filled with stories about people He'd spoken through—stories about people who'd witnessed His power. I wanted to be one of them. I believed in them. Hell, my mom did it, so it had to be true, right? And she would have been so proud. I remember thinking, 'If I could just walk on water, she'd be so happy. She'd really love me.'

"Walk on water. Did that even happen? Don't answer that. Don't ruin Jesus for me. Anyway, one time I fell down in church, and I was doing what I normally did—what everyone else did. Shaking. Tossing my head around. Arching my back. You pretty much just make it look like a seizure. Mom snatched me by the arm, yanked me up, and said, 'No one likes a fake.' Oh, I could have died. And I knew I'd never be able to fool her, and she'd never be okay with her unrighteous daughter. This empty thing that God wanted no part of."

"She sounds like a nut job," Kinzer said.

"Maybe. Just funny now. To think what she'd say if I told her I was having the devil's baby. That'd send her over the edge. Probably even make sense to her. Her daughter, who was so incapable of feeling the Holy Spirit, would totally be the mother of the Antichrist."

Kinzer glanced around nervously. "Can you keep it down?"

Her eyebrows pulled close together. "Are you kidding? Hey everyone, I'm the mother of the Antichrist!"

"Shut up, bitch!" one of the flannel and denim guys shouted from the corner booth.

"You wanna die, asshole?" she replied. "Listen, Kinz-ar, or whatever, no one believes any of the bullshit you're talking about. I could hold up a sign on the side of the road and spit on and on about this crap and no one would give any fucks. You think you're the first person to start talking about God and Satan being up to something?"

She had a good point, but there still wasn't any reason to be making a scene.

"What am I supposed to think about this?" she asked. "My mind isn't even letting me think about it. I think it's some sort of defense mechanism to keep me from losing my shit. Doesn't feel real. That doesn't mean much. Some things just don't. Had a lot of things happen that never felt real. Keep telling myself that it's just a hallucination...or a dream. But it's not."

She took another sip of her drink.

"So why don't you want to talk about your boyfriend? What's that about?"

"It's complicated."

"Unlike everything else?"

Kinzer didn't respond.

Maggie whirled her finger around the rim of her glass.

She giggled. "Mom really was full of crap, wasn't she?" A sad look in her eyes made her seem as if she was a kid that had just discovered Santa wasn't real. "So what happens?" she asked.

"Huh?"

"This kid? What happens to it?" Her voice had lost its harshness. It was soft, soothing to Kinzer's ears.

"We take care of it."

"We as in…"

"The Leader's Allies."

"You gonna take my kid from me?" She stroked a hand against her stomach.

Kinzer hadn't really thought any of this through. Everything was happening so fast. Too fast. He didn't know how the Leader would want to handle the Antichrist or if he'd want Maggie to be involved in its life.

"Did you want to be a part of its life?"

Maggie's gaze drifted behind the bar, settling on a poster of a pinup girl stretching across a motorcycle.

"No. I'm not a fucking mother. Probably be shitty at it anyway. I got my own life to live."

"What life is that?"

"You got a problem with me?"

"It was just a question."

"A life where I get to do what I want. Live how I want. You can't do whatever you want when a kid's involved. It's all about the kid. At least, that's the way it should be." Her gaze sank to her belly. "I had a boyfriend…" She teared up. "…well, I called him a boyfriend. He used to say, 'Life's not worth living if you ain't feeling good.' He was an asshole, but I agree. You find the things in this world that give you something—that make you feel the way you want to feel, and you gotta hold on to them. You don't ever let them go. They're what'll keep you strong. They're what'll keep you wanting to live another day. Can't do that with a kid. They need you. Depend on you. It's all about them. Well, I think so."

"Lessons from an addict?"

"Lessons from someone that's lived life."

"Well, Maggie, I've lived a long one, and I gotta say, that doesn't seem like a way to live. That seems like a way to die."

"Well, that's what I've got. I can feel pleasure. That's real. That's mine. Isn't that what Hell's all about anyway?"

"No. Like I said—"

"Right. All that shit about how it's the reverse of what I think. Whatever. So you demons are all a bunch of prudes? Well, that *fucking* didn't sound all that prudish."

She wore a scornful expression, like the one she'd had when he'd first seen her back at Dedrus and Treycore's. Kinzer knew there was no point in arguing. Not while she was like this. She'd been through a lot. She just needed to adjust to all the news that she'd been bombarded with.

She turned toward the other side of the bar so Kinzer only had a view of ratty waves of dirty-blonde hair.

"Don't you fucking judge me," Maggie said. "I'm okay with a lot of things, but a hypocrite isn't one of them."

\*\*\*

*Feels like a fucking sauna*, Kid thought. He stumbled through the thick, humid air.

Sweat created a rim around his shirt collar. The sun burned against the back of his neck. Treycore didn't appear to be nearly as affected by the climate. Kid presumed this was a benefit of being an immortal.

He and Treycore had been walking through the jungle since dawn. Now midday, it was becoming unbearable.

Kid was already on edge. What little sleep he'd managed to get the night before had been laced with nightmares—flashes of his time at Jerry's. He was tending to clients. He was being ravaged by them. Then there was Daddy. His fingers wrapped around Kid's throat. His belt slapped against Kid's ass. His dick invaded his hole. Kid, just a child, screamed out, begging him to stop.

As Kid had roused from the hellacious sleep, he'd felt that even though he would never have to live like that again, it still would always be a part of him. It would haunt him until the day he died.

Black gnats danced around Treycore as he slapped a stick against a branch in his path. One flew at Kid, landing in a layer of sweat that steadily thickened on his forehead. Its wings were bound to the sticky moisture. As it struggled to get free, Kid brushed his fingers over it, unthinkingly smashing it into his skin. He flicked its remains to the black soil at his feet.

*How long are we gonna keep walking? We've been doing this for hours.*

A question stirred in Kid's mind. For a while, he'd been worried that it would sound moronic. At this point, he didn't care. He'd been walking through the stupid jungle for too long already.

"Can't you just fly us out of here or use your power to—"

Treycore tossed a harsh gaze back. The tension in his jaw and the furrow of his brow made Kid feel like he'd insulted his dead mother.

Treycore's lips opened, but closed just as quickly. He turned and pushed a frond out of his path. "No," he said curtly.

*Touchy subject.*

"What's the point of having wings," Kid began, "if you can't fucking use them? Your ex-bitch can fly."

"I don't want to talk about this," Treycore said. "I can't fly, so just leave it alone."

*Why are you so fucking mad at me?* Kid thought. *I'm not the one who dated the psycho who put us out here!*

Kid was pissed. Treycore was being so dismissive, as if just because he was mortal, he didn't matter. He'd already been made to feel that way by too many people, and he was tired of it.

"Must be pretty useless if it can't even get us out of here," Kid muttered.

Treycore stopped again. He turned around. His wincing eyes narrowed even further. He was giving a look that made Kid think that he was about to leap on top of him and pound into his face.

"Kid," he said, "you should just stop talking, because in a second, I'm gonna make you."

Kid rushed him and stood tall, pushing his chest out.

"Come on." He knew that Treycore's impressive physique, combined with his immortal strength, could easily overpower him, but he wasn't going to let Treycore get what he wanted with threats and a pissy attitude.

Treycore stepped toward him. Kid didn't budge.

"We don't have time for this," Treycore said. "We need to get back to Kinzer, so just follow me and keep the fuck out of the way." He turned back around and started back through the foliage.

"You don't have a power or something like that disappearing girl?"

"No," Treycore snarled.

"So, what I'm hearing is that you're like the most useless angel...or higherling...or whatever-the-fuck...in the world."

Treycore threw his stick into nearby shrubbery. He charged Kid. Grabbing him by the arm, Treycore twisted Kid around and shoved him against a tree.

"Mortal," he hissed into Kid's ear. "I'm not in the mood."

"And I'm not your slave." Kid didn't show anger. He was matter-of-fact. Treycore could condescend all he wanted, but Kid didn't have to sit back and take it. Not anymore. He wasn't going to feign shame and humility just because that was how Treycore preferred it.

Treycore flipped Kid around and pressed his shoulder blades against the tree. His grip was severe. Kid wondered if he was intending to cause him that much pain or if, in his frustration, he had forgotten his own strength.

"Who do you think you are?" Treycore asked, staring into Kid's eyes.

Kid felt as if he was trying to tear his soul out with his rage.

"You're nothing! I carry divine authority. You're lower than the lowest fallen. I'm older than the earth. The trees in this jungle are older than you. I can live forever. You have to die. Have you seen me? Have you seen my body's perfection? That's my birthright. Compare that to your disgusting figure, covered in the imperfections of mortality. The scars of your pathetic, disgusting life."

Kid imagined how he looked in the mirror. The welts, the dents in his flesh, many of which were a product of his time at Jerry's.

"Oh, and you smell!" Treycore continued. He grimaced, as if just being this close to Kid was unbearable. "I wish you knew how fucking bad you smelled. Any immortal can smell you coming from miles away. It'd be like if you had to wander the jungle with a pile of shit. And I think that'd still smell better than you do to me."

A tear formed in Kid's eye, but he wasn't going to show weakness.

"You're not even very attractive. I can't imagine how it feels to be lowly, even for a mortal."

"Feels pretty good." Kid struggled to keep his voice from cracking. He held eye contact with Treycore. If he avoided his gaze, Treycore would know that he'd won. But the more he looked into Treycore's eyes, the more he imagined his immortal senses could detect his vulnerability, his hurt. Was Treycore fueling his inner terror so he could stand there and take pleasure in his misery? The longer Treycore stared into his eyes, the more Kid hated him. He didn't just hate him, he despised him. How could some supposedly angelic being be so cruel, so brutal, so uncaring?

Treycore's anger—intense, severe, and filled with fury—came at Kid.

Kid's fists popped up. He pressed his back against the tree and pushed off, projecting himself toward Treycore. He knew he couldn't win in a fight against an immortal, especially one filled with such unquestionable contempt for him, but he wasn't going to lie limp and take it. He'd already had too much of that.

He launched a fist at Treycore's cheek.

Treycore snatched it. Kid threw his other fist, but Treycore snatched that one too. He shoved Kid back against the tree, lifted his arms into the air, and pinned them against the bark.

Kid struggled, but Treycore was too strong. Sweat rushed down Kid's forehead.

The tear in his eye slid down his cheek. Kid was embarrassed. Now Treycore knew that he was getting to him.

Treycore pressed his lips against Kid's, stirring a surge of heat that combatted the heat of his fury and rage.

Kid's mind told him to attack, but all he could do was kiss Treycore back. Treycore's hot breath rushed across Kid's upper lip and tickled the tip of his nose.

*No,* Kid thought. *I don't want to fuck you. You're an asshole! I hate you!*

But as much hate as he felt for Treycore, he couldn't stifle the inexplicable sexual pull that made him want to be fucked by this beautiful creation. His penis filled, expanding rapidly. Treycore's monstrous bulge stroked against the jean barrier between them. Their lips opened wider. They pressed their lips closer together.

Treycore nibbled on Kid's bottom lip. It was painful—so painful that Kid thought it would bleed.

He wished it hurt more.

He moaned.

Treycore released Kid's wrists. He wrapped his arms around him, pulling him into a tight embrace. Attempting to gain some control over the kisses, Kid set his hand on Treycore's cheeks, caressing his thumb against the tiniest of bristles.

Treycore's lips retreated. His nose slid along Kid's cheek. Moisture and breath mixed across Kid's earlobe as Treycore's tongue assaulted it.

Kid rolled his head back, slamming it against the tree. A rush of pain ran from the point of impact to his upper back. It was intense, almost immobilizing. It wasn't the sort of pain he desperately wanted Treycore to force on him, but he wasn't going to allow it to separate him from the passion of this moment. He wanted Treycore. He *needed* him.

Treycore left Kid's ear and offered intense kisses down his neck. Biting, sucking, licking. He pressed his pelvis against Kid's, squashing him against the tree.

Kid ground his teeth. The combination of the pain from his ass being smashed into the hard surface and the immortal pressure that was crushing his pelvis—making his penis feel like it was a nearly bursting balloon—was brutal. He released Treycore's face and balled his hands into fists. He could endure the pain. He'd done it plenty of times before. And this was a pain he wanted...a pain he ached for. It stirred a rush of electricity that ran from his hips to his chest, exciting him.

Treycore slid his hands under the back of Kid's T-shirt. He stroked up and down, digging his fingers into his flesh. The pressure was so intense that it rubbed Kid's skin raw. Kid rolled his head against the bark and groaned through clenched teeth.

Treycore pulled one hand back out from under Kid's shirt. He snatched Kid's neck, stifling his breath. It snapped Kid out of his pleasure.

His eyes flashed to a red-faced, jaw-clenched Treycore. What was happening? Had he done something wrong? Was Treycore mad at him?

Treycore's lips covered his.

Kid's face turned scarlet. As much as his body urged him to breathe, there was something so erotic about Treycore controlling his breath, his life, and he didn't want it to end.

Treycore gripped even tighter around his neck. Now, Kid couldn't breathe at all. He felt light-headed. If Treycore maintained his grip, he was going to pass out. Spots danced around the jungle and Treycore's head as Kid felt his consciousness steadily slipping away.

The spots grew larger and darker.

Treycore released his grip.

Kid instinctively pulled away from Treycore's lips, gasping for air.

Treycore's fingers wrapped around the back of his head and pulled him back into their embrace.

Kid pulled away. He didn't have a choice. His instincts wouldn't allow him to put himself in danger again, even though he wanted it so desperately.

Treycore maintained his control, keeping his lips right before Kid's as he sniffed. Kid felt disgusting. He knew he smelled foul to higherlings.

As Treycore's lips returned to his, that thought vanished. This time, Treycore's kiss was soft. It was a relief to Kid's lips, which were starting to feel numb from the intensity of Treycore's previous oral assaults.

Heat and pressure built in Kid's chest. His penis was hard...painfully hard. It felt like he'd been blue-balling for months and needed relief.

They stroked their pelvises against each other. The stimulation only made the sensation even more unbearable. His body, in an attempt to save him from pain and torture, urged him to escape, prodding him to the side.

His heel hit a root stretching out from the bottom of the tree trunk. He fell back. The tail of his spine slammed against a pointed rock.

He shouted. Another surge of pain. Not the sort he craved from Treycore. Just wildly uncomfortable.

He wasn't going to let it interfere with this moment. He unfastened his belt and wiggled his still-buttoned jeans and boxers down to his heels, exposing his fully erect penis, the skin taut against his muscle. Kicking his shoes off, he collected the clothes together in a pile beside him.

Treycore pounced on top of him. They kissed and rolled across the jungle floor. Rocks and branches stabbed into Kid's ass, sides, and shoulder blades. In an effort to lessen the discomfort, he dug his fingers into Treycore's back.

Treycore straddled Kid's pelvis. He ripped Kid's t-shirt off over his head.

He grimaced down at Kid's pecs and abs, his gaze lingering on the cuts and scars that tainted the mortal's otherwise perfect flesh.

Kid was ashamed of them. He didn't want Treycore to see those vulnerabilities. In an effort to distract Treycore's attention, he forced another kiss on him.

Treycore lifted his pelvis off Kid, grabbed his hips, and flipped him onto his stomach. He stroked Kid's ass crack with the bulge in his jeans. Kid pressed his butt into Treycore's pelvis, feeling that absurdly large bulge. He remembered how big it was. It was going to be far too much for him to handle. Kinzer wasn't nearly as big as Treycore and that had seemed nearly impossible.

Still, he wanted it inside him.

"Please..." Kid begged. His body ached with hunger—hunger for Treycore's torture.

Treycore grabbed Kid's hair, covered with sweat. He intertwined his fingers in the locks and yanked back.

The sting in Kid's scalp sent a jolt of excitement racing down his back.

Treycore put his mouth against Kid's ear. His breath rushed just behind Kid's lobe, reminding Kid of their first sexual encounter. "The more you scream, the more it's gonna hurt." Treycore didn't sound angry like he had when he was yelling at Kid. He sounded playful, teasing.

A swirl of desire stirred in Kid's chest. Kid didn't figure Treycore would deliberately give him a serious injury, but he was worried that Treycore would underestimate his own power or overestimate Kid's.

It was a risk he was willing to take.

Treycore unzipped his jeans.

Kid gulped.

Treycore rolled off him. "Get over here and suck on me," he said, lying beside him.

When Kid realized that he wasn't going to have to immediately take Treycore's immortal cock up the ass, he was relieved. He wanted to hurt. Not to die.

Treycore undid the top button on his jeans and slipped them and his briefs halfway down his thighs.

That desire in Kid's chest stopped. Even time seemed to stop as he stared at Treycore's massive girth. Kinzer's had been large for a human. It was bigger than anything he'd ever had to take, even when he was forced to fuck for Jerry. But it could still reasonably fit in his ass without making him worry that it might tear into major organs.

Treycore's had to be at least fifteen inches, but the length wasn't what intimidated Kid. It was so wide around that he figured he couldn't even get one hand all the way around its circumference. And although Treycore's mushroom-shaped head suggested that there would be some subtle help in adjusting to the massive shaft, there was no way it would be able to get inside Kid without some serious effort. Even the idea of *sucking* on it seemed like an exhausting challenge.

Treycore stroked his cock with one hand. His longest finger wrapped around a little over half of its girth. Kid got on his knees and crawled to him. Treycore's fine, blond locks spread across the black soil as he pleasured himself with his hand.

Kid ran his tongue along the rim of Treycore's cock's head, slowly, carefully. His stomach knotted anxiously as his concern about taking that monstrous cock in hixs mouth intensified.

A translucent droplet formed at the tip of Treycore's penis. Kid sucked it and swallowed. He slid his lips over the head, rocking back and forth. He was trying to gauge how easy it was going to be for him to get this bit in his mouth at least. The first quarter of the head was reasonable, and the sides were like slides, welcoming Kid's lips farther along. After that, he had to open his mouth as wide as possible to shove the engorged edges of the tip in. He folded his lips over his teeth. His nervousness about teeth intensified. He didn't want to hurt Treycore. He didn't want to do anything that would make him want to stop. He set his worry aside as he followed the edges of the tip with the first bit of the shaft. He licked around the head, swirling broadly, exhausting his tongue as it collected a thick film of pre-come. He massaged the head of Treycore's penis with his lips, moving up and down, up and down. In moments where he was back at the narrower part of the head, he gulped Treycore's pre-come and continued to slide his lips along the engorged edges of the head of his cock.

"Oh!" Treycore groaned.

Kid gripped both hands around Treycore's shaft and synced his lips and his hands in a broad, continuous, stroking motion. A thick, heavy load of pre-come spewed from the tip of Treycore's dick. Kid sucked it in and pulled his head back, swallowing the treat and licking his lips.

Treycore tossed Kid a satisfied glare. Kid had only seen the foul, unpleasant, condescending side of Treycore. This side was frisky, playful, and fun. He liked it.

Kid lowered his head to Treycore's balls and licked between his nuts. The hairs lining the flesh of his sac were coarse and scraped against his tongue.

It didn't stop Kid. He assaulted Treycore's testicles, licking desperately at the blond-covered sac.

He pumped Treycore's cock with his hands, eyeing a blue web of veins just beneath the flesh of his balls. He licked along one and followed it to another, using it for navigation until he came to the edge of his sack. His mouth moved to the flesh under Treycore's testicles. He kissed it lightly, then pressed his lips firmly against the skin and sucked as hard as he could.

He released Treycore's cock and wrapped his arms under Treycore's legs so he could press his lips even tighter into his flesh. A fit of passion rushed through Kid's body, and he impulsively pulled away from Treycore's balls and threw himself on top of him. Their mouths locked, and Kid slipped his tongue past Treycore's lips. Treycore ran a hand up Kid's back, feeling with his finger along his spine. Kid slipped a hand under Treycore's button-up. Treycore had those wonderful abs! Kid hadn't thought he could get any stiffer, but the moment he felt those abs, his cock grew painfully harder. He broke his passionate kiss with Treycore to catch a breath.

Treycore wrapped his free hand around Kid's neck and pulled him back into an embrace. Kid tried to pull back, struggling to breathe, but Treycore pressed kisses against Kid's lips. He ran his thumb along Kid's cheek. His other hand continued stroking his back. Treycore's finger pressed against where Kid's spine had hit the rock. Kid whimpered like a fox with its leg caught in a trap. He twitched. His body attempted to convulse away from Treycore. Treycore gripped even tighter to Kid, his fingers digging into the spot that had stirred the reaction.

A rush of pain ripped through Kid, like shards of glass stabbing into his back. He balled up his hand and slammed it into Treycore's cheek. Treycore's face inched to the side. He clenched his jaw and grabbed Kid by the throat, staring him down. Kid's face flushed. He wanted to explain what had happened—that he had just been so overwhelmed with pain and acted instinctively. What was Treycore going to do to him now? He could effortlessly snap his neck if he wanted to. Or worse, he would just end this pleasurable experience.

Kid's eyes filled with fear. Sweat poured off his forehead and ran down his cheeks.

Treycore pulled Kid down so their faces were millimeters apart. Treycore's jaw relaxed. He moved his face closer to Kid's and brushed their lips together. He didn't kiss him, though. To Kid, it seemed as if Treycore was testing him to know if Kid wanted to continue. If Kid kissed him back, he would accept that as approval. If not, he would cease entirely. Kid didn't hesitate. He placed a soft, reassuring kiss on Treycore's lips before pulling away. Treycore glared at him suspiciously, as if he was still trying to read Kid—like he didn't understand him. Kid planted another soft kiss on his lips.

Treycore released Kid's neck and stroked the back of his fingers against Kid's face. Kid breathed heavily. Treycore kissed him again.

They breathed into each other.

Kid's erect cock slid under Treycore's button-up and moved against the grooves in his abs. The harder he pushed his penis against Treycore's abs, the more relief he felt, and he wanted relief so much. At the same time, he desperately wanted Treycore inside him. He didn't know how. He knew it wouldn't be physically possible—or at least, it might be the most unbearable experience of his life, but he wanted Treycore inside him. He wanted him to swell in his ass. He wanted to scream while Treycore forced it in him harder and harder, not giving him a moment to recover. He wanted Treycore to explode inside of him so his whipped cream load spewed out through the space between his asshole and Treycore's pulsating dick.

Kid's thoughts were getting him too close to climax, and he wasn't about to let that happen until Treycore had had his way with him—even if that left him paralyzed or worse. He pulled his pelvis back, so only the tip of his cock grazed up against Treycore's immortally perfect abdomen.

Treycore reached his hands into the placket of his button-up and gripped the material. With a swift rip, the buttons popped off. One smacked Kid between the eyes.

Kid shook off his surprise.

"Fuck." He stared in awe at Treycore's flawless body.

It wasn't actually flawless. Now that Kid could see it under daylight, though his abs were jagged and ripped, they were obviously lopsided. His pecs were massive, but he had incredibly small nipples. As hairless as his chest was, he had the faintest of happy trails, which Kid was so enamored with that he dove his head straight to Treycore's waist to lick between the thin, blond hairs. He trailed his way up to his navel. Swirling his tongue into the shallow dip, he did his best not to miss any crevice.

His hands massaged Treycore's magnificent abs. They felt like smooth pebbles, cushioned by slightly dampened flesh. As Kid licked, he worked to get as much of Treycore's sweat inside him. Kid didn't know what had possessed him. The sweat didn't taste particularly great, but he felt this compulsion to consume as much of it as he could, as if it was water and he had gone days without a drink. In reality, it'd just been a few hours.

Treycore grabbed Kid by his hips. He sat up, bringing them face to face.

"I'm gonna come in you," he said, his expression serious.

It was an expression that concerned Kid. He was hoping that Treycore was considering the logistics of sex. Clearly, it was all that he wanted too, but there was no way Treycore was going to be able to come inside him with ease, even having had all those men at Jerry's loosening him up for the past few years. However, Kid couldn't think with his rational mind. All he wanted was for Treycore to be in him—even if that meant that he was going to be ripped in half.

Kid pulled away and flipped on his stomach, exposing his smooth ass. Treycore flashed a smile that made Kid want to satisfy him even more.

*Tear me open. Destroy me.*

His erection stirred against the dark earth.

Treycore kicked his shoes off and slid his now ankle-high jeans onto the jungle floor. He crawled to Kid and kissed his ass with soft, tender kisses. He cupped his ass cheeks in his hand and kneaded his fingers into them. His mouth found its way to Kid's asshole. His tongue danced around the edges.

Kid closed his eyes, savoring the tingly sensations that rushed from his ass, through his abdomen, and into his chest.

"Ow!" Kid shouted.

Treycore had slipped a finger into his ass, fast and hard. Kid thought that perhaps it had been a painful warning for what their anal sex was going to feel like. He relished the sting.

Treycore slipped his finger in and out of Kid's ass.

The painful rubbing and ripping at his crack wall reminded him that they didn't have any lube, which meant it would be an even more painful experience than he had previously considered. Kid wasn't sure that was such a bad thing.

"Ah!" Kid groaned.

Treycore had forced, not one, but another two fingers in. Kid dug his fingers into the damp ground.

"No, please..." he whined, but what he meant was, "More!"

Treycore kissed the base of Kid's spine softly as he continued forcing his fingers inside him. He lowered his head, collected saliva in his mouth, and spit a thick wad onto his fingers. As his moistened digits continued penetrating Kid's ass, they provided him with at least a modest form of lubrication, making the experience somewhat less painful.

Treycore pulled his fingers out. Kid took a breath of relief, but as he caught a glimpse of Treycore's shadow moving up him, he tensed and simultaneously wished that he hadn't. He felt soft flesh at his ass crack.

Kid wondered if Treycore had ever had sex with a mortal before. It didn't seem like he would have, considering his clear disdain for them. However, if he was having sex with him now, it seemed more than likely that he'd encountered this before and would be able to take the right things (like his inhumanly large cock and Kid's very humanly asshole) into consideration.

Kid glanced over his shoulder. Treycore looked worried, like he knew how much pain Kid was about to experience and like if there was anything he could do, other than not stick his penis inside him, he would be more than willing to help.

Kid nodded to Treycore. He wanted this arousing creature to know that he was fully aware of the consequences of what they were about to do and that he wanted to do it more than he'd ever wanted anything in his life.

Treycore put his hands on Kid's hips and lifted.

Kid took this as his cue and rose to his knees.

Treycore wiped the head of his dick against Kid's asshole.

Kid couldn't imagine how this was going to happen, and he really didn't want to. The more he tried to, the more impossible it all seemed.

Treycore leaned down and kissed behind Kid's ear. Kid whipped his head around and kissed him as Treycore pressed the tip of his cock against his ass crack. He pressed harder and harder.

Kid closed his eyes. A part of him hoped that Treycore wouldn't be able to get it in and would just give up. Another part of him wanted the whole thing in, destroying him.

The pressure against Kid's asshole built. The combination of the pain and the uneasy anticipation of the impending pain made his body squirm. He crawled forward.

Treycore grabbed him by the shoulder and pulled him back. With his other hand, he finagled the tip of his dick into Kid's hole.

Kid squinted. It didn't feel any worse than having the three fingers inside him, but he knew there was much more to come. Treycore massaged Kid's shoulder. He slid the head of his penis in.

Kid's breath caught in his throat.

"I can't," he said, realizing, despite his desire to have Treycore inside him, the extent of his limitation.

Treycore slid his cock's head farther inside.

"Ah!" Kid cried.

Treycore slid back out slightly. Then slipped it in just a little farther—until the bottom of the mushroom forced its way into Kid's ass.

"No!" Tears filled Kid's eyes. He pushed forward.

It was incredibly painful, but as his body attempted to reject Treycore's massive weapon, all Kid could think about was how much he wanted it.

Treycore maintained his grip on Kid's shoulder and kept him from moving.

"Please," Treycore said as the base of his cock's head slid back out.

Kid's legs trembled. His breaths were quick, erratic. He dug his fingers even deeper into the ground.

Treycore worked the tip of his monstrous member back inside Kid, who tried to maneuver his ass to delay the sting of Treycore's spear. He was going to have to find a way to keep his body from rebelling against this massive intrusion.

He bit on his lip as he pressed his ass back, allowing the base of the head back in. He kept going until he was back at the place he'd had it in before.

"Stop, stop," Kid whined. Tears mixed with his sweat and showered over the earth before him.

Treycore pulled out...just a little. He wiped his hand across Kid's back and slid his hand down to Kid's ass, massaging it gently.

As Kid's breathing settled, Treycore slid his shaft farther in.

Kid screamed out. He crawled forward. Treycore's eyes widened. His hands snapped to Kid's sides, and he crawled on his knees right behind him so his cock remained inside.

"Careful, careful." Treycore wrapped an arm around Kid's chest and pulled him back until his shoulder blades pressed against Treycore's chest.

Kid's body convulsed, and his pec and ab muscles twitched.

*Stop fighting him!* he yelled at his body. *I need this.*

Treycore kissed the back of his neck.

"You have to be careful." His hot breath rushed against the back of Kid's ear. Kid whipped his head around and planted another kiss on Treycore's lips. Treycore pulled his arm up from Kid's chest and locked it around his neck. He pushed his hips forward, not managing to get his cock any farther in.

Kid cringed. He pulled back and screamed out again. "Fuck!"

Treycore pecked Kid's shoulder and rubbed his nose against Kid's neck. Kid gripped his hands onto the arm Treycore had around his neck and squeezed as he tried to distract himself from the intense, swelling pain inside him. He hoped the distraction would lessen his body's struggle.

Treycore took deep, heavy breaths. Kid's abdomen rose and fell in frenzied spams. As Kid's breathing steadied, Treycore pulled his ass back, his cock steadily moving out. He pushed back in.

Kid's breathing became even more spastic. His survival mode took control again. He ripped Treycore's arm away from his neck and scurried to get away. Treycore crawled on his knees to keep up with him.

Kid came to a tree trunk. He pressed his hands against it as he struggled to endure the pain.

*You can take it! Just take it!*

Treycore put his hand back at Kid's shoulder, massaging lightly. He pulled his ass back, letting his cock slide out slightly, giving Kid that same sweet relief. Kid wrapped his arms around the tree trunk. His chest and cheek scraped along the rough bark.

A vine crawling around the tree touched just above his abs.

Treycore released Kid's shoulder, grabbed the vine, and pulled it back. The vine clung to the tree. Blue veins bulged out of Treycore's bicep and forearm. His neck tensed. He ground his teeth.

RIP! RIP!

Kid worried that the sound might have been coming from his ass, but as the vine's clinging roots snapped, releasing the vine from the trunk, he was assured this was not the case.

A few pulls and a quick yank and several feet of the vine were loose.

Treycore grabbed Kid by his hair and tugged. Kid released the trunk and fell back so his shoulder blades pressed up against Treycore's chest. Treycore secured the vine around Kid's neck, as if keeping Kid as his prisoner.

"Oh, fuck yeah," Kid said, throwing his head back. He let his hands fall behind him and rested them on Treycore's love handles. Treycore grabbed his hands and forced them to the base of Kid's back, putting one wrist over the other. He held them in place with one hand, and with his other, he snatched a long, dangling tendril off the vine and tied Kid's wrists together. He accidentally slid farther into Kid.

"Ah!" Kid cried. But Treycore's slave reveled in his bindings. "Fuck me!" he begged.

Treycore slid his cock in and out very slightly, very quickly.

Kid struggled wildly about, fighting the vine and tendril, both of which were too strong for him to free himself. Treycore hadn't even put in a quarter of his cock yet, but it was nearly unbearable.

He was glad he couldn't get free. It would keep his body from fighting. "Godfuckingdammit!"

Treycore continued pressing in and pulling out. Kid could feel the flesh in his ass tearing. He knew Treycore's pre-come wasn't providing him with enough lubrication, but he didn't want it to stop. He tensed his wrists against the vine's tendril and leaned forward so the vine constricted around his throat—another desperate attempt at distracting himself from the pain Treycore was putting him through—the pain that a part of him kept reminding him was too much for any mortal to handle.

Treycore's hand caressed across Kid's thigh, then up to his navel and across his torso. He grunted into Kid's ear. His ass rocked steadily back and forth with subtle precision.

Kid's cock was flaccid. The pain was just too much for him to stay aroused, but despite appearances, the whole situation was deeply gratifying and the intense, trembling pain that surged through him was delicious. He wanted to reach around and touch Treycore. He wanted Treycore to kiss him. He wanted to feel Treycore's hands all over him. Despite how impossible he knew it was, he wanted even more of Treycore inside him. His longing for more was intense, but he was going to have to be satisfied with what he was getting.

Red streaks streamed down Treycore's shaft. He pushed in and came back out, the blood covering his cock as droplets dripped from Kid's hole.

Kid leaned farther forward. The vine constricted even more around his neck. His face was dark red. The veins exposed above and below the vine were bloated. He made a constant wheezing sound as Treycore continued pleasuring himself in his ass.

Treycore's hand made its way to Kid's nipple. He gripped onto it with his thumb and index finger and moved them together, as if he was turning a screw. His pelvic thrusts became even quicker.

Kid's eyes rolled back. He was seeing spots again—large, circular spots.

"Oh!" Treycore moaned, his movements becoming even quicker and more intense. "Oh, yeah!" He released Kid's nipple and wrapped his arm around his chest. He wrapped his other arm around Kid's lower torso. He wiggled his shaft in what felt like farther than he'd been able to before, though Kid was sure he still hadn't taken more than a few inches.

Kid tried to scream again but he just started choking. He couldn't breathe. He was really choking.

*Please don't let me die*, he thought, wishing he could communicate that to Treycore.

Treycore leaned so that his mouth ran along Kid's cheek. His hot breath pressed against Kid's burning, red flesh.

*I'm gonna die.*

Treycore sped up even more. His hand moved up to Kid's neck. His fingers slipped between the vine and his neck as he held on for support.

It strangled Kid even more.

*Yes!*

"Yes! Oh, yes!" Treycore cried.

Despite Kid's unbearable suffocation and the throbbing in his ass, his body wasn't fighting anymore. He was delirious, lost in a blissful rapture that delighted in the experience, unable to feel any pain at all.

Rushes of sensation stirred through his limbs. He shivered in ecstasy.

Kid heard a sound and glanced over his shoulder, seeing white feathers erupted behind Treycore, fanning out on either side of him. He closed his eyes and grunted as his shaft shifted only slightly farther within Kid.

The back of Kid's skull felt like it was about to pop off, and Kid knew he didn't have but a few moments of consciousness left.

If this was how he was going to die, he was satisfied. The spots blurred together, transforming his vision into a bluish-green blob.

"Oh...oh..." Treycore moaned. His cock swelled inside Kid's ass. He ripped at the vine around Kid's neck. It snapped.

Kid fell forward. He gasped desperately for air. His arm scraped across the side of the trunk, and his face plowed into the ground.

Treycore followed right behind, continuing to ride him. His body convulsed.

"Ah. Ah."

Even though his cock moved deeper, Kid knew it had to have still been just a fraction...maybe four inches max...that was inside him. That was as much as was physically possible.

Kid felt the sharp, intense pain, but his body was too busy re-stimulating his lungs for him to be able to scream. It was a horrifying feeling, but something about it sent his mind reeling with delight.

Streaks of white rushed over Treycore's reddened cock. His milk-white, immortal load spewed out of the edges between his cock and Kid's hole. It slid down to the pubes on Kid's balls and dripped onto the jungle floor.

## CHAPTER EIGHT

"You sure we can trust this guy?" Kinzer asked.

"I'm sure," Dedrus replied.

They sat at a table in a cafe.

In a corner booth, a few teens flipped through comics. A woman at a table stacked with interior design magazines fussed at her stroller-bound infant as she picked its pacifier up off the floor. Several homeless people, with carts and bags, slept in cushioned chairs. A girl who couldn't have been more than seventeen bustled behind the counter, running between baked goods and the espresso machine.

"Dedrus," Kinzer said, "someone ratted me and Janka out. It could've been anyone. Maybe even Fie."

He sipped from a white coffee mug.

"I know we can't trust everyone, but between the Raze being after us and us having the Anti—"

"Could you keep it down?"

Dedrus lowered his voice. "We have..." He eyed Maggie. She stood in the adjoining bookstore, between two aisles of magazines, flipping through a copy of Vogue.

"That's an even better reason to keep our fucking mouths shut."

"We just won't mention her, okay?"

A woman in her seventies, trembling with a walker, made her way through the café. She approached their table.

"Freddie," she said to Dedrus in a scratchy smoker voice. "Those bathrooms are disgusting. Will you help me, dearie?"

"Of course, grams." Dedrus hopped out of his chair and helped the crone into the chair beside Kinzer.

Fie's gift was shifting, so his misleading appearance didn't surprise Kinzer. However, it was an unpleasant-looking disguise. The crone's face was as wrinkly as crumpled aluminum foil. Scattered around the wrinkles were moles and warts of varying sizes. She wore a muumuu of a dress that did nothing to suggest the sort of figure that Fie'd shaped into.

Fie positioned his crone-form in the chair. "Oh, thank you," he said. He leaned toward Dedrus. "Okay, seriously, what's he doing here?"

Kinzer assumed that when Fie had finally returned his call, Dedrus had told him about what had happened to him and Janka.

"He's trying to help," Dedrus said.

"Considering what happened to Janka, I don't think it's a good idea to trust him."

"I lost my wings, too," Kinzer said.

"Could be a diversion. Convince us you're still one of us. You never—" Fie held up a shriveled finger. He turned and pushed out a phlegm-filled cough. "Oh, lordie!" he proclaimed, still in the scratchy, smoker voice.

"We need," Dedrus said, "a place to hide out."

"I can't help you." He wheezed, struggling to move phlegm out of the crone's windpipe.

"What? Why not?"

"Everything's gone to shit. After you told me about Janka and Kinzer, I tried to warn Donna and Krimson. Can't get ahold of them. As far as I know, they're off the grid. They're my contacts to all my resources."

"I couldn't get ahold of them, either," Dedrus said.

*Bad news*, Kinzer thought.

Based on what had happened the night before, he doubted they'd been warned, and it was likely that the Raze had gotten to them.

"The Raze came to our house," Dedrus said. "Tried to kill us."

"It's a fucking bloodbath," Fie said. "All bets are off. Just get your asses hidden and wait for this shit to blow over."

"Where?" Dedrus asked.

"Fuck if I know. I got to cover my own ass."

"Listen," Kinzer said. "This is bigger than the Raze infiltrators being outed."

Fie followed Kinzer's glance as he looked to the magazine stand in the bookstore.

Maggie rested a magazine on her bloated belly. She looked to a few racks away. A blond kid, on his knees, pulled stacks of crossword puzzle magazines off the rack and set them beside him. She smirked.

Fie fell into a fit of coughs. "Shit…that's…not…" he said, struggling to push the words through phlegm-filled spams.

Dedrus nodded.

"Oh, fuck. This is worse than I thought." He balled his hands into fists. "Okay. I've got a place in the mountains that I was planning to go to. I'll head back to my place now and get some—" He stopped. His mouth hung open.

Kinzer looked to see what had distracted him. Through the cafe window, Craetis walked down the sidewalk.

"Fuck, fuck, fuck," Kinzer said.

He scanned the scene. His eyes flashed to the adjoining bookstore. Just a few yards behind Maggie, Mika skimmed through a book on a rack labeled "Paperback Bestsellers." He pursed his lips. The dip in them became even more defined.

"We have to get her out of here," Dedrus said.

As Craetis approached the cafe door, a man, who'd just let his family out, politely waved him in.

"Thank you," Craetis said, glancing over the cafe patrons as the door shut behind him.

Kinzer stared at Maggie.

*Look up*, he thought. *Come on, bitch. Look up!*

Maggie flipped to a page in her magazine. She tucked her thumbnail between her teeth and arched her back.

Fie, still in crone-form, shook as he got on his feet.

Dedrus rose, pushing the walker toward him. "What are you gonna do?" he asked.

"I'll distract them," Fie replied. "You guys just get her the fuck out of here."

*Look up!* Kinzer continued thinking at Maggie, wishing his gift had been telepathy.

Maggie's glance flitted from her magazine to the table where Kinzer was. As she saw Kinzer staring her down with a penetrating, deliberate stare, she stared back, as if waiting to receive a psychic message. His eyes shifted to behind her, and she followed his line of sight slowly, cautiously, until she saw Mika tucking a paperback on the rack behind her.

She turned back to Kinzer, shrugging ever so slightly, as if saying, "What the fuck am I supposed to do?"

Kinzer threw his glance to the bookshelves on the other side of the magazine aisle.

Tucking the copy of the fashion magazine under her arm, she speed walked toward the cafe, slipping around the magazine stand and turning down the row of bookshelves. She was out of Mika's view. Unfortunately, she was also out of Kinzer's.

"Well, well," Craetis said, approaching Dedrus and Kinzer's table. "Funny running into you here."

"New leg?" Dedrus asked.

"Like it? You can thank Vera. She made a few deals. Got us some new limbs."

"I'll bet she did. So how did you find us?"

"A little birdie."

*That rat*, Kinzer thought. He knew Fie couldn't be trusted. No wonder he was so eager to get away.

"Where's the girl?" a voice asked. Vera was suddenly sitting in Fie's seat.

She'd changed her look dramatically, sporting wavy, light brown hair that fell just past her shoulders. She also had a new arm, subtly showing off a manicure as she massaged her new fingers against the table. She wore an elegant, yet plain, beige dress with matching platform shoes. A string of pearls dropped to her bust. For Vera, it was a very modest look, likely because she was trying to blend in with the average mortals that surrounded her.

"Hidden," Kinzer said, "somewhere you'll never find her."

"Oh, I doubt that," Vera replied. "Try that clever act all you want, but I don't believe for a second that you're able to just tuck her away somewhere safely. Whom would you turn to? Certainly not Donna or Krimson. Certainly not Janka."

The mention of Janka's name sent waves of heat rushing to Kinzer's face.

*"Leave him alone!" Kinzer had cried out. "It's me. I'm the one you want."*

*Craetis undid the ropes binding Janka and removed his gag.*

*"Oh no," Veylo said. The back of his almond-colored hair waved down to his shoulders, his bangs just barely passing his nose. He had a wide forehead that cut sharply as his eyes collapsed into his skull, enabling the overhanging lights to obscure them in sharp shadows.*

*Veylo ran his thumb across the sword he held. It was Kinzer's sword. "We've discovered that both of you have been doing a little reconnaissance for the Leader, and I'm afraid we can't have traitors like yourselves believing that we will let these sorts of transgressions go unpunished."*

*Mika grabbed a cluster of feathers on Kinzer's wing and yanked them out.*

*Blood rushed down Kinzer's back.*

*Deter did the same with the other wing.*

*Kinzer ground his teeth, feeling the intense sting.*

*"Are you ready to watch the one you love die?" Veylo asked.*

*Janka moaned as he writhed about. Craetis grabbed Janka by his button-up collar and punched him in the face.*

*"Stop it!" Kinzer cried. Mika and Deter continued plucking his feathers. The pain was so intense, like someone was setting fire to him or stabbing knives into his back.*

*But that wasn't his concern.*

*Craetis slammed his fist into Janka's face again and again and again.*

"Touchy subject?" Vera mocked, dragging Kinzer's thoughts back to the present.

Kinzer's attention flitted to the adjoining bookstore as he scanned to make sure Maggie was out of sight. Her round belly caught his attention. She was heading up a flight of stairs to the second floor of the store, the fashion magazine tucked close.

*What are you fucking doing?* Kinzer thought.

Mika, who'd abandoned the paperbacks, paced by a series of spinner racks filled with bookmarks and mini giftbooks. His gaze wandered until he glanced up the stairs and froze. The usual M in his lips thinned across a smile. He walked toward the steps, taking his sweet time.

Vera followed Kinzer's stare. She smirked. "Somewhere we'll never find her?" she asked. "The romance section, perhaps?"

Kinzer flashed Dedrus a knowing glare.

They swept under the table, snatching up their swords, which had been resting at their feet, disguised in brown packaging paper. They ripped the paper apart.

Kinzer sliced at Vera. "Tapping out," she said with a wink. She disappeared.

Kinzer whipped around. Deter was behind him, his sword jabbing at him.

Kinzer twisted his sword around, blocking the attack.

Dedrus slashed at Craetis, who grabbed a chair and used it as a shield. Dedrus's sword cut right through it.

Their movements were so quick, it took the cafe patrons a moment to realize what was going on. When they finally did, they stirred with panic. The woman with the strollered baby hopped out of her chair and hurried across the cafe. The teens with the comics watched in shock and horror, but couldn't seem to pull their attention from the spectacle. The homeless sleepers roused, full of bewilderment as they rushed to their feet and scurried for the door, like a light flicking on in a cockroach-infested apartment.

Dedrus struck at Craetis again. He dodged the attack. Kinzer and Deter's swords clashed.

*Gotta get to the second floor*, Kinzer thought, *before it's too late*.

As Deter pulled his sword back, Kinzer grabbed his cup of coffee and chucked it at Deter.

The coffee exploded like a grenade across his face.

"Fuck!" Deter cried, smoke rising around the scalding coffee.

Kinzer made haste. He dashed into the adjoining bookstore and up the stairs to the second floor.

Wide-eyed patrons gasped and screamed as he passed them, his sword bobbing about as he ran.

The second floor was a labyrinth of bookshelves. Kinzer caught a glimpse of Mika. He had an arm around Maggie and his hand over her mouth as he pulled her around a shelf in Home & Gardening. She slapped at him with her magazine.

Kinzer raced around the shelf. "Stop right there!" he ordered.

Mika whipped around, maintaining his hand over her mouth. He chuckled. "Sloppy, sloppy," he said, shaking his head.

"Thank you, Kinzer," Vera said, walking alongside Kinzer, making her way to Mika, "for watching her for us."

She flashed beside Mika and Maggie, wrapped her arms around them, and disappeared.

"No!" Kinzer exclaimed. This didn't just mean the end of Maggie. It meant the end of the Antichrist...which meant the end of the resistance against the Christ...which meant the end of the world.

In a single moment, he felt like everything that he and Janka had worked so hard for had been stripped from him.

He hurried back downstairs to find Dedrus. His heart ached. Dedrus met him at the bottom of the stairs, sweat sliding across his temples.

"Vera just teleported Deter and Craetis outta here."

"She got her," Kinzer said, his heart steadily sinking.

Dedrus panted as he tried to catch his breath. Sirens blared outside. Through the front windows, Kinzer saw cop cars lining the sidewalk. Officers filed out like they were clown cars. Blue and red lights blazed.

"We gotta get out of here," Kinzer said.

From a nearby bookshelf, Maggie stepped out, her eyes wide.

"They gone?" she asked.

"What the—" Dedrus started.

"Fie!" Kinzer exclaimed. He felt bad that he'd been so hasty in assuming that he'd sold them out. "He must've...but...where's your magazine?"

"That old lady you were talking to took it," Maggie said.

The doors to the cafe and the entrance to the bookstore burst open. Policemen stormed in.

"We can chat about this later," Dedrus said.

"Can you get us outta here?" Kinzer asked.

"I sure fucking hope so. Get in front of me and run."

"Drop your weapon!" an officer screamed as the other policemen streamed through the doors and positioned themselves around the front and side of the store.

"Sir, don't move, and drop your weapon. Sir, move and I will be forced to fire."

Dedrus's wings fanned out, effectively concealing Maggie and Kinzer.

"Fire! Fire!"

The sound of gunshots filled the air.

Bullets ricocheted off Dedrus's wings as he, Kinzer, and Maggie bolted up the stairs. Maggie held her baby bump as if her movement was about to make the baby drop out of her.

"The window!" Dedrus exclaimed.

On the other side of the store, a window stretched out, looking out at a shopping center across the street.

As they raced toward it, Dedrus's wings tucked close. He slipped between Maggie and Kinzer. His wings fanned out again, curling in a ball around him as he threw himself into the window.

The glass broke into large chunks that crashed to the ground, hitting the pavement outside with a—

CRASH!

Dedrus flapped his wings, circling back into the bookstore.

The officers raced up to the second floor. Dedrus wrapped his arms around Kinzer and Maggie.

"Hold on," he ordered.

"Oh, fuck this!" Maggie exclaimed.

Before she could object any further, she, Kinzer, and Dedrus were soaring through the air, gliding toward the shopping mall across the street.

## CHAPTER NINE

Kid splashed the warm spring water onto his abdomen and rubbed it into his muscles. He stepped deeper into the spring until his ass was fully immersed. He dipped his fingers in the water, reached around, and gently massaged his asshole. His chin quivered as a sting of pain raced through him. He grunted.

*Fuckin' ass could've been a little gentler.*

Of course, he wouldn't have wanted it that way. That had been the most pleasurable experience he'd ever had—even better than sex with Kinzer. He hadn't gotten off, but he'd still had a fucking great time, and he already wanted more. He didn't know how he was going to be able to continue journeying with Treycore when all he was going to do was want to fuck him.

It was so painful at times, he thought he couldn't take anymore, but it was so fucking hot. He'd never been so horny, never wanted to fuck so bad, never wanted someone to come inside him so much.

As he stood in the spring, his thoughts lingered on their intensely painful encounter. His penis was full, throbbing. If only there was a way he could get Treycore's entire dick in him.

"Make sure you get up in that ass."

Kid's defensive instincts kicked in. He whirled around. Treycore stood on a nearby rock in just his jeans. His hands rested on his hips.

A big, obnoxious grin curled into his sickle-shaped dimples as he stared down at Kid.

"I'm getting it right now." He stopped massaging his hole. He wasn't going to do that in front of Treycore.

"You'd better if you want me up in that shit again."

"With that dick, you'll probably end up in some shit."

"Won't be the first time." Treycore winked. He undid his jeans and slid them down his thighs.

There was that absurdly large, immortal cock again. Saliva flooded into Kid's mouth. His ass loosened and quivered as he battled between taking the pleasure and fighting the incredible pain.

Treycore stepped out of his jeans and dove off the rock. His back muscles flashed Kid just before he disappeared into the water, leaving an explosion of droplets behind him. He swam toward Kid, his flesh shimmering as the sunlight beamed through the water onto his back. As he swam into a shallower part of the spring, he came to Kid, he reached around and grabbed him by the legs. His face moved right into Kid's pelvis as Treycore consumed his dick. Kid threw his head back.

Treycore rested his knees on the bottom of the spring and pumped Kid's cock with his hand and mouth.

"Oh fuck."

Treycore's tongue swirled around the tip of his head. With his free hand, he reached back and grazed his finger against Kid's hole.

Kid felt the same stirring of pain that he'd felt while he'd been rubbing it. He cringed and hissed, but it was nice. Very nice.

Treycore deep-throated Kid's cock and slipped his middle finger inside his hole.

Kid's pelvis pushed forward.

Treycore pulled his lips back, sliding his tongue side to side as he slowly released Kid's cock. He kissed just above Kid's dick and pulled his finger out of his hole, moving both hands over his ass cheeks. He sprung out of the water, his hands sliding up to Kid's waist. He kissed up his abdomen to his chest. He tugged at a nipple with his teeth.

Kid stroked his fingers through Treycore's soaked hair with one hand and set the other on his shoulder.

Treycore slid his hand down to Kid's submerged erection and stroked it, his thumb massaging his shaft. His teeth released Kid's nipple and he kissed across his pecs. His lips felt their way across the smooth terrain. Occasionally, his tongue would slip out from between them and caress Kid's muscles.

Kid enjoyed the sensation of Treycore's wet tongue traveling across him, leaving a trail of saliva in its path that dried quickly under the sun's heat. But even after it dried, the sensation lingered, and Kid felt like Treycore had marked him.

Treycore's tongue found its way to Kid's other nipple and encircled it over and over again.

Kid arched his spine, pushing his abs forward. Treycore kissed down to just above his abs. He stopped, his lips just barely touching Kid's flesh, his breath gently rushing against his skin. It was torture for Kid, who wished that Treycore's mouth would just run up and down every part of his body at once.

Treycore pulled back. The hand on Kid's cock stilled.

"About earlier," he said. "I'm not looking for anything serious."

"It's cool," Kid said. "I mean…it's just fucking."

Although, it was so much more than that to Kid, and he wondered if Treycore had said that because he could tell Kid was enamored with how Treycore made him feel…because maybe Treycore knew he had this powerful effect on mortals.

Treycore stared into Kid's eyes, as if trying to stare much farther. A broad grin stretched across his face.

"Good. Now it's time to get you off."

As much as it pleased Kid to hear that, he really didn't care whether or not he got off. He really just enjoyed being tortured by, and pleasuring, Treycore. Besides, it had been being on the brink of death that had left Kid in such intoxicating pleasure.

Kid lunged at Treycore, wrapping his legs around his waist and throwing his arms around his neck. Their lips met in a frenzied fit of kisses. They weren't the careful kisses from their first encounter. They were sloppy, thoughtless, and out of sync. As their lips clashed without rhyme, they soon developed an awkward rhythm together.

Treycore pressed the head of his dick against Kid's ass crack. Kid's cheeks instinctively twitched and tightened, despite his deep longing for more.

Treycore pulled away from Kid's lips and kissed his way down to Kid's chin. He moved his hands up and down Kid's back, much softer than the first time.

Treycore kissed up to Kid's ear.

"Take a deep breath," he whispered, his breath tingling against the hairs just behind Kid's ear.

Kid did as he was told. Treycore pulled back and returned to Kid's lips. Kid surrendered to Treycore as he collapsed on top of him. Air swept across his back. As they hit the water, droplets flew into the air. The spring water consumed them as they dropped off the shelf in the spring Kid had stood on.

Treycore's blond locks waved about rapidly in the settling water. His wings fanned out. They fluttered quickly, subtly, preventing the two of them from floating upward.

Kid worried that if Treycore wasn't very careful, he'd drown him, but considering how thoughtful he'd been with the vine in their previous encounter, he opted to just trust him. Although he might bring him to the brink of passing out, in the end, he would do what was best for him...or at least, what would keep him alive.

Treycore's fingers tickled up Kid's torso, moving through the grooves in his abs. Their kisses softened. It was an odd experience for Kid, considering their last fuck had been anything but sensual. It was odd, but it felt just as good. Kid felt a stirring in his chest and heat building in his pelvis. He pressed his erect dick into the dip between Treycore's abs.

With his free hand, Treycore cradled Kid's ass, steadily pressing his fingers into his flesh.

The longer they remained underwater, the more uneasy Kid felt. But he played as if he was fine. He didn't want to ruin the moment with his insecurity.

Treycore's lips left his and trailed down his neck. Kid peered back at the specks of spring debris that clouded the water around them, glistening in the sunlight. They sank deeper and deeper into the spring, making their way steadily to the bottom—a luminous cluster of flat rock formations. Their slow, steady motion made Kid feel as if time had slowed, giving him just a moment where he didn't have to think about his past, Jerry's place, fallens, or any of this Antichrist shit. He could just savor the intoxicating feeling that rushed through him as Treycore's body moved against his. He could let Treycore take control and let his own responsibility slip away. Despite how cruel this higherling had been to him, how spiteful and cold, something in him trusted him just enough. He hated that part of himself, considering how long he had worked to develop a deep distrust for mankind. But he couldn't deny that ever since his first fuck with Treycore, he had felt some deep trust that even though he might abuse and torture him, he was only doing it for the sake of ecstasy and pleasure.

Treycore kissed to the dip at the base of Kid's neck, and then licked it tenderly. His fingers made their way up to Kid's waist, his thumb stroking back and forth.

Kid's penis got even harder. He started seeing spots, just as he had when Treycore had strangled him with the vine. He had to go back up for air, but he didn't want this moment to end. He grabbed the edges of Treycore's wings. They were hard and slick. He slid his hands back and forth against them. They pulled out of his reach as Treycore kissed down his abdomen.

Treycore's thumbs stroked Kid's sides as he licked and kissed at the pulsating muscles. His tongue dropped into his navel, and he kept it out, brushing over Kid's flesh, as he made his way down to Kid's pelvis. As he came to his cock, he glanced up at Kid, who was looking right back at him. He ran his tongue over the head and licked up and down the shaft.

Kid's body was desperate for oxygen, and his head felt swollen, like it was about to erupt.

Treycore sucked Kid's dick into his mouth. He swirled his tongue about rigorously. His hands tightened against Kid's ass as he moved his head up and down. Kid wanted to call out. He wanted to let Treycore know how good he was making him feel, but all he could do was continue to hold his breath and writhe with pleasure.

Treycore's lips touched the base of his cock, and he jerked back up, his lips freeing Kid's shaft as his tongue assaulted the head.

Kid knew he wasn't going to make it much longer. He looked to Treycore, hoping to try and psychically convey his agony, but Treycore was so absorbed in tickling the head of his cock with his tongue, Kid was starting to worry that he was going to pass out.

Treycore's wings did a quick flap. His body rushed over Kid's until they were face to face. Treycore kissed Kid's lips. Kid couldn't kiss back. He was too busy straining to hold his breath. Treycore wrapped his arms around him, and with a quick maneuver of his wings, they shot up.

SPLASH!

Treycore's wings scattered water every which way. They continued to flap subtly. Droplets flung about.

Kid gasped desperately for air, but it was still in vain because as he attempted to force air into his mouth, Treycore kissed him passionately. He breathed through his nose, but his body had been so deprived of air, it wasn't enough, and he had to pull back to sneak a breath. Before he could get very much, Treycore's lips would be back at his. He felt continuously torn between his body's desperate need for air and his deep longing to have Treycore's lips against his.

Treycore's wings flapped about, pushing Kid and himself through the water until he was against a rock at the edge of the spring. Treycore pushed Kid's back against the rock and continued forcing kisses on his oxygen-hungry body. Every so often, their lips would separate just long enough for Kid to take a heavy, much needed breath.

Treycore's cock pressed against Kid's leg.

*Please*, Kid thought. *Oh please, more.*

Treycore pulled his lips from Kid's and pressed them against his cheek. His tongue toyed with his skin.

Kid gasped nearly as desperately as he had when they'd first come back up for air. He trembled from ecstasy and exhaustion. He stroked his hand against Treycore's back, the back of his hand tickled by Treycore's feathers. He tightened his other hand against Treycore's dense bicep.

"*Fuck me*," Kid groaned.

Treycore pulled away. His wings' subtle movements died down. "What?" he asked, his expression filled with confusion.

"Please."

"But, you're hurt...from earlier."

"I want you inside me."

"No!"

"Do it!"

Treycore grabbed Kid by his biceps and flipped him around. He pushed his cock against his ass.

"Yes," Kid moaned.

Treycore grabbed him by his hair and tugged.

"Oh!" Kid groaned. He reached his hand back and brushed his fingers across Treycore's face. Treycore's hot breath hit Kid in the back of the neck. Goosebumps rippled under Kid's flesh, scurrying up his legs and across his back.

Treycore positioned the head of his dick on Kid's hole and pushed forward.

"Ah!" Kid didn't actually feel any pain, but the anticipation, though wildly arousing, was frightening. Every muscle in his body tensed. Once again, his cheeks tightened automatically, his body's attempt at fighting against his perverse, masochistic impulse.

"Do it!" Kid ordered.

Treycore grabbed his cock by the shaft and pierced the tip of the head into Kid's hole.

Kid's eyes glistened. A tear slipped out of one eye and rushed down his cheek. His ass tightened even more.

"Wait, wait!" Kid exclaimed.

Treycore started to pull his dick back out.

"No! Back in!"

"No," Treycore snapped.

"I want it."

They stared into each other's eyes. Kid bit on his tongue and took deep, tense breaths. Treycore shook his head sternly. Kid took another breath and nodded. Treycore gulped. Despite it being Kid whose ass was most in jeopardy, it seemed that Treycore was the more concerned of the two.

Treycore pushed his dick's head a little farther into Kid's ass. Kid's legs convulsed. Tears poured uncontrollably from his eyes. Treycore pushed in a little farther.

Red rushed up to the surface of the spring water.

Treycore pulled out.

"What are you doing?" Kid asked belligerently.

"You can't...not now."

"Yes, I can!"

"No, you can't."

Kid's face turned red, just like it had when he had been out of breath.

Treycore's wings pulled into his back. He swam across the spring, sliding out onto a nearby rock. He flipped onto his back and sprawled out, letting his hard cock fall to the side.

Kid's face was still red. He swam rapidly to the edge and pulled himself out beside Treycore. He grabbed Treycore's cock by the shaft, held it up, and licked it with a furious passion.

"Oh yeah!" Treycore groaned.

Kid deep-throated the dick until he got about a quarter of the way down the shaft. He gagged on the tip. It didn't stop him. He continued trying to take as much as he could.

"Holy shit!" Treycore watched Kid as he choked his way down a little farther, then farther still.

The sides of Kid's mouth stung. His jaw muscles tired quickly. He forced breaths through his nose. A thick wad of pre-come shot out of Treycore's dick and hit the back of Kid's throat. Kid popped his head back and coughed until the pre-come shot out onto the rock.

"You okay?" Treycore asked.

Kid didn't respond. He forced his lips back over Treycore's shaft. Treycore grabbed him by the head and stroked his fingers through his hair.

Kid's tongue massaged the tip of the dick's head and sucked gently. He could feel the entire immortal masterpiece swelling against the insides of his cheeks. It was a satisfying feeling that he reveled in. Something about stimulating Treycore this much made him feel so satisfied. And it only challenged him to take it even farther. He pulled off the shaft and forced his lips against Treycore's balls, jacking Treycore's penis with his hand.

Treycore grimaced as Kid sucked and tugged at his testicles.

Kid flicked his tongue about, feeling its way through his pubes. His tongue ran down to the base of his balls, followed by his lips. He sucked just under Treycore's balls.

"Ah!" Treycore called out.

Kid sucked even harder. He released Treycore's dick and slid his arms under Treycore's thighs, tilting them up so Treycore's hole lifted into his face.

Kid hated the sight of an ass, but he couldn't wait to get his face in Treycore's. He slid his tongue around the rim. He stuck his middle finger in and curled it up, rubbing along the wall of Treycore's ass. Treycore's pelvis jolted about. It was clear he'd hit some sort of nerve in the immortal's anatomy. He took advantage of it and flicked his finger about even harder on the spot that seemed to be pleasuring Treycore so much. Treycore groaned and moaned as his ass bounced on the rock. He grabbed his cock and stroked it rapidly.

Kid licked around his finger. Occasionally, he rubbed his nose against the top of Treycore's hole. He slipped his ring finger in with his middle finger and continued putting pressure on the spot that was clearly driving Treycore crazy. Treycore's ass bounced even quicker against the rock. His abs tightened, making his muscles appear even more ripped than they already were. Every line in his torso stood out more pronounced than usual. Feathers pushed out from behind him. They bent and twisted as they struggled between the rocks and Treycore's shoulder blades. Treycore ground his teeth and groaned as even more pre-come spewed from his dick's head.

Kid was pleased that a mere, disgusting mortal such as himself could get to Treycore like this.

Kid's tongue vacillated between tickling and licking around the rim.

"Oh...I'm gonna..." Treycore panted, stroking his cock even faster. His thumb vigorously massaged the head.

Kid pulled his fingers out of Treycore's ass and sprung to his feet. He positioned himself over Treycore's cock and bent his legs so he could try to sit on it. Blood continued leaking from Kid's ass, covering Treycore's dick.

Treycore's eyes widened. He pulled his hand away from his dick. Kid slid Treycore's dick into his bloody hole.

"Stop, stop!" Treycore begged, closing his eyes and forcing his shaft into Kid.

"Ah!"

"Please...stop!"

Treycore grabbed under Kid's thighs and pushed up. He tossed him back into the spring, gripped onto the rock, and took a deep breath.

Kid's face was red again as he stood in the spring.

"What the fuck?" he shouted, enraged.

"You know *what the fuck*!"

"I want you to come in me!"

"Your ass is in bad enough shape as it is. You need to let it heal!"

"Don't tell me what to fucking do with my ass!"

Treycore shook his head and rose to his feet. Kid swam back to the rock and pulled himself up.

"You scared of a little blood?"

"What?" Treycore asked. "No."

He turned and started to walk away. Kid grabbed him by the shoulder and pulled him back around.

"Then what?"

Treycore grabbed Kid's biceps. He held them gently and looked into Kid's eyes. "I don't want to hurt you," he said.

"But I *do*."

Treycore grabbed Kid's ass cheeks and hoisted him up. His erect cock rubbed between Kid's cheeks.

Kid smiled.

Treycore smirked back. He shook his pelvis back and forth, creating friction with Kid's flesh as blood continued leaking out onto his dick.

Kid kissed him softly, taking time to savor Treycore's plush bottom lip. Their noses touched gently, and Kid let them linger together for a moment. He wrapped his legs around Treycore's waist.

Treycore knelt on the rock. He leaned forward. He tilted his head back, slipping from their embrace.

Treycore gazed at him.

Kid stared into his eyes, trying to read him, attempting to anticipate what Treycore would do next, but at the same time, hoping he wouldn't be able to figure it out.

The corner of Treycore's mouth curled upward. He pulled his pelvis back so that his erect dick slipped out in front of Kid. He caressed his hands up to Kid's sides as he lowered him onto the rock. The rough edges of the rock dug into Kid's shoulder blades.

Treycore pressed his hard cock between Kid's pelvis and himself. His ass bobbed up and down.

Kid groaned as his ass squeezed between the rock and Treycore's hard shaft. Pre-come slid down the head of Treycore's cock and dripped onto Kid's skin. As Treycore's cock slid over the pre-come, it and Kid's blood mixed, acting as lubrication, making it even easier for him to slide his cock back and forth over Kid's skin.

*Tear me apart*, Kid thought.

Treycore pressed his hands against Kid's pecs. He rubbed his thumbs against his nipples. Kid grabbed onto Treycore's forearms. As Treycore's frottage became more rapid, Kid gripped on even tighter.

Treycore leaned down and kissed him. As Kid kissed back, Treycore slipped his tongue in his mouth. Kid reciprocated with his tongue, and soon, their tongues were swiping across each other, saliva sticking and sliding in strands into each other's mouths.

Treycore's eyes rolled back.

Kid pushed against Treycore's biceps. Treycore took this cue and flipped on his back beside Kid. Kid rolled on top of him and straddled him so Treycore's dick was right behind him. He rolled his ass circularly on Treycore's abdomen. Treycore grabbed his dick and jerked it about.

"I'm so close," he whispered.

Kid leaned down to his ear. "Will you come on my ass?"

Treycore nodded.

Kid pushed off the rock and positioned himself over the head of Treycore's dick. His thighs tensed, the muscles and veins bulging as they held Kid up.

"Come on," he begged.

"Oh, yeah. I'm gonna….I'm gonna…"

Kid slid his pelvis back so he could see Treycore's cock.

"Here it…"

Kid sat just over Treycore's dick and lowered himself until the head was right at his hole. He lowered himself even farther. Treycore shook his head violently.

"No. You're gonna hurt yourself." His pelvis convulsed so that it pushed the head farther into Kid.

"Fuck!" Kid called out as tears rushed from his eyes and blood leaked down Treycore's shaft.

"No," Treycore argued, yet he continued. He grabbed Kid by the waist and tried to force his penis deeper into him.

Kid groaned in agony before Treycore's body twitched and convulsed, assuring Kid that he had his come inside him. Kid's body convulsed as he stroked his own hard cock until he shot all over Treycore's upper torso and chest.

"Ah…ah…oh…"

It was so delicious...so amazing. And there was something so much deeper to it than Kid had experienced with any of the fucks he'd ever had before. Something intimate. Something beyond just their physical expression. As he looked into Treycore's eyes, he felt like he could see through the hard shell he'd been showing him, to something so much more.

He couldn't explain the power that rushed through him, but it was so strong that it scared the shit out of him.

\*\*\*

Kid lay on Treycore's chest, stroking his fingers up and down Treycore's solid muscles. Treycore had ripped various fronds off exotic trees and arranged them on the jungle floor so they'd be able to rest for a while before continuing their journey back to Kinzer and the others.

Treycore wrapped his arm around Kid's neck and rested his hand on his hip.

A flutter of excitement rushed through Kid. Being that close to Treycore felt good. He liked fucking him. And as much as he didn't want to admit it, there was something else he felt for him...something much stronger. Although, he continued to wonder if this was an effect that all immortals had on mortals. Although, he hadn't felt anything like this with Kinzer.

*You don't even know him!* he thought, angry with himself for feeling so much, so soon.

It had to be something about him being immortal, though. Some feeling they could rouse within them. That was the only explanation.

"You have a lot of nightmares?" Treycore asked.

Kid was completely thrown.

*Where'd that come from?*

"What?"

"Last night, you were muttering to yourself. Kept crying out *no* over and over again."

He hadn't realized that he'd been so vocal in his sleep. He was embarrassed. It wasn't something he wanted to talk about. Not to Treycore. Not to anyone.

"Probably just from sleeping in this shitty place."

Treycore stroked Kid's arm as if he knew better and was consoling him. He nestled his mouth beside Kid's ear.

"You like to read?" Kid asked, attempting to change the subject.

"What?" Treycore asked, clearly just as confused as when he'd asked Kid about nightmares.

"Reading. When I was in your room, I saw all these books on your floor."

"Just there to pass the time."

Kid tossed his head back, glaring at Treycore skeptically.

"Mortals read because they're desperate to escape reality for a moment. Immortals read because we're trying to escape eternity. Your wounds, your pain...they have an ending. Ours don't. Our scars, our mistakes, our grief is everlasting."

"It can't be that bad. Come on, you have it pretty easy. You have powers. You have wings. You have eternal life."

"My wings are clipped," Treycore said. "I don't have any of those things."

"What?"

"You asked earlier about why I couldn't fly. It's because my wings were clipped."

"Like Kinzer's? But I've seen them. You—"

"Not like Kinzer's. During the war, I was a spy for the Leader. I collected intel from the Almighty's generals and swapped information with my contact. Some of the Leader's warriors attacked a camp I was in. Several of us were captured. Back then, it was common to clip the enemy's wings and take them to POW camps, where they'd torture us for information. But they couldn't clip us entirely. If they did, we'd lose our ability to cross between immortal realms, and they wouldn't be able to take us to their camps without a special serum. So they clipped us just enough so we lost our ability to fly. Unlike Kinzer, we retained most of our immortal traits."

"Wait. The Leader's men captured you?" Kid asked. "I thought you worked for the Leader."

"I did. I was a spy, but the warriors that had attacked our camp didn't know that. They assumed I was just another higherling that they could pry information from."

"Then how did you get out?"

"At the time, Vera was also part of the Leader's underground spy operation. When she discovered that I'd been captured, she had the Leader fake an escape for me. They had to fake it to look like I broke free. Otherwise, the Almighty would have questioned it. Questioned my loyalty, and I would've been at even greater risk."

As Kid looked into Treycore's eyes, he didn't see the anger and hate he'd seen before. He saw pain and sadness. He saw weakness and vulnerability. He wished he could wrap his arms around Treycore and console him. But he knew how stupid that would look. They'd known each other for less than a day, and he was just a smelly mortal, as Treycore had continually reminded him. As much as he wanted to believe that Treycore was sharing this because he was having strong feelings too, he knew it was more likely he just wanted someone to share it with...like Kinzer had done at the diner.

Treycore's wince-of-a-look fixed on him.

Kid felt as if it was probing for a secret, searching for more. He glanced to the side.

There wasn't anything good in Kid's past. Nothing worth sharing.

"Why?" Kid asked.

"Why what?"

"Why fight for mortals if you're at such risk? The way you talk, it sounds like you hate us. But here you are, protecting us."

"Well, I'm not a huge fan," Treycore said with a smirk. "You've seen what I do. I don't exactly see the best side of you guys."

Kid knew what he meant. He'd seen how those men looked at him and the other boys at Dick Dongs. It was so similar to the way Jerry's clients had looked at him.

"Exactly," Kid said. "How can you look at those greedy, selfish bastards—who just see you as an object, who would break you and rip you apart without another thought about what they'd done—and think that there's anything here worth saving?"

Kid snuck a look at Treycore. He could tell by the way Treycore glared back at him that he'd said too much.

Treycore appeared troubled, as if he was trying to see what in Kid had evoked his question, and Kid desperately didn't want him to know. He wasn't proud of his past, and he would rather Treycore not know about it.

"I've seen a lot of that," he said. "I've seen centuries of torture, blood thirst, and rape. But every so often, you see some puny mortal do something that surprises you…sacrificing something so precious for the sake of another. For their child. For their lover. I was created to be aesthetically pleasing. It's a quality higherlings venerate, but when you've had that advantage as long as I have, it doesn't impress you. You come to see the beauty of things unseen. Like those things I've seen in mortals. Will, honor, love. When you see things like that, you realize that somewhere inside of these creatures is something beautiful. Something worth saving."

Kid couldn't believe what he was hearing. Even with all that rage and anger, there was an optimistic side of Treycore. It was beautiful. A feeling stirred within Kid that was so powerful it scared him. He couldn't handle this anymore. He had to get away. He couldn't let Treycore detect it. He wouldn't let him see the surge of feelings that were raging within him.

"I guess we'd better start back up." Kid hopped to his feet.

## CHAPTER TEN

Dedrus soared through the air.

"Fuckers! Fuckers! Fuckers!" Maggie screamed out as she hyperventilated, her arms strangling Dedrus. Her face was nearly as white as Kinzer's.

Dedrus had been flying for some time. He wanted to get as far from the bookstore as possible, so when Vera discovered that she had the wrong Maggie, she would have a difficult time finding them. By now, they were flying over industrial warehouses, well outside the city perimeter. Dedrus, his energy waning from carrying Kinzer and the ample-sized Maggie, had begun his descent.

As they neared the ground, Kinzer dropped his sword and released Dedrus's chest. Bending his knees as he hit the asphalt, he rolled across the ground.

Dedrus's wings reared back, catching the wind so it propped him and Maggie upright. Concerned about the landing and the safety of Maggie and the unborn Antichrist, he tossed his sword aside.

"Get ready for a little bump," he warned.

Their feet hit the ground. Maggie's foot didn't land right, and she dragged Dedrus to the ground with her.

"Fucker! Fucker! Fucker!" she wailed. She kicked him in the stomach and punched him repeatedly in the arm.

"Ow! What the fuck?"

She pulled back and ran her hands up and down her body, spasming in a fit of shivers.

"Oh my fucking God!" she exclaimed. "Oh my fucking God!"

*Crazy bitch*, Dedrus thought.

He pressed off the asphalt, starting to his feet. A kick from his side, much stronger than the one Maggie had given him, sent him rolling onto his back.

Kinzer's face was fire red, his sword at Dedrus's throat.

"What the fuck?" Dedrus asked.

"What are you doing?" Maggie's gaze vacillated between them.

"You're the fucking rat!" Kinzer exclaimed.

"What?"

Dedrus was bewildered. They'd just fought the Raze together. How could Kinzer possibly think that he was in league with them?

"I didn't tell anyone about where we were, and I'm sure as fuck that Fie didn't, considering they're probably chopping him up as we speak. And we're the only ones who knew we were gonna be there, so that narrows it down to you and you."

Dedrus could see his point. It didn't make it hurt any less.

Had Kinzer forgotten their past? Did he really have no clue how much he still adored him?

"*You* came to *me*—remember?"

"That doesn't mean shit."

"There are a million ways that they could have found us. For all we know, they could have a Tracker."

Kinzer's sword pressed even tighter against Dedrus's flesh. "You know as well as I do how hard it is to find a Tracker, especially now."

Kinzer was right. Janka was one of the few Trackers to survive the war. The Leader had sent Morarkes to destroy them first because their gift made it easy for the Almighty to hunt and kill their greatest warriors.

"I don't know how they found us. Maybe they tapped Fie's phone. Maybe they've been keeping an eye on him. Fuck if I know. I get if you want to kill me right now. But Kinzer, I swear to our Leader that I have never sided with the Raze. I'm on your side, and I want to help. You need help. We both do."

He wanted to say so much more. He wanted to tell Kinzer that he worshipped the ground he walked on and would never have done anything to hurt him. Now wasn't the time for that.

Kinzer stared into his eyes.

Dedrus reared his head back, giving Kinzer permission to slice his throat open if that was what he thought he needed to do.

Kinzer ground his teeth, groaning as he tossed his sword aside.

"Fuck!" He stomped to the side of a nearby building and smashed his fists against the wall, his sleeve appearing as if it were straining to contain his flexing biceps. "Fuck, fuck!"

Maggie helped Dedrus to his feet. He made his way to Kinzer.

"Kinzer." He rested his hand on his shoulder. "I would never betray you. Please believe that."

"I know," Kinzer said, his chin quivering as he spoke. "With all this going on, it's just hard to know who to trust. I don't know what I was thinking. I'm sorry."

Dedrus wrapped his arms around him.

They embraced.

"You assholes need to get your shit together!" Maggie fussed.

Dedrus chuckled. "So where we gonna take this bitch?"

"I know a place."

***

Kid pushed through the brush.

Since his last jungle fuck session with Treycore, he hadn't bothered to put his shirt back on. Sweat flowed like a waterfall down his rigid rock-wall-of-an-abdomen. His legs convulsed. It still felt as if Treycore was inside him.

"You...think...I'm gonna die out here?" he asked, panting heavily.

Treycore snickered as he pushed a branch out of his path. "I'm not gonna let you die," he said. For a moment, Kid imagined he was saying it because he actually had feelings for him, but he knew better. It was just because Kinzer had asked him to protect him.

"Well, it'll be nice when we finally get out of here," Kid said, exasperated.

Treycore threw a glance over his shoulder.

"It hasn't been that bad," he said with a cocky smile.

A rush of excitement welled in him. He liked that, despite being a mortal, Treycore had thought they'd had a good time. Maybe that meant he did like him.

*No. Shut up! That's ridiculous,* he thought, mentally chastising himself.

"In fact," Treycore said, whirling around, picking Kid up, and slamming him against a nearby tree. "I wouldn't mind being stuck out here a little longer."

Kid blushed. His heart skipped a beat.

Treycore moved in to kiss him, when a sound caught their attention.

A rumbling. Like a car engine.

Just a few yards ahead, what looked like a bus moved between the cracks in a cluster of fronds.

*There must be a road*, Kid thought.

Treycore and Kid broke away from each other and bolted toward the bus.

*We're saved!*

\*\*\*

Kinzer hit the gas in a compact car he'd stolen from a garage near where Dedrus had landed.

Branches and saplings slapped against either side of the windshield as the car bumped and jerked down an overgrown path that had been overtaken by the neighboring forestation. The car bounced into a clearing, where a cabin emerged from a cluster of woods, as if growing from them.

Trees hung over the roof. Kudzu hooked around the rails and steps on the front porch. Patches of stray boards and shingles lay at the foot of the cabin.

"Cute," Maggie muttered facetiously. She sat in the backseat, her hand on her belly, as if preventing it from bouncing with the rest of the car.

"We sure those crazies aren't gonna find us?" she asked.

"This was one of Janka's hideaways," Kinzer replied. "We always said that if there was an emergency, this is where we'd go. No one knows about this place. Not even the Leader's Allies."

"Hold up," Maggie said. "I'm not having my baby in some cabin in the woods! I want to have it in a hospital. Doped up, eating good food, watching soaps."

Dedrus chuckled. "We'll take care of you, Maggie."

Kinzer pulled the car up alongside the cabin, and he, Dedrus, and Maggie headed inside.

It was a mess of dust and cobwebs. On a wooden beam just below the ceiling, a squirrel chewed on an acorn. As Kinzer shut the door, it scurried across the beam and hopped through a crack in the wall. In the opposite corner, a brown bat was affixed to the wall, clearly having decided it'd found the perfect place to take its daylight rest.

Dedrus flicked a light switch by the door. "No electricity."

"Generator's out back," Kinzer said.

He scanned the debris, recklessly spread across the floor—newspapers, magazines, table legs, and toppled bookshelves. Shitty as it looked, it only evoked good memories in Kinzer. He and Janka had spent several romantic nights in this cabin, groping each other by the fire, tearing through walls and furniture during their lovemaking, penetrating each other until the pain was too great for either to keep going.

They worked to clean up the pigsty, piling the garbage on the front porch and scavenging anything they could make use of.

Kinzer took the one mattress in the cabin and set it up in a bedroom for Maggie. Attempting to make the room a little more livable, he put a side table beside the bed and stacked magazines on it so she'd at least have something to read. It wasn't going to be easy being in the middle of nowhere, but Kinzer knew it was what they had to do.

\*\*\*

"Y'all about ready to eat?" Dedrus asked.

He stood at the kitchen stove, a slab of meat sizzling in a skillet.

Behind him, Kinzer and Maggie sat at a table that had a chunk taken out of its side. It'd also had a broken leg, which Kinzer had repaired with two chair legs.

"Hell yeah," Kinzer replied.

Dedrus lifted the skillet and walked over to the table, emptying the meat onto a chipped china plate between Kinzer and Maggie.

They didn't have any more dishes or silverware, so they were going to have to make do.

"What is it?" Maggie asked.

"Deer," Dedrus replied.

"When did you get a deer?" she asked, bewildered.

"About two hours ago."

After they'd straightened up the house, he'd grabbed his sword out of the back of the car and trekked into the woods to find them something to eat.

Maggie eyed it with apprehension.

Kinzer shoved a bite in his mouth. "It's perfectly healthy," he assured her.

Reluctantly, she grabbed a piece and tore it off, nibbling at the edge.

"You're eating for two," Kinzer said. "Remember?"

"I know." She chewed on it. Her expression transformed from concerned to impressed. "Not too bad."

"Thanks," Dedrus said with that adorable smile.

Kinzer loved that smile. So innocent, so fun, so dorky.

This was the life that he'd wanted with Dedrus. These simple, magical moments.

Why hadn't Dedrus wanted these sorts of moments with him?

Bzzz. Bzzz.

Kinzer and Dedrus leapt out of their chairs. They grabbed their swords, which had been lying at their feet, and scanned the room.

Bzzz. Bzzz.

Dedrus gasped. "Oh, shit!"

He reached into his pocket, pulled out his cell, and pressed it to his ear.

"Treycore? You fucking ass. I've been worried as fuck!"

***

Kid was giddy with excitement.

A web of telephone lines zigzagged between orange, red, and blue buildings on either side of a street, which bustled with cyclists and yellow, SUV-looking taxis.

*So this is what it's like to be in another country*, Kid thought.

Judging by the sidewalk, littered with trash and construction debris, they weren't in the best part of Peru, but it was still thrilling to Kid, who'd never been anywhere outside of the U.S. And more importantly, he was glad that he got to share the experience with Treycore.

"Yeah, yeah," Treycore said, a payphone receiver pressed to his ear. "Okay, Dedrus. I'll be there as fast as I can...You don't worry about how..."

*He may not have to worry about how, but I sure as fuck do,* Kid thought.

He didn't have a passport or any money for an airplane ticket. What was he supposed to do? He wondered if Treycore was just going to ditch him. He supposed that since the fate of the world was at stake, that was very likely.

"...I will be," Treycore continued. "Let Kinzer know Kid's fine...Uh huh...yeah...okay. Bye."

He hung up, picked the phone back up again, and mashed his thumb on the dials.

*Who's he calling now?* Kid wondered.

"Lero, it's Trey. Yeah. Got a favor to ask."

## CHAPTER ELEVEN

"She has the baby here," Dedrus said. He knelt before the fireplace and struck a match against the flint of the box. "Then what?"

Maggie had retired to her makeshift bedroom for the night. Kinzer and Dedrus had moved into the living area.

Dedrus tossed the lit match between crumpled up newspapers that surrounded stacked logs.

Kinzer sprawled across a couch that he'd slid before the fireplace.

"I don't know." He gazed at the flame that morphed slowly into a building fire.

"We need a plan." Dedrus rose to his feet and set the matchbox on the mantel. He slipped back to the couch, falling onto the cushion opposite Kinzer. "That baby isn't going to just walk out and be able to take on the Almighty. It's gonna be a long time before it can even defend itself. And you know the Almighty will do everything in His power to destroy it. That's a lot of things against us."

Kinzer nodded. "I know. But we can't really plan for the next fifteen...maybe twenty years. We gotta plan for tomorrow."

Dedrus knew he was right, but there was so much more to this than either of them were considering. As his mind wandered in that direction, it became so overwhelming that he had to stop. He couldn't bear it.

"So what do we do tomorrow?" Dedrus tucked a bang that had settled in his face behind his ear.

"Get some supplies. Try to give the Antichrist the best delivery we can."

Dedrus sighed. What did higherlings and fallens know about delivering an immortal child from a mortal? For all they knew, the labor would kill Maggie. And she was close...too close for them not to be considering those sorts of things.

Dedrus was tired of his mind being ravaged by those kind of thoughts.

He needed an escape. He assumed Kinzer felt the same way.

*We can just fuck.*

He knew that wasn't true. He could never just fuck Kinzer.

He wanted to be close to him, though. He needed to be close to him again.

He crawled across the couch and rubbed his nose against Kinzer's cheek, pressing his lips softly against his chin.

In the light of the fire, Kinzer's eyebrows cast shadows over his eyes, making him appear almost menacing. Kinzer pushed off the arm of the couch and firmly kissed Dedrus. He wrapped his arms around him, swapping places as he forced Dedrus on his back.

Dedrus's neck dragged across the fabric lining the arm of the couch. He savored Kinzer's hot, wet mouth, sliding his hands under Kinzer's shirt, feeling his way across his abs. The dips between his muscles were jagged, as if he was feeling across a jagged rock covered in a thin layer of cushioned flesh.

Kinzer grabbed one of Dedrus's wrists and pulled it over his head, pressing it against the arm of the couch. He did the same with the other. Pulling from their embrace, he moved his lips close to Dedrus's. Not close enough to kiss him. Just close enough for Dedrus to be tormented by the thought.

Dedrus's mouth instinctively attacked.

Kinzer withdrew.

This had always been their relationship—him attempting to show Kinzer his affections, and Kinzer pulling away.

Though the deprivation was cruel, it was also erotic.

He lay there, waiting for Kinzer to kiss him, hoping, praying to the Leader, that it would come sooner rather than later.

Kinzer's lips hovered over his.

Dedrus thought of it as a test. If Kinzer kissed him, it meant that he wanted to be with him—it would give him hope that they might actually have a future together. If he just fucked him, then he was just using him for his body.

Kinzer planted a hard, deep kiss on Dedrus, his tongue slipping between his lips, tasting as it wished. His mouth made its way down Dedrus's chin and slid across his neck.

Dedrus delighted in the warmth and the confirmation of Kinzer's affection.

Kinzer sucked softly between Dedrus's jaw and neck. His teeth tugged at the flesh.

Without warning, Kinzer pulled back.

They locked eyes.

Kinzer looked sad. Did he regret the day he'd rejected Dedrus's love? Surely not. He wouldn't have met Janka if he hadn't. Dedrus wanted him to regret it, though. He wanted Kinzer to look back and see the foolishness of his mistake— to feel for him as he'd always felt for Kinzer.

Kinzer's gaze stirred a rush that crawled from the base of his spine to his neck. Dedrus pulled, practically tore, out of his shirt.

Kinzer did the same, revealing his muscular body, sharp shadows amplifying the grooves in his abs.

Dedrus licked through the grooves, savoring the taste of his flesh.

Kinzer gripped onto the button on his jeans and stepped off the couch, making a quick effort to get them off. Dedrus was right beside him, working far more effectively, because his were at his ankles twice as fast as Kinzer's.

Before he could turn around, Kinzer tackled him from behind, driving them both to the wood-paneled floor.

Kinzer lay across Dedrus, his dick between his cheeks, his abdomen pressed against his back, his lips at his neck.

Heat radiated off Kinzer's lips, sweeping between locks of Dedrus's hair, kissing the tiny hairs that strayed across the back of Dedrus's neck. They tickled and stood on end, though they were nowhere near as erect as Dedrus was in that moment.

Splinters in the wood scratched at his shaft's flesh as he strained from the pressure between the floor and Kinzer's pelvis.

Kinzer stroked his cock between Dedrus's cheeks.

Dedrus savored the feeling. He wondered how something was capable of causing him such excruciating pain and such intoxicating pleasure at the same time.

Dedrus pushed his ass back, begging for Kinzer to just put him out of his misery and enter him. He wanted to feel that cock forcing its way in.

Kinzer pressed on the floor, pushing up. He spit in his hand, offering modest lubrication before he navigated the head of his cock into Dedrus's ass.

*Get it in!* Dedrus thought.

He needed Kinzer to be close to him. He needed Kinzer to be with him as he had so long ago, if only so he could pretend they'd never parted.

Kinzer raised his hand to his mouth.

"No!" Dedrus snapped. "I don't need anymore spit! I want it like this."

He just wanted to feel the raw rub, the tear inside of him, the burning sensation that let him know that Kinzer and he were one.

Kinzer's eyes shimmered in the light from the fireplace. He jerked his hips forward.

Dedrus squinted. The sharp sting was intense, but he knew it could be worse.

"All the way!" he demanded.

Kinzer obliged.

Dedrus tried to scream, but it caught in his throat. The pain was so intense, so severe. He couldn't breathe. Jerking his head back, he hit and punched at the floor, desperately attempting to distract himself from the pain.

Tears rushed from his eyes, dripping onto the floor, glistening in sparks from the fire.

Despite the clear pain Dedrus was in, Kinzer didn't stop. He thrust back and forth with a violent passion, groaning like a warrior striking for the kill.

It was just how Dedrus liked it—how Kinzer knew he loved it.

Dedrus wondered if his hole was bleeding because each stroke felt so rough, so dry. He figured he might as well have had Kinzer shove his fist inside him.

Kinzer stroked his hand up across his back, petting him, as if supporting him through this difficult time.

Another thrust from Kinzer, and Dedrus was done. The pain was too intense.

"I can't!" He slapped his hand against Kinzer's ass. "I'm sorry. Please."

Kinzer started to pull out, just as he'd always done when it was truly too much for Dedrus.

However, the thought of Kinzer exiting him seemed a worse prospect than the severe pain he was in already. Dedrus shoved his ass back to the base of Kinzer's shaft. He threw his hands around Kinzer's ass and clung desperately to his cheeks, gnashing his teeth as he absorbed the pain.

Kinzer continued his assault. He slipped his hands under Dedrus's arms and wrapped around his neck. He interlocked his fingers as he shoved Dedrus's forehead against the floor and thrust into him repeatedly.

"Ah! Ah!" Dedrus called out, thinking Maggie had surely heard them.

Kinzer's hands released each other and found their way around to Dedrus's chest. In a quick maneuver, Kinzer pulled his legs forward, positioning himself on his knees, and rolled back, taking Dedrus with him, landing so that he lay across the floor.

Dedrus remained over him, squatting at his pelvis, Kinzer's girth still inside.

Dedrus threw his hands behind him and set his palms on the floorboards. He arched his back and whirled his ass in circles.

"You feel so fucking good," Kinzer muttered, still caressing his back as his ass bobbed up and down, as if trying to force his cock deeper into Dedrus than physically possible.

Dedrus risked a glance over his shoulder. He could see Kinzer's exhilaration, his arousal, as he plowed in, seemingly without regard for Dedrus's enjoyment.

Dedrus tossed his head back, closing his eyes to savor the sensation. His crouched legs quaked, but he was used to this. It was just a particularly low lap dance, something that Dedrus considered himself to be an expert at.

Kinzer's hands fell to Dedrus's hips, gripping on to his love handles as they forced Dedrus's ass to the base of his shaft. He was so deep, hitting that spot that sent ripples of ecstasy rushing through Dedrus's brain. His skin felt like it was being pricked all over. His pelvis felt like it was being consumed by fire, possibly just a bodily reaction from having to endure Kinzer's cock. He hissed through his teeth as the pain became almost too much for him.

"Fuck yeah!" Kinzer called out.

Dedrus could tell Kinzer was about to come. He could feel it in the way his dick was pulsating. It was a familiar feeling.

But he wanted to top Kinzer. He hadn't done that yet, and he knew if he did, Kinzer wouldn't be able to help but recall their time together.

He was going to top him, even if it killed him.

He grabbed Kinzer's wrists and ripped his hands from his love handles. Dislodging Kinzer's dick from his ass, he sprang forward.

"No, no, no!" Kinzer cried as the head of his dick slipped out of Dedrus's hole.

Dedrus crawled to freedom.

"Not this time," he mocked.

Kinzer's eyes filled with rage. He snatched Dedrus by his ankle.

Dedrus tossed a glance back and kicked at Kinzer's shoulder with his free foot. But Kinzer grabbed that one, too, and reeled him back in.

*Not happening, asshole.*

Kinzer released Dedrus just long enough to restrain him by his calves. He clenched down so hard, Dedrus thought his skin might tear off.

But Dedrus was determined to win.

He closed his eyes. His wings shot out of his back, startling Kinzer as he pulled his hands back to defend against the oncoming feathers.

Dedrus rolled across the floor and leapt to his feet, lunging at Kinzer.

Kinzer grabbed him by his shoulders, and they went rolling across the floorboards. Dedrus could feel the splinters grazing across his wings.

As Dedrus landed on top, he wrapped his arms around Kinzer's thighs and clamped tightly around them, lifting them up.

Kinzer struggled. "You bastard!" he shouted.

Dedrus didn't pay any attention. He provided a spit for his dick, then pushed his hips forward, letting the tip of his cock taste Kinzer's hole as he made sure he was in a good position to drive in.

He was, and he did.

He didn't let Kinzer off the hook, either. He shoved as deep inside as he could, without regard for the modestly lubricated walls in his ass.

The veins in Kinzer's neck streaked from his jawline to his chest. He screamed out. Not as if the experience was slightly uncomfortable. He screamed as if it was the most unbearable pain he'd ever experienced in his life.

Dedrus didn't stop his assault. He pushed in and out with a furious passion. After all, that was what Kinzer would have done.

"Harder!" Kinzer demanded, despite appearing to be in excruciating pain.

Dedrus complied. He leaned down and snatched Kinzer by his jet-black hair, pulling back sharply, as though he were a vampire about to bite into his prey. "How hard do you want me to fuck you?" he asked.

The whites of Kinzer's eyes were red, his breathing sporadic. "Rip my fucking ass apart!"

Dedrus pulled back and forced Kinzer's face against his chest. "Show me you want it."

A part of what he was unleashing was that rage—the rage that he'd felt toward Kinzer all this time—the rage that, at one time, he had unleashed all alone, knowing that Janka had taken from him the only thing that had ever mattered.

Kinzer touched the tip of his tongue against Dedrus's nipple. He licked lightly, deliberately.

Dedrus couldn't tell when his nipple would feel that sensation again, and it drove him insane.

His balls felt like they were about to explode.

He cried out. "Oh, fuck. Fuck, no. I'm gonna—"

He had to stop himself. He wasn't going to let Kinzer off that easy.

He started to pull out. But Kinzer grabbed his hips and drove him back in.

"You bitch!" Dedrus cried.

"You started this," Kinzer said through gritted teeth. "Now finish it like the fucking higherling I know you are."

Dedrus pushed on Kinzer's legs, struggling to get out of him, but Kinzer's grip was too strong, and he was too close.

He didn't have much time left, and his hips' movements were beyond his control, reaching deep into Kinzer, feeling that pressure around his shaft, as if Kinzer's ass was just begging to be come inside of.

Then, he cried out, a deep, guttural cry, as he felt that jolt of fluid rip into Kinzer.

Kinzer screamed out at the same time, a stream of come soaring through the air and sprinkling translucent white splotches from his abs to his chin.

Dedrus smiled. He gazed into Kinzer's eyes. Kinzer wore a smile.

For a moment, he was transported back to their tent—to the days when they'd fuck. Kinzer looked so at peace, so at ease.

A flash of worry washed over Kinzer's face.

*What was it?*

He already had his guesses. Kinzer was thinking about Janka. He was thinking about how wrong it was for them to be doing this. He was remembering that he didn't love his immortal fuck buddy...that he'd never loved him...could never love him.

\*\*\*

Maggie lay across the mattress, feeling as comfortable as if she'd decided to sleep on a concrete slab.

The moans and groans had finally settled outside her door.

Moonlight streamed through the window, illuminating her room with a blue light.

She'd occupied her attention with a crack just under the ceiling, trying to imagine what kind of creature would have lived inside it. Bat? Cockroach? Spider? The thought of a spider left her feeling small prickling sensations all over her body, so she had to pull the sheet down to ease her paranoia.

Her belly now held her attention. It was too big to ignore, unlike the early days, when she had known what it was and tried to act as if it wasn't.

It took her back to a day many years earlier.

"A whore isn't fit to be a mother!" Mom had shouted.

Having noticed Maggie's continual weight gain, her mother had forced her to take a home pregnancy test. The result had sent her into a fit, screaming and fussing.

"Who is it? Who is it, slut? Where did you take his poison? Did you eat it, too? I bet you did. I bet you sucked it right out of his snake. You loved it, didn't you? Whores always love it. They need it. Is that what you are? Is that what you want everyone to think you are?"

One humid afternoon, her mom, seeming unusually pleasant, told her she needed a haircut and they headed off. As the drive stretched far beyond the usual for the hair salon, and Maggie's mom didn't seem any more inclined to reveal the whereabouts of their destination, Maggie became suspicious.

Her mom didn't have to discuss her plan. Somehow, she just knew, and as they arrived at the city clinic, Maggie was certain she only had two options: stay with her mother or with this thing that was inside her.

An alley lined the side of the clinic. As her mom crept inside without her, she stared at it, thinking, *That's my choice.*

It was uncertainty. It was terrifying. But she felt that it was the right thing to do, and a powerful urge pushed her down that alley, into her future.

Years later, she was sure that God was punishing her. Her mom was the closest she'd ever been to God. Everyone had told her so…constantly. Surely, they were right. Satan's path had been compelling, and it had led Maggie into darkness.

*Bunch of crap*, Maggie thought, her eyes still on her belly, but her thoughts on her mom's communions with the divine.

A part of her had always wondered—imagined, "What if she's just making this all up?" Even as a kid, she had this deep suspicion for her mom, but she was sure that it was just ignorance—her naivety about God. Had it been a lie? Had her mom been insane? She knew she'd never know the truth. What she knew was that whatever her mom experienced on those mornings on the linoleum floor of the local Pentecostal chapter was not what it had seemed to be.

Nothing was what it seemed.

Still, her mom had been right about one thing: "A whore isn't fit to be a mother." Maggie had always known that, and it was why she'd wanted to terminate this pregnancy. This wasn't a way to bring a child into the world. A child deserved better than that. The world was cruel enough without having to grow up so disadvantaged, so crippled by societal boundaries.

*I'd be a terrible mother*, Maggie thought. *They just need to take it, so I can get on with my life. I didn't ask for it anyway. It was forced on me. I would have never done this to myself. No. It deserves better. I'd be the worst thing for it.*

Her thoughts wandered to a boy at the bookstore Dedrus and Kinzer had taken her to. He played on the floor, pulling crossword puzzles off the rack and setting them at his side.

*Where the fuck is his mom?* she'd thought. *Fucking irresponsible bitch.*

She studied him. She wondered if she'd be capable of taking care of something like that.

*No, no, no,* she'd thought. *It's a rodent. It's horrible. Why would anyone want something so careless, with such disregard for everyone else?*

But she hadn't been able take her eyes off him.

Now, she wasn't able to take her eyes off her belly.

\*\*\*

As Dedrus smirked, his bristly beard scratched against Kinzer's cheek.

Dedrus's stomach lay flat across his. His arm framed Kinzer's face as he tickled Kinzer's scalp with light strokes through his black locks.

Guilt ravaged Kinzer's mind. He'd thought he could just fuck Dedrus. He'd thought he'd be able to distance himself from those feelings from the past, but at the culmination of the act, he'd realized that he'd forgotten about his Janka entirely and was only thinking about his feelings for Dedrus. He'd wanted him. He'd needed him—the way that he'd needed him so long ago.

He'd thought, *Could he love me? Does he love me?*

When he saw that glisten in Dedrus's eyes, he could have sworn that he knew the answer, but he'd believed he'd understood that same look back in the days before Janka.

Janka. Oh, how Janka would rage knowing that Kinzer's feelings for Dedrus had returned so quickly.

*I'm disgusting,* Kinzer thought. *How could I? How could Dedrus, knowing how I feel? Knowing what I've been through?*

He started to feel violated. What if Dedrus had plotted this? Had wanted him to fall back in love with him, only to reject him again?

*No! Dedrus wouldn't do that.*

He'd been a good friend. He'd been more than that.

Kinzer massaged his fingers through the vee above Dedrus's ass and offered a soft kiss.

Kinzer's cock brushed across Dedrus's leg hairs.

Dedrus set his arms on either side of Kinzer and propped himself up on the cushion beneath them.

His serious expression let Kinzer know that Dedrus had something he wanted to talk about.

He knew that look. It was the same one he'd seen when Dedrus had confessed his feelings to him.

What was he supposed to do? Dedrus had clearly just been caught up in the moment. He didn't want him, and as soon as someone else came along, he'd find them equally appealing.

No. Dedrus just *thought* he wanted him. For this moment.

Maybe if he was quiet, Dedrus would bail.

He outlined the grooves in Dedrus's back, offering a smile, ignoring Dedrus's struggle.

"I know you're going through a lot right now. This probably is too soon to ask."

*Fuck. We're totally talking about this. Goddammit, Dedrus.*

"I just keep wondering if maybe..."

Kinzer watched Dedrus's thumb trail up his side and slide under his pecs.

Dedrus took a breath and looked back into his eyes. "Do you think there could ever be something like we used to have?"

"Friendship?"

"Is that what you think I mean?"

"Isn't that what we had?" Kinzer knew better. His comment was a cruel jab that he hoped would hurt Dedrus. If it didn't, then it would just hurt him.

"No. I know what we had. *You* know what we had."

Kinzer's thoughts returned to their nights together, but those memories only brought him pain, and Kinzer wasn't willing to go back there anymore.

"Whatever we had, it's not there anymore."

Dedrus's beard quivered with his cheeks. His mouth fell open. Sparkling orbs of fluid stirred at the corners of his eyes.

He pushed his arms into the cushion, his legs shuffling over Kinzer as he stood.

"Fine." He scooped his briefs off the floor and slipped them on. The band snapped against the dip in his waist and clung to that finely curved ass.

*This is what he deserves*, Kinzer thought. *For what he did to me.*

"Why have you been doing this?" Dedrus whirled around, his face bright red.

Kinzer crawled up the cushion until he was sitting. He flashed a gaze back to Maggie's room. "Can you keep it down?"

"You were leading me on."

"What?"

"You knew what I wanted. You *know* how I feel about you." Dedrus clenched his fists. They trembled at either side of his briefs.

"How do you feel?"

"I love you!" Dedrus's eyes stared into Kinzer's with confidence, certainty, as if he wanted to make sure there was no doubt about the sincerity and conviction behind his confession.

*How dare he say that to me!*

Heat rushed to Kinzer's face.

"No, you don't." Kinzer leaned over his legs. He grabbed his boxers off the floor and wiggled them on.

"Are you telling me what I feel?"

"I just don't want to hear this bullshit." Kinzer hopped to his feet, stepping to Dedrus so they were face to face. If he was finally going to confront this, then Kinzer wanted the truth.

"Bullshit? I told you that I loved you. You knew that."

"Do you really think I believed it?"

The creases in Dedrus's forehead twitched with his eyebrows. "We were together. I told you I wanted to be with you. I told you I wanted you to be the one—"

The more he spoke, the more it hurt Kinzer. How could he say these things? How could he act like he actually cared about him?

"I was very clear," Dedrus insisted.

"Why don't we ask Ryson how clear you were?"

Dedrus's gaze shifted wall to wall. "Ryson? What about him?"

"Why don't you tell me?"

"Nothing happened with—"

Kinzer lost it. He lunged forward, gripping Dedrus by his neck and shoving him against the wall beside the fireplace.

This wasn't like the playful wrestling of their sexual escapades. It was pure, vicious rage.

"Don't you fucking stand there and lie to me!" His jaw clenched.

He wanted to rip Dedrus apart. No matter how good of friends they'd been, no matter how much they'd been through together, no matter how much he'd helped him these past few days—he couldn't bear Dedrus's lying to his face.

"Don't you fucking dare," Kinzer continued. "I deserve better than that. You look me in the eye and you tell me the truth."

Tremors vibrated from Dedrus's neck, through Kinzer's hand.

*Is he scared?*

Dedrus hesitated, like he was being careful not to speak too soon. His gaze sank. "I didn't do anything wrong."

Kinzer's nostrils flared. His fist rose, but he stopped it before it built up the necessary momentum to throw a punch. He released him and stepped back, turning away.

"You knew how I felt about you, and I thought I knew how you felt about me."

The tears from Dedrus's eyes rushed down his cheeks, catching in his prickly beard. "You should have said something back then."

"What? That I knew you were fucking Ryson behind my back?"

"They moved me to another troop."

"Honestly, you didn't do anything wrong. We'd never talked about any sort of commitment. And when I found out about him, I just assumed I knew why. You didn't want to commit to me. If that was the case, I wasn't gonna waste the rest of my life."

"Is that what you think it would have been? A waste?"

Not a waste. A tragedy. He knew that when he discovered that Dedrus didn't love him back, he'd be devastated, and he feared that he wouldn't be able to handle it.

"I thought I needed to move on."

"Well, I'm glad one of us could."

"You're so full of shit. You're a fucking liar."

"A liar?"

"Acting like you were *so* into me back then. Playing like you didn't know what I was talking about when I brought up Ryson. This whole 'woe is me' shit right now."

"You don't know what you're talking about." Dedrus hurried past Kinzer and scooped his jeans and shirt off the floor. He slipped into the jeans, pulling them up his legs.

"I wanted to be with you," Kinzer said.

"I wanted to be with you, too, you fucking idiot!" The waves of his hair bobbed over his shoulders as he shouted. He buttoned the top button of his jeans and headed for the door.

Kinzer grabbed his arm and pulled him back.

"Admit it! You didn't want me until I was with Janka, because you were jealous. Suddenly, I mattered because I was with someone else who mattered."

"You're insane." Dedrus yanked his arm from Kinzer's grip.

He walked to the door, set his hand on the knob, and froze. He wiped his hand across his face, freeing a tear that had settled in his scruff.

"Why?" Dedrus asked.

"Why *what*?"

"You could have told me this back then. You could have confronted me, and I would have told you how much I loved you. How much I wanted to spend the rest of eternity with you. How much that didn't even matter."

Kinzer's rage settled. He didn't know if what Dedrus was saying was true, but it evoked honesty from him. "I loved you. I thought you were different than all the others. When you went away, I didn't see anyone else. I didn't do anything...for a long time. Not because I had to stop myself. Because I couldn't imagine being with anyone other than you. When I heard about Ryson, I knew you'd never feel for me the way I felt for you."

Dedrus's gaze softened as he scanned Kinzer. He opened his mouth like he was about to say something, but stopped himself.

He opened the door and stepped outside, closing the door behind him.

Kinzer's thoughts went wild.

What if Dedrus really had loved him? What if, all this time, he'd made such a big deal out nothing?

He returned to the couch, collapsing onto his face. The fabric scratched at his arms as tears collected on the cushion.

## CHAPTER TWELVE

Kid stepped into the hotel room, his nostrils savoring a sweet, pine aroma. It was the best thing he'd smelled in a long time. This was also the nicest place he'd seen since he'd first arrived at Jerry's.

Between the main living area and the adjoining bedroom, Kid thought the room might have been as big as the workout room at Jerry's. The living area divided into two parts. On one side was a white-tiled kitchen, complete with a fridge, microwave, and coffeemaker. A black, marble counter separated it from the living area, where Kid and Treycore stood. A red leather sofa and cushioned chairs faced a wall-mounted flat screen TV.

Treycore went to the kitchen counter, and picking up a pen and a notepad that were placed on it, scribbled something down.

Kid meandered into the adjoining bedroom.

"Whoa!" he exclaimed.

A king-sized bed took up most of the room and faced its own flat screen TV. On the other side of the bed, a window stretched across the wall, looking out at the ocean, which glistened in the moonlight.

Kid raced up to the window, his eyes fixed on a beach as waves crashed against the shore.

Treycore came up behind him, wrapping his arms around his chest and tucking his nose against Kid's face.

"You like it?" he asked.

"It's beautiful!" Kid exclaimed, beaming.

"Maybe once we figure all this out, we'll have to come back. You know, for a visit."

Shivers rushed up and down Kid's body. The thought of getting to spend more time with Treycore was exhilarating. He giggled with excitement. Spinning around, he planted a firm kiss on Treycore's lips.

Waves of heat rushed through his body. His thoughts scrambled. He couldn't pull Treycore close enough. He wanted Treycore to be inside him. He wanted to never let him go.

Treycore kissed his way down to Kid's neck.

Kid became so lost in the moment that he muttered, "I love—"

Treycore pulled back sharply.

"—Kinzer," Kid finished. He was relieved that he'd managed to catch himself before saying "you."

The words he'd almost uttered had startled Kid, but they were how he felt. Oh, what a dumb mortal he must've been. It was a trick of the mind, surely. Of course, after everything he had been through he would have believed that he was in love with the most beautiful man...well, immortal...he'd ever encountered.

It must have been something Treycore emitted—some magnetic power that betrayed Kid's senses. Made him think they were more than they possibly could have been.

Treycore would have laughed—mocked him, even—if he knew how he felt. Even worse, he might never be allowed to fuck him again.

Treycore's arms withdrew from around Kid. His face appeared frozen, stoic.

Kid couldn't tell what he was thinking. Maybe he was just relieved that he hadn't said his name. Or, maybe he knew that he was about to say his name and was horrified.

"Who was that guy you called?" Kid asked, desperately trying to get out of what felt like a wildly uncomfortable situation.

"Um...uh," Treycore stammered.

Kid was surprised. He'd never seen Treycore at a loss for words.

Treycore headed back into the living area. Kid followed after him.

"My ex-girlfriend," Treycore said. "You remember the bitch who—"

"Oh, I fucking remember."

Treycore returned to the counter. He tore a page from the notepad and scribbled on the next page. Kid leaned against the doorframe between the two rooms.

"Well, this guy's got her same gift. He's a very old friend. Went into hiding during the war. That's not exactly accurate. I guess you could say he was forced into hiding. The Leader created a weapon. A very powerful weapon known as Morarkes. They were designed to kill immortals, particularly higherlings. Their first targets were Teleporters and Trackers, the two greatest threats to the Leader's army, considering he had very few of either in Hell. As far as I know, there were only a handful of Teleporters in Hell. Heaven had nearly twenty."

As he spoke, he didn't look back up at Kid. Kid worried that it had something to do with when he'd said those stupid words, "I love…" Treycore must have known how he really felt and was sweet enough to not tell him why he could never like a stinky mortal.

"When Lero, the higherling I called," Treycore continued, "discovered that his Teleporter friends were being killed off by this weapon, he came to earth, went into hiding, and tried to blend in with mortals. I wish I could say that after the war, he found out he liked earth so much that he decided to stay. Truth is, he's always been paranoid about another war breaking out and him being the first target. And for good reason. The war really never ended, and his kind are at the top of the Leader's hit-list."

"Thank you, Trey."

A man, appearing out of nowhere, like Vera, was suddenly sitting on the counter beside Treycore. Kid assumed this was Lero.

Lero wore a stark-white suit that contrasted nicely with his skin, which was nearly as dark as the Brazilians' at

Jerry's. His hair was black, like Kinzer's, but meticulously combed so that it sheened. He had a thick, inch-long beard. His head seemed too large for his body, and his nose seemed too large for his face. Even with his odd features, Kid still found him incredibly attractive.

Lero's palms pressed down on the counter as he leaned back, kicking his feet out before him.

"I appreciate you reminding me why I shouldn't have come," Lero continued.

"Come on," Treycore said, flashing a smile. "For old time's sake."

Lero's eyes shifted to Kid. "Now, who's this little guy here?"

"Kid," Treycore said, hardly acknowledging him.

Lero smiled. "Hey there, Kid."

Kid tossed him a wave and as friendly a smile as he could fake.

"Damn, he fucking stinks," Lero said. "Even for a mortal."

*Douche*, Kid thought. But as he inspected Lero's expression, he didn't detect an insult. His eyebrows were cocked, his stare fixed. His mouth hung open, as if he was about to drool. Kid knew that look. He'd seen it on so many of Jerry's clients.

"Don't mind him, Kid," Treycore said, throwing Kid a brief glare. "He's just been around mortals too long. Lost his immortal manners."

Kid knew he was just making a joke, but by that point, he knew of quite a few immortals, and he couldn't help but observe that they didn't really have very good manners.

"What do you think of my hotel?" Lero whirled his hand in the air, clearly indicating far more than the little room they were in.

"What do you mean?"

"This is mine. Well, one of many. We have hotels in countries across the globe."

"During Lero's mortal years, if you will," Treycore began, "he hit it big in the luxury hotel industry."

"This was, of course," Lero expanded, "after a few years as a struggling stage actor, a loathed opera singer, a migrant farmer, a war vet, and a series of other dead-end jobs. Of all my occupations, I think robber baron is my favorite."

Treycore snatched the page he'd ripped from the notepad and handed it to Lero.

"Can you take us there?"

Lero didn't even look it. "I *can* take you anywhere. The question is: *will* I?"

"You seriously gonna be an ass about this?" Treycore asked.

"Trey, you realize that every time I teleport, I leave a scent behind that the Leader and the Almighty can trace, right?"

"I know. I was with Vera, remember?"

"Unfortunately. In fact, this is where my problem lies. I can smell that bitch on you right now, so I don't imagine that your little excursion outside of the States was for sightseeing. You're dancing with the Raze, and if I take you somewhere and she finds you, she's gonna be able to smell me on you, just like I can smell her on you."

Lero looked to Kid. "It's the shitty part about being a Teleporter," he explained. "When we travel, we give off this scent, like burning rubber, that only other Teleporters can smell. There are so few of us that, over the years, we've easily been able to distinguish the nuance in each other's scents."

His eyes snapped back to Treycore. "That said, if that bitch hunts you down and smells me, then I'm the one who's fucked. Word'll get out that I'm still alive and posing with a bunch of mortals, and I think you can imagine how thrilled the Almighty will be. You know how He feels about deserters."

"Dude, I *need* your help."

"And I would *like* to stay alive" Lero said. "I don't know what fucked up shit you're in with the Raze, but I'd recommend you just leave it."

"I can't. Dedrus and Kinzer are in trouble. I have to help them."

Kid thought Treycore should just tell Lero about the Antichrist, but he figured he had a good reason for keeping that to himself.

Lero's eyes shifted back to Kid. "Well, Treycore, as you know, I'm a businessman. I might be willing to make an arrangement...negotiate."

He licked his lips.

"Negotiate?" Treycore asked. "What do you mean? I don't have anything. I have some cash back at our place, but..."

"Oh, I'm not talking about money."

The crotch in his pants protruded forward.

*Damn*, Kid thought. *He might be as big as Treycore.*

"Give me a little time with that foul-smelling kid, and I'll take you wherever the fuck you want to go."

*What kind of fucked up fetish does this guy have?* Kid thought, wrapping his hands around his elbows, as if trying to defend his body from Lero's gaze.

"That's not happening," Treycore said.

"Then enjoy your stay in Lima."

"I'll do it," Kid said.

He knew what he had to do. His mind flashed back to his nightmare.

He was back at Jerry's. He was trapped behind that chain-link fencing. He was trapped under clients...under

Daddy. He'd hoped that he'd ridden himself of that sort of life. But he knew the only way he could help the person who'd freed him from all that pain was by temporarily returning to it.

"Fuck no!" Treycore said. "No, he won't."

"Yes, I will," he insisted.

Red rushed across Treycore's white flesh. His dimples sharpened. His eyebrows came together. "Kid, stay out of this!" he barked.

Kid ignored him. "I'll do whatever you need me to." He stepped into the living area, dropping his arms to his side as he surrendered to Lero.

Lero's lips curled into a smile.

"No," Treycore snapped. He grabbed Kid's shoulder and pulled him into the bedroom. "Kid," he hissed. "You're not a fucking whore."

"Yes," Kid said matter-of-factly. "I am."

It hurt Kid to say it, but it was true.

Treycore's face softened. He looked at Kid, as if pulling from his pupils the painful memories of his past. Kid let his immortal gaze pierce into his soul, hoping it would reveal his shameful, humiliating past so Treycore could understand.

"Kinzer saved my life," Kid said. "He's done more for me than I can ever repay him for."

Treycore's gaze wandered.

"I don't care if his immortal cock kills me," Kid continued. "This is what I know. This is what I'm good at. This is something that I can do to help."

He pushed past Treycore and approached Lero, grabbing him by the hand, just as he'd done with so many of Jerry's clients before.

***

Kid left the door cracked open, as Treycore had requested. Treycore had been willing to let him follow through with this, but he'd repeatedly told Kid to shout the moment he started to have second thoughts.

Lero sat on the bed. He scanned Kid. He smiled. "Wanna get a little more comfortable?"

Kid looked around uneasily. It wasn't that Lero was unattractive or that he wouldn't have fucked him even without a proposition. He'd just hoped that he'd never have to live the kind of life he'd lived when he was trapped at Jerry's.

"Come here," Lero said.

Kid approached him.

Lero sat up, wrapped his arms around Kid's waist, and pulled him back so he was lying on top of him. He stroked his thumb across his temple.

"I won't hurt you," he said. "I just want to pleasure you."

He gently kissed Kid's lips.

A wave of heat swept through Kid's face. It felt so good.

Kid touched Lero's soft beard, the prickles massaging his fingertips.

Lero's fingers slipped under Kid's shirt as he pulled it off over his head. He rolled over. Setting Kid on his back, he kissed his way down the canal between Kid's pecs.

The heat that Kid had felt on his face now swirled like a hurricane in his chest.

Lero's fingers combed softly across his belly, his fingers trailing through the rifts at the edge of his abs, down to his jeans. Undoing his button, he grabbed either side of the jeans and Kid's underwear and pulled down, sliding them off his legs.

As he returned, he pressed that gargantuan nose of his against Kid's sack, stroking it, groping it with his most obnoxious, and for Kid, most erotic, feature.

Kid felt Lero's tongue as it licked across his balls. It swept up quickly and then widened so that it could suck Kid's entire cock in his mouth.

Kid's cock swelled.

The tip of Lero's tongue flicked about as his lips moved up and down his shaft.

Kid writhed in the sensation as tickles massaged up and down his body.

Lero pulled back from Kid's cock, a beautiful grin stretched across his face.

He stood and undressed, removing his suit and shoes.

His body was far more impressive than his face. His muscles were bulkier than any of the other immortals he'd seen. His pecs were like boulders. They twitched as he stacked his clothes. And the way his ass bobbed up and down as he stepped to the dresser, setting his clothes down, made Kid even harder.

Even as Kid appreciated Lero's body, still savoring the delicious sensations from Lero's mouth, his mind couldn't help but wander.

*What is Treycore going to think? Does he think I'm tainted? Will he not fuck me again because of this?*

Lero crawled over Kid, stroking through Kid's pubes with his massive cock as he pressed their abs together and planted another gentle, burning kiss on Kid's lips.

Lero's fingers encircled Kid's thighs. He gripped around them, pulling Kid's legs into the air. He pulled his cock back and lined it up with Kid's hole.

"That's a beautiful ass," he said.

He released one of Kid's legs, pressed his hand to his mouth, and hurled a juicy wad of spit in it. He wiped the spit over his cock and returned his hand to Kid's thigh, propping it up as he navigated the head of his dick to Kid's hole.

Kid threw his head back. He gulped.

Lero slid the head of his dick inside him.

Kid could tell that Lero had far more experience fucking mortals than Kinzer or Treycore because of how slow and carefully he moved.

Lero lost his balance slightly on the bed and forced his dick farther into Kid's hole.

"FUCK!" Kid wailed. It'd been too much for him to handle.

"Sorry," Lero whispered, stroking his hand up and down Kid's thigh. "Are you okay?"

Kid nodded. "Yeah, yeah. I'm fine."

But he wasn't really fine. The awful sting just made him think of his Treycore. And as good as Lero felt inside him, he was sure that after this, Treycore would never respect him again. He'd just think of him as a tainted whore. The thought that Treycore would never force himself inside him again, never wring his neck and leave him begging for air, never send him into rapturous ecstasy again, tortured Kid. Tears streamed down his face. He tried to stop them, but they just kept coming.

*I want him,* he thought. *So bad. But I can never have him.*

"Are you okay?" Lero asked.

\*\*\*

*Why would he do that?* Treycore thought. *For Kinzer? What the fuck's so special about Kinzer?*

He sat on the couch in the room beside the bedroom, his ears anxiously anticipating any sign that Kid needed help.

He couldn't believe that Kid had agreed to do that for Lero. He shouldn't have. They could've found another way home.

*What did he mean when he said he was a whore?*

There was so much he didn't know about Kid. But he wanted to know. He wanted to know everything about him.

He couldn't believe how obsessed he was with a mortal—a mortal that was so hung up on Kinzer, he didn't even think about him. But fucking him, touching him, was better than anything he had ever experienced in his lengthy life.

He was under Kid's spell—totally hypnotized by him.

He'd felt it ever since he'd met Kid at Dick Dongs. He could reason that this boy was just a horrid, flawed, foul-smelling mortal, but everything about him mesmerized Treycore. The sound of Kid's voice. His humble eyes, ever evasive. His timid smile. Treycore adored this boy so much that he hated him, and he hated himself for being incapable of controlling his desire, for being powerless against his want for a lowly, nothing of a mortal.

What he felt was more than lust. He'd known lust time and time again. He'd had eons of it.

The chemistry he felt with Kid was so much more. It allowed him to see beyond the façade Kid put up. Treycore could see past it all, could hear what Kid desired and needed in every movement he made. He could feel him in a way he'd never been able to feel another.

He didn't know his life, his story, yet he wanted this nothing of a mortal to be his everything. But why? How could he have felt this infatuated with a creature that he hardly knew?

He had loved since the dawn of creation. He'd loved Vera with his whole heart. He would've surrendered his immortality for her. He would've sacrificed everything. There was a time when she was good. He remembered when she cared for the mortals, when she fought for them. He remembered the days when the scent of her breath, her secretions, stimulated him. Her eyes lit the fire in his immortal loins. Her words were finer than the greatest of songs. When she giggled, he felt at ease. She was flawless.

But during the war, she'd been trapped in a terrible battle, one that left her mutated, deformed. Her face was scarred. Her body was tainted.

"Am I hideous?" she would continuously ask him.

The answer was always no. He'd never seen her form as hideous. Vain as angels were created to be, he couldn't see anything but the magic in her soul.

But Treycore knew by her repeated need for affirmation that nothing he could say would give her peace. And he remembered when she returned to him one day, her body uncorrupted, as flawless as it had been when she'd been first created.

"Look, Treycore," she'd said. "I'm beautiful again. Now, you can love me."

Try as she did to convince him that she had done it for him, he knew that she had only done it to please her own vanity, and as her beauty came at the great expense of siding with the malicious Almighty, whom they'd sworn themselves against, he could no longer set his immortal spirit alongside hers.

He left her. Left her to simmer with the decision she'd made. Left her to dwell on her loss.

Yes, he'd loved Vera. And yet, who couldn't have loved as perfect a creation as she? She had been meticulously forged to be the embodiment of seduction and desire, so his attraction had made sense. And they'd had such an expanse of time together before they united.

Kid wasn't anything like that.

He was so far from the Almighty's ideal and he hadn't known him even a week, but Treycore's senses craved him more than he had ever craved his greatest love.

*Why does this boy haunt my mind?* he wondered.

And if Treycore felt such strong desire, how could Kid be so oblivious to it. Surely Kinzer couldn't fuck him...couldn't understand him...the way Treycore could.

"FUCK!" came from the bedroom, ceasing Treycore's musings.

He sprang to his feet, rushing to the door and peering through the crack.

Lero was inside Kid, who had tears streaming down his face.

*That's it!*

Treycore forced the door open and barreled at Lero, fists clenched.

He pried Lero off Kid.

"What the fuck?" Lero yelled.

Lero was a punching bag as Treycore thrust his fists at him again and again. He knew he had to get them in since Lero could vanish at any moment.

"Stop!" Kid shouted. "Treycore, stop it!"

Kid snatched his arm.

"Treycore, he didn't do anything wrong!"

As Kid pulled Treycore off him, Lero disappeared.

"Fuck!" Kid cried. He smacked Treycore's shoulder. "Are you outta your fucking mind?"

Tears were still rushing down his face.

"You screamed!" Treycore exclaimed.

"It wasn't like that."

"Then why are you crying like a fucking baby?"

Kid wiped the back of his hands across his face. "None of your fucking business," he snapped. He groaned. "Goddammit! Now what the fuck are we supposed to do? Huh?"

Treycore didn't understand why Kid was being such an ass. "I was just worried."

"Well, now you fucked up our chances of getting back to Kinzer."

*If you say his name one more fucking time*, Treycore thought, *I'll turn you over and pound the shit out of you, and I won't fucking hold back.*

Kid collapsed onto the mattress.

KNOCK KNOCK!

Lero, still naked, tapped his fist against the open door. His boulder pecs jiggled. He cowered as he entered the room. "Kid, if I did something—" he began.

Kid shook his head. "No, no. I'm sorry. It was just a misunderstanding."

"Trey, if I pissed you off—"

"My bad. I just thought...I don't know what I thought."

*I thought I might actually matter to this asshole.*

"Well, let's get you guys back to the States."

## CHAPTER THIRTEEN

*Kisses trailed around Kinzer's belly button as Janka worshiped his torso, massaging his thumbs against the sides of his abs, trailing them down his perfectly arched hips.*

*"Oh yeah!" Kinzer cried, throwing his head back.*

*Janka slid his nose down the rift in Kinzer's abs, breathed softly across his flesh, down to the head of his cock. He flicked it with the tip of his tongue. His hand glided across Kinzer's abs, stroking, groping. He combed the very tip of his teeth down the bulging vein in Kinzer's cock, the tip of his tongue slipping out infrequently, surprising Kinzer each time.*

*Kinzer just wanted Janka to take his cock, to bury his face against his pubes. He wanted to feel the embrace of Janka's lips, the warmth of his saliva lubricating his flesh.*

*"Suck me!" Kinzer begged.*

*Janka's lips arched into a smile against Kinzer's shaft, as if he was enjoying torturing his lover.*

*He wrapped his hands around Kinzer's ass, kneading just for a moment before gripping onto them and flipping him onto his stomach.*

*He sprang to his knees, separated Kinzer's cheeks, and pressed the head of his cock against Kinzer's hole.*

*Kinzer's hole dilated.*

*"Fuck me, please! Fuck me hard!"*

*Janka offered some spit before he pressed the tip of his cock into Kinzer.*

*A little spit wasn't going to do much more than get it in. It wasn't going to go in easy on his body.*

*A thrust of Janka's pelvis sent Kinzer crawling. Janka grabbed him by his wrists, forcing him to remain still. Another thrust of his cock pushed the walls of Kinzer's ass open.*

*"AH!" Kinzer cried.*

*Another thrust and Kinzer felt like he'd sat on a flagpole. He gritted his teeth and groaned, squinting as he tried to take in the massive, swelling pain.*

*Janka's pelvis was wild with excitement, slapping against Kinzer's cheeks over and over.*

*Kinzer gripped onto the boards in the floor, doing his best to absorb the pain that throbbed through him.*

*Janka wrapped his arm around Kinzer's neck and pulled him back.*

*Kinzer's back arched, the rifts in his abs stretching, his belly button flattening against his tense muscles.*

*Janka wrapped his other hand around Kinzer's head, forcing him to turn back, and planted a kiss on his lips.*

*His tongue invaded Kinzer's mouth, sliding about, tasting everything in its path.*

*Kinzer's tongue eagerly met his. Sweat drenched his hair and rushed down his forehead. His fully erect shaft sprayed pre-come onto the floor.*

*Janka continued shamelessly forcing himself into Kinzer's tense, resistant hole.*

*As Janka broke from their kiss, he slid his lips across Kinzer's face until they were beside his ear.*

*"I love you," he whispered.*

*"I...love..." Kinzer cried out, struggling against the nearly unbearable pain, "...you!"*

BANG!

Kinzer, not even fully conscious, rolled off the couch, grabbed his sword, and sprang to his feet.

As he came to, he scanned the room.

It was pitch black. The fire that Dedrus had started had gone out.

"Dedrus? That you?"

He felt a jab at the back of his neck.

"Move," a voice whispered, "and I'll slice your fucking head off."

Kinzer recognized the voice. It was Craetis. The Raze had found them.

But how?

\*\*\*

Treycore pushed a door open and peered into a bedroom. The blue morning glow showered through a window, cascading across a mattress set against the wall. Next to it, a table that appeared to be substituting for a nightstand had magazines scattered across it.

"Dedrus? Kinzer?"

Lero had teleported he and Kid to a cabin with the coordinates he'd given him, but where was everybody? Surely, they wouldn't have just up and left without them.

Treycore walked back into the main living area, where Lero was waiting. Kid stepped out of the kitchen, looking puzzled.

"Is this the right place?" Treycore asked.

"It's the right place alright," Lero said. "You can't smell that? I would've thought as long as the two of you were together, you would've been able to pick up on it a bit. She's been here. Very recently."

"So you should know where she is."

"Oh no," Lero insisted. "It's not that recent."

In the same way Teleporters were able to differentiate each other's scents, they were able to follow one another's paths, especially if they'd teleported recently. It was a bit of information Treycore'd gleaned in his relationship with Vera.

"Are you bullshitting me, Lero?"

As Lero made eye contact, Treycore knew that he was.

"Seriously, Treycore?! You know that bitch would be so eager to pass along intel to the Almighty about where I am. I don't need that. I'm doing good for myself. I'm happy."

"You have to take us there. Please. I can't tell you why. You just have to trust me on this."

Lero's head shifted in spasms, clearly struggling to make a decision.

"Please," Kid begged.

Lero's attention shifted between them. "I'll take you as close as I can without her being able to detect me, but that's it."

\*\*\*

Kinzer's face hit a concrete floor.

Craetis stood over him, laughing.

Support beams lined the chipped, concrete walls. White stripes scattered across the raked floor. They were in an empty parking garage, surely abandoned.

Dedrus had snuck back into the cabin while Kinzer was sleeping and had been captured with Maggie and him. After Vera had teleported them to this location, she'd teleported again, presumably to retrieve Veylo.

"Ow!" Maggie shrieked. She stood behind Kinzer, her hand on her belly.

Deter had shot her up with a syringe that Kinzer assumed was to force her into labor.

Mika and Deter restrained Dedrus.

CHEW! Went a stairwell door as it opened a few yards from them.

"Kinzer!" a voice exclaimed.

Kinzer didn't look up. He couldn't look into his enemy's eyes. All his rage. All his hate. And yet, what could he do with it now that he was powerless?

Footsteps crept up to him.

"What's the matter? You aren't still mad about that whole me killing your boyfriend thing, are you?"

That day ravaged Kinzer's thoughts.

*Janka had crawled across the concrete, his limp legs dragging behind, leaving a trail of blood in their wake.*

*He leaned in to Kinzer, blood shimmering in the whites of his blue eyes.*

*Kinzer's vision blurred as tears rushed down his face.*

*Janka coughed. Blood flooded out of his mouth and slid down his chin.*

*"I..." he said, struggling to speak, "love...you."*

*"I love..." Kinzer fought to say through tears.*

*A sword, Kinzer's sword, wrapped around Janka's neck and slipped across his flesh.*

*A river of blood pooled onto the floor.*

*"No!" Kinzer wailed.*

*Janka collapsed into a puddle of his own blood.*

*Veylo stood over him, wiping his finger across Kinzer's blade, across Janka's blood.*

*Kinzer drowned in a fit of tears. He tried to reach down and hold his lover, but the chains held him back.*

*"I'm so sorry," Veylo said. "But this is the price you pay when you mess with the Raze."*

*He stepped around Kinzer, alongside Deter, and raised the sword.*

*SLASH!*

*Kinzer tried to scream, but it caught in his throat.*

*Mika released the bone of his wing. It dropped to the floor just as quickly as Janka.*

*Another quick slash and what remained of his wings, his gifts, joined the other.*

*Deter unlocked his cuffs, freeing Kinzer's wrists. He collapsed on top of his now-deceased lover, his tears collecting in Janka's immortal blood.*

*Veylo traipsed around him.*

*"Oh, Kinzer," he had said as he'd stood over him, still wielding Kinzer's sword. "You think you're suffering now?"*

Kinzer used the pain and horror as he leapt to his feet, ready to tear Veylo in two. But just as quickly, Craetis had his arms.

Veylo was dressed in a tailored navy blue suit with a matching bow tie. The bangs that usually dropped below his nose were combed to the side. His shoulder-length hair curled sharply around his neck. The garage lighting reached back into his deep sockets and sparkled across his pupils.

"I suppose I should thank you for bringing the child right to me."

"Fuck you," Kinzer said, struggling against Craetis's grip. Craetis squeezed Kinzer's biceps. The grip burned against his muscles. Kinzer took it as a warning not to try it again.

"Don't be upset," Veylo said. "We were bound to find you sooner or later." He turned to Deter. "Did you bring their swords with you, like I asked?"

Deter motioned to two swords, laying on the ground behind him.

"What are you up to?" Kinzer asked. "Why don't you just kill us?"

"Oh, I will," Veylo assured him. "But you know me. I'm all about theatrics. Which is why I'd rather not blow my wad. You see, I've been working on a little project that I'd like you to test out for me. It's a very special project that I'm hoping you and Dedrus will be able to appreciate."

He reached into his pocket and pulled out a long, aluminum cylinder. He pressed his lips against the end of it and blew.

A high-pitched sound stung at Kinzer's ears. Dedrus groaned.

*What is Veylo up to?* Kinzer thought.

There was a sadistic gleam in Veylo's eyes.

STOMP! STOMP!

Tremors ravaged the concrete floor, shaking the support beams.

A ripping sound came from the side of the garage.

A green tentacle punctured through the wall. Another punctured just a few feet from it. And then another.

"No fucking way," Dedrus said.

Kinzer gasped.

The tentacles flailed about, tearing through the wall, creating a dust-filled cloud.

A chunk of the wall pushed forward, breaking open like a baby chick pushing its way through its shell.

SMASH!

Chunks of wall collapsed onto the floor, and an orb slid through the fresh hole.

It was a Morarke. There was nothing else it could have been.

As its tentacles squirmed across the garage floor, as if feeling before it, a giant, rhinoceros-sized foot slipped through the hole. Another foot was right behind it.

Its flesh was green, laced with gray from the wall debris. Its dome-shaped head had two holes. Its mouth was a gaping crater filled with swirling, razor wire teeth. Just a few feet above that was a slit of an eye. Halfway down its bulky body, eight tentacles swung every which way, feeling before it, as if trying to make sense of its surroundings.

"Fuck!" Dedrus exclaimed.

The floor cracked into webs as the Morarke's mammoth feet stepped toward Veylo's assembled meeting.

"Isn't it beautiful?" Veylo asked.

"If the Almighty or the Leader find out that you have that—" Dedrus began.

"And how will they find out when you're both dead? Besides, I have this one perfectly under control. Trained him myself. I call him Hoddy. Quite spectacular, isn't he?"

The Morarke growled. It stopped until it was a few feet before them, its tentacles relaxing, caressing rather than flailing.

Craetis's fingers shook against Kinzer's arms. Kinzer knew it was because he was scared as shit. As he should have been.

"You see how good it's being by not attacking you without my instruction? Just because we were too lazy to understand how truly remarkable these weapons really are, doesn't mean that we can't find a way to utilize them."

"Oh, ah!" Maggie squealed. She hobbled over. "Fucking Jesus! I'm having a baby. Will someone just get me to a doctor?!"

"She's right," Veylo said. "We really should be off now."

"If you think," Dedrus said, "we're just gonna let you prance out of here with the Antichrist, you're dead wrong."

Veylo looked up to the Morarke. "Hoddy, kill these disgusting creatures."

Deter and Mika tossed Dedrus on top of the swords. Craetis pushed Kinzer on top of him and joined his fallen allies as they ushered Maggie to the stairwell door. Veylo followed behind.

Kinzer and Dedrus slipped their swords off the floor, leapt to their feet, and hurried to the stairwell.

One of Hoddy's tentacles rushed in front of them, slamming against their bodies, projecting them across the parking garage. Dedrus slammed into a fire extinguisher box mounted to a support beam. Kinzer hit the concrete wall, his sword rattling as it hit the floor.

"Fuck!" he cried. He dropped, his arms smashing against the concrete.

Hoddy paced toward them.

"Shit," Dedrus said. In a moment, he was back on his feet, holding his sword out before him.

Kinzer spotted another stairwell on the other side of the garage.

"Follow me," he ordered. He limped alongside the wall. Dedrus hurried behind.

## CHAPTER FOURTEEN

Kid tailed behind Treycore, down a hallway. What few working fluorescent lights were on flickered sporadically.

Lero had dropped Kid and Treycore off outside an abandoned hospital and pointed them toward where he'd felt Vera's teleportation. As they'd entered the hospital, they'd heard moaning and followed the sound.

Treycore and Kid peered into a security mirror. Kid saw that giant, Craetis, who he'd fought with at Dedrus and Treycore's place. He dragged Maggie along with some guy in a suit, heading into a room.

"Veylo has Maggie," Treycore said before turning to kid. "Okay, I'm gonna take these assholes out. You hide somewhere and just stay safe. Got it?"

"I wanna help."

"You'll help by staying out of my way. I can take these assholes. I've taken on worse. The whole battle between Heaven and Hell, remember?"

Kid nodded. He was disappointed, but he knew there was no way he could help Treycore fight immortals. If anything, he would be an inconvenience, like he felt he'd been all along.

Treycore grabbed Kid's arm and pulled him close. He kissed him softer than he'd ever kissed him before. Kid savored his sweet, immortal taste.

As Treycore pulled back, he returned for another kiss—long, passionate, deep. He pulled away again and looked into Kid's eyes. It was that same soul-piercing gaze—the one that made Kid feel so naked, so vulnerable.

"I won't let anything bad happen to you," Treycore said.

Kid smiled. It sounded like something someone would say to someone they loved. He wanted to tell Treycore how he felt. He wanted to say that he loved him. But that was ridiculous. They'd known each other for such a short time.

He clenched his teeth and headed down the hall, taking sanctuary in a nearby restroom.

\*\*\*

Treycore glanced around, making sure the coast was clear. He darted down the hall, readying his sword.

Maggie's labor screams echoed all around him.

Approaching the door at the end, he set his hand on the knob. *Bunch of fallens*, he thought with disgust. *No sweat.* He turned the knob and burst in.

Maggie lay on the hospital bed, her soaked hair shining under the lights. She clasped onto the sheets, tensing her grip.

"I need a fucking epidural!" she wailed, hissing breaths, sweat dripping off her bangs.

Veylo and Craetis's attention jerked to Treycore. Veylo whipped out his sword and lunged at him. Treycore sliced into Veylo's thumb, forcing his sword to the floor.

"Fuck!" Veylo roared, massaging his wound. Craetis barreled at Treycore.

Treycore sliced his sword through the air. Craetis halted just before its tip.

"Just a little farther," Treycore mocked.

"If you didn't have your sword," Craetis snarled, "I'd fucking tear you in two."

"If you think," Veylo began, his fresh blood spewing onto the floor, "you're walking out of here with that baby—"

"I don't *think*," Treycore replied. "I *am*."

"Fuck no!" Maggie shrieked. "I am not fucking going anywhere! I am having this baby. Ah! Pain! Fucking pain! Someone get me an epidural *right now*!"

"Everybody back the fuck off!" Treycore ordered.

Craetis didn't move.

Treycore stared him down. "Today is not the day to test me."

Craetis and Veylo retreated into the far corner. Treycore maneuvered around the bed, holding his sword out.

"Now," Treycore said. "We're all going to get through this nice and—" Something pushed him into the wall. "Fuck!" he called out.

While he'd been fixated on Veylo and Craetis, Deter had snuck behind him and tackled him. Deter grabbed Treycore's wrist and rammed it against the wall. Treycore's hand froze up, and his sword slipped free. Bouncing off the linoleum floor, it landed a few feet away from him. Craetis leapt over the bed. Treycore elbowed Deter in the face and threw himself at his sword. Just as his finger grazed the tip, Craetis landed with one foot on the sword's hilt.

"Fuck no," Craetis growled, looking down at the now-helpless Treycore.

"Hey!" a voice came from the hall.

All eyes turned to Mika, who had Kid by the arm, a dagger to his throat. "Look what I found in the restroom."

Treycore's face went white.

"Now," Veylo said. "What to do with you, Treycore?"

***

Kinzer plowed through the stairwell door. Dedrus was right behind. They hauled ass, practically throwing themselves down a set of concrete steps. What sounded like an explosion came from behind them as the monster's tentacles shredded the stairwell entrance apart like it was made of cardboard.

"Just like old times," Kinzer said, hopping on the platform of the second floor.

"You know what that means?" Dedrus said.

"I'll distract, and you kill the motherfucker."

Three tentacles wrapped over the rails above them. As they reached the bottom of the first floor, Kinzer pushed through the door. He raced across the asphalt. Dedrus's wings sliced like knives through the back of his shirt. He bounded into the air and flapped to the top of a neighboring building. The Morarke's tentacles ripped through the garage's brick wall. Its razor teeth crushed bricks and pipes into dust. Kinzer waved his sword about.

"Come here, you fucking dick!"

The creature shrilled as it stomped toward him, leaving a trail of prints in its path. Dedrus dive-bombed off the roof, tucking his wings close, pointing his sword out, and aimed at the eye-slit above Hoddy's razor-mouth. One of Hoddy's tentacles went right for Kinzer. He leapt over it. He thought he'd cleared it when five mini-tentacles shot through the side of the main one and grabbed him by the ankle.

*Fucking hurry*, he thought.

Dedrus was less than a foot from the monster's eye-slit. He maneuvered his wing ever so slightly. The tip of his sword was almost there. A tentacle came from his side, wrapped around his waist, and barreled him to the ground.

"Fuck!" he cried.

The tentacles around Kinzer released him.

*Oh no*, Kinzer thought. *It picked Dedrus. Why? It totally had me.*

A realization struck him. He didn't have his wings…or powers. Dedrus must have been giving off a stronger immortal scent than he was.

*Shit. I'm gonna take it out myself. Without anything.*

*\*\*\**

*Is this how I'm gonna die?* Kid wondered.

Mika tightened the tip of his dagger against his neck.

"Move it!" Craetis barked as he kicked through a door, holding Treycore in a headlock.

He tossed Treycore on the floor and kicked him in the stomach.

"Aw, fuck!" Treycore groaned.

Craetis kicked him again. "Bet that turns you on, doesn't it?"

The room they were in was just a few halls from Maggie's, as made apparent by the still-audible screams that reached it. With a clean, black desk, black leather chair, and shelves still stocked with medical books, at some point, this room must've been one of the hospital doctor's offices. Judging by the room's pristine appearance and perfectly functional fluorescent lights, one wouldn't have even known that they were still in the abandoned hospital.

Craetis hopped on top of Treycore, pinning his arms to the floor.

"What do you say we have a little fun time, just you and me?" He licked Treycore's cheek.

Treycore turned his head and bit into Craetis's tongue until it bled. Craetis snapped back, letting the blood drip onto Treycore's cheek.

"You always did like it kinky, didn't you?" he said with a wink. He released one of Treycore's hands and slapped him across the face.

Mika pulled Kid around Craetis and stepped into the adjacent corner. Deter entered and closed the door behind him.

"I think I would like to get a little something in," Craetis said.

He flipped Treycore on his stomach and sat on his hamstrings. Treycore reared back, his fists slamming into Craetis's arms in vain. Craetis yanked his jeans down, revealing his naked cheeks.

Kid's chest tightened. He wanted to tear Craetis's face off. "Leave him alone!" he shouted.

Mika slammed Kid's head into the wall. "Shut your fucking trap."

"Damn! Mika," Craetis said. "Look at that ass! Been a long time since I've had a higherling."

As Mika watched with eager eyes, he stroked his hand up and down Kid's chest. It reminded Kid of so many other hands that had violated him and of the only hand that he wanted to touch him that way.

"Get on the floor," Mika whispered into Kid's ear.

Kid did as he was told and sprawled out on the floor. Mika pressed his dagger against the back of Kid's neck as he unzipped his suit pants. Being that Mika was immortal, Kid knew it was going to hurt, but he was determined to take it without showing weakness.

"Well, well," said a familiar voice.

All eyes went to the desk.

"If it isn't my dear, sweet love."

The chair behind it swirled around.

It was Treycore's psycho ex-bitch, Vera. Her hair was straightened, except for the ends, which curled at her shoulders. A sleeveless, white dress molded against her immortal, modelesque figure, complimenting her cum-white flesh. Her eyes met Treycore's.

"So glad to see you made it to our little event," she hissed.

Through a slot under the desk, Kid watched as she tapped a five-inch gray heel on the tile floor.

She rose. The leather on her chair squeaked. Her heels clicked as she came around the desk.

Maggie's cries grew louder in the hall.

By the sound of it, Kid thought she might be giving birth...or being violently tortured. Vera didn't seem to notice. She rested her hip against the edge of the desk.

"You're not going to win," Treycore said.

Craetis grabbed him by the hair and smashed his forehead into the floor.

Vera smiled. "Oh, Treycore. Can't you see?"

Maggie cried out again.

"We already have."

Craetis twisted his arm. Treycore's face turned red. He grunted.

"Cut it out!" Kid cried.

"Shut up, faggot," Treycore barked.

Kid was shocked by Treycore's severity. *Why was he being mean to him? Weren't they in this together?*

"That's so cute," Vera said. "I think the mortal's developing a little crush."

Treycore stared at her, expressionless.

Her thin lips curled into a smirk. "You seem different, Treycore. You seem...troubled."

She stepped toward him and knelt until her face was just above his, as if trying to illustrate her superiority through their positions.

"What's wrong?" she asked. "You used to be so open with me. It doesn't matter. You, Kinzer, and Dedrus have failed. We have the mortal woman, and we have the child. Mika, release the mortal. We have no business with him."

Treycore remained expressionless. Mika grabbed Kid by the back of his collar and forced him to his feet. Keeping his dagger tight against Kid's neck, he led him to the door.

"No, no!" Kid protested.

Treycore's jaw tensed. "Just get the fuck out of here, Kid."

"They're gonna kill you!"

"You care for Treycore?" Vera asked.

Kid looked to Treycore. He wasn't sure if he should answer.

"Don't worry. I can tell you do. I apologize if we haven't been previously introduced. I'm Vera. Kid's your name, right? I'm assuming it's not just a descriptor. Mika, you can let him go. He won't try anything. Will you?"

Kid shook his head.

"Let him go."

Mika released him. He tucked his dagger into its sheath and zipped his pants back up.

"You don't know me," Vera said, "so I can understand why you don't feel that you can trust me. But I'm a fallen that keeps her word. Treycore can vouch for this. Can't you, Treycore?"

"Kid, don't listen to her."

"Have I ever gone against my word?"

"Kid..."

"As you can see, even Treycore, who in this moment despises me, cannot deny that I'm a fallen of my word."

"Kid..."

"Shut him up," Vera said.

Craetis's hand rushed over Treycore's mouth.

"Treycore," she continued, "I'm sorry, but this is between me and Kid."

Kid's eyes moved uneasily between Treycore and Vera.

"If I told you that you could save Treycore's life, would you be willing to make a deal?"

Treycore muttered behind Craetis's hand, but it was clear that he was saying, "*You fucking cunt.*"

"Would you?"

Kid nodded.

"Don't be shy. I need a yes or a no."

"Yes." His voice rose uneasily.

"Don't you fucking do it!"

Craetis pressed his fingers tighter together.

"What if," Vera went on, "instead of taking his life, I agreed to take yours, however I choose."

"Don't be stupid, Kid."

Kid's gaze drifted to the floor. Could he give up his life for this immortal that he'd known for such a short time? Was he willing to sacrifice himself when he didn't even know how Treycore felt about him? What if Treycore didn't even love him? What if Treycore couldn't have cared less about him? His thoughts spiraled through a labyrinth of doubt and confusion, but despite all the doubt, Kid couldn't stop himself from muttering, "Yes."

"No!"

"Treycore," Vera said. "I don't see what your issue is. I asked him, and he agreed. That's how deals are made. And in the end, he's sparing your life, so I would think you would be wise to listen to your own advice and not be stupid."

CLICK CLICK!

She walked behind the desk and sat in her leather, swivel chair. She pulled one of the desk drawers open.

"Take a seat."

\*\*\*

Kinzer watched in horror as the tentacle around Dedrus tossed him against the side of the building adjacent to the garage. Feathers exploded like a grenade as he hit the wall wing-first.

"Ah!"

Kinzer looked up the one-story-tall creature, fixing his focus on its eye-slit.

*How the fuck am I gonna get up there?*

He didn't know, but he had to hurry before it ripped Dedrus apart.

A ladder rose up the side of the neighboring building. He sprinted to it, and scaled it. Dedrus crawled to his feet. His wounded wing trembled before tearing off the bone and collapsing onto the ground. A tentacle wrapped around his ankle and yanked him across the asphalt.

"Fuck!" he cried as the flesh on his arm peeled off. The asphalt dug into his muscles, leaving a blood trail behind him.

As Kinzer stepped onto a rung at the monster's height, he looked back. Hoddy was several yards away.

*I can't make that.*

He hadn't even considered that, without his wings, he wasn't going to be able to get over to the Morarke.

*Shit.*

He eyed a window ledge a few feet from him. Grabbing onto the side of the ladder, he swung over to it and crouched down. With the hilt of his sword, he smashed a hole in the window and climbed inside.

\*\*\*

Dedrus's arms were restrained in Hoddy's tentacle as it pulled him toward its razor-wire mouth. The Morarke shoved his remaining wing inside. Blood and black feathers showered across his face. Dedrus shouted, his cry bouncing across the sides of the buildings, echoing through the alley. A window by the creature's head exploded into shards. Kinzer, his arms over his face, his hands grasping his sword, soared through the air.

\*\*\*

Kinzer threw his arms forward, sticking his sword out so it would drive into the creature. Hoddy lowered Dedrus and turned its eye-slit to Kinzer. The movement was just enough to spoil Kinzer's plan. His sword pierced nearly a foot away from its target.

*Fuck!*

Hoddy shook its head about, dislodging Kinzer and his sword. Kinzer tumbled to the ground, his back slamming against the asphalt. Hoddy pulled Dedrus back to its razor-mouth and shoved his arm in.

"Ah!"

It was painful for Kinzer to hear, but he couldn't do anything about it. The blow to his back was so intense that it had left him temporarily paralyzed. From the edge of the tentacle that was wrapped around Dedrus, several mini-tentacles popped up. At their tips were sharp, blade-like claws. They slashed deep, penetrating wounds into his face.

"Holy fuck!"

Kinzer struggled to his feet. His sword was a few feet from him. He hobbled over to it and picked it up, turning to the creature, defeated.

One of Hoddy's highest tentacles came crashing down.

*Now or never*, he thought.

Just before it struck, Kinzer leapt into the air and mounted it. As it swirled around to the back of Hoddy, Kinzer kicked off. He flew through the air and landed on his knees on the beast's head. Kinzer cried out, summoning as much strength as he could. Raising his sword, he fell forward and drove it into Hoddy's eye-slit.

Hoddy's razor-filled mouth unleashed a loud shrill. Its tentacles flailed around it. It tumbled forward. Its tentacle released Dedrus, and he went soaring through the air.

Knowing he would be crushed if he didn't get out of Hoddy's path, Kinzer bounced off the monster's head. As he hit the asphalt, he tucked his sword close to his chest, closed his eyes, and rolled for his life.

CRASH!

The asphalt cracked open as Hoddy slammed into it. It was like a semi-truck had fallen from the sky.

\*\*\*

Kid approached a chair before the desk. Vera sifted through a drawer, pulled out a stack of papers, and set them on the desk. Maggie's screams and cries continued outside.

"Come on," she said. "We don't have all day."

Kid sat. She slid the papers to Kid.

"This is our agreement. It's just as I said. Agree to it, and our dearest Treycore keeps his life, and you lose yours."

Kid gulped. He'd made a hasty decision, but something in him assured him that it was the right one. Treycore probably didn't love him, but that didn't matter. He loved Treycore, and he didn't care if Treycore didn't feel the same way.

Vera placed a black fountain pen on top of the papers. "It's your choice. Sign the last page, and it will be done." She gazed into his eyes, giving him a look that he'd only ever received from immortals—a look that stared into his soul. "Don't, and I will rip Treycore limb from limb right in front of you."

His eyes turned to Treycore, who shook his head violently. Kid picked up the pen. Flipping to the last page, he closed his eyes and signed on a dotted line.

Vera retrieved the stack and skimmed through it. As she came to the last page, she stroked her finger across his signature. "Oh, mortal," she said. "It's so sweet seeing how much you care for my love." She turned to Treycore. "He really does stink, though, doesn't he?"

"Just let him go," Kid said, resigned.

Her lips curled into that familiar smirk. She opened the desk drawer and tucked the papers inside. "In a moment. It says in your contract that I get to see this through as I desire, and it's my desire for him to watch."

The matter-of-fact, serene look in her eyes switched to something else—something twisted, like when he'd first seen her.

"Bind them."

Mika reached into his sack and pulled out a strand of rope with barbed wire twisted around it. Craetis pulled Treycore's hands behind his back while Mika tied the rope around his wrists, fastening it so tight that the barbs drew blood.

"You always did like it kinky, didn't ya, Treycore?" Craetis mocked.

Mika approached Kid's chair, grabbed him by his shirt collar, and tossed him to the floor. He pulled another strand of barbed rope from his sack, knelt down, and bound Kid's wrists behind his back. As the barbs punctured into Kid's flesh, he gritted his teeth. Vera rose from her chair and stepped around to Kid, who lay on his side, blood dripping off his wrists, on the floor. She knelt and grazed her fingernail under his chin.

"Uncertainty might perhaps be the cruelest thing a person can endure," she said. "So I want to set your mind at ease."

She leaned closer to him until her lips were right next to his ear, her breath rushing into it. It reminded Kid of his passionate, delicious encounters with Treycore—something he was sure he'd never get to experience again.

"I promise," she whispered, "not to kill you until you regret the deal you made." Pressing her thumb against his chin, she licked up his cheek.

Seeing Vera's more sadistic side left Kid feeling completely vulnerable. He hadn't realized the extent of the position he'd put himself in. He'd agreed to let her torture him in the most perverse ways she could possibly imagine. And being that she was an immortal from Hell, that was probably far worse than he'd considered.

Treycore struggled with his barbed rope. Blood splattered across the back of his shirt.

Vera took a step back. She nodded.

Craetis released Treycore's mouth and wrapped his arm around his neck. He pressed his lips to Treycore's ear. "I'm gonna enjoy this," he said.

Deter stepped up to Kid.

Kid glanced up at him. Fear ravaged his mind. Graphic depictions of violence from horror movies tore at his emotions. How were these immortals going to kill him?

Deter grabbed him by his shirt collar and threw him against the wall.

Kid's back slammed against a modern acrylic. As he hit the floor, the frame of the painting rammed into his side, tearing his shirt.

Vera rested her hands on the desk and leaned back.

Deter snatched Kid by his throat and lifted him off the floor. He slammed Kid's head into the wall. Once. Twice. Three times. It happened so fast that Kid didn't have time to react, and the blows left him immobilized. Deter threw him against the wall and pummeled him in the stomach. Kid moaned just as he had when he was being pounded by Treycore. Blood streaked from his temple to the corner of his mouth. He wanted to fall to the ground, but Deter's punches kept him pinned to the wall.

Deter finally stopped, and grabbing Kid's shirt collar, ripped it down the middle. He pulled it off and slung him onto the desk. He gripped the back of his jeans and ripped down. The denim rubbed Kid's skin raw. His ass was exposed, awaiting punishment. Vera opened another drawer and pulled out a paddle. As she came around the desk, she eyed Kid's ass.

She tossed a glance to Treycore. "Looks like you've already done a bit of damage." She handed Deter the paddle.

"No!" Treycore cried. "Deter's too strong! It's too much for him!"

Deter chuckled. His eyes were alight with enthusiasm. He held the paddle high in the air and thrust it down. Kid tightened his jaw, attempting to will himself into silence. But as the paddle slammed into his ass with immortal strength, he couldn't help but scream out.

The pain was so severe, so intense. He knew that his body wouldn't be able to handle much of this. Deter didn't give him a moment to recover. He smacked the paddle against his ass again...and again...and again.

Tears showered from Kid's eyes.

*Don't cry, you fucking pussy*, he scolded himself. *Don't let them see you cry!* But the pain was far too intense.

"Ah!"

"Stop it!" Treycore called out.

Vera's fingernails dug into the desk. Her look wasn't as sadistic as before. It was aroused. As Deter intensified his next strike, Kid tightened his wrists against the barbed rope, hoping to distract himself from the pain. Another blow to Kid's ass sent him into a fit of screams just as Maggie unleashed another cry from the nearby room.

## CHAPTER FIFTEEN

Kinzer rolled onto his back, his chest rising and falling, sweat rushing down his face from his forehead. It was like he'd had the most intense fuck of his life. He sat up, looking around anxiously. Several yards away, near a few packed dumpsters, blood gushed from Dedrus's forehead and pooled onto the asphalt. He shook feverishly.

Kinzer sprang to his feet and ran to him. Kneeling beside him, he assessed Dedrus's shredded body. It reminded him of the last time he had seen Janka. The last time he would ever see Janka.

"Kinzer." Blood rushed from his mouth, dripping into his pool of blood.

It pained Kinzer to see his ex-lover in this suffering state. There was a time when all he wished upon Dedrus was pain—pain for hurting him so much. Right then, he would've given his life to take that pain away.

"You have to get to the child," Dedrus continued. "You have to protect it from the Almighty."

Here he was, with his last dying words, still concerned over the fate of mortals. It reminded Kinzer of all the time they shared together, discussing morality, equality. It reminded him of all those things that he had worshiped about Dedrus—those things that had been his reasons for falling in love with him.

"I will."

Dedrus eyed his sword on the other side of the alley. "Take it. Find them. Put a stop to all this."

Kinzer nodded.

"Promise me."

Kinzer wrestled with his request. How could he promise that he could put a stop to this? For all he knew, Veylo had already killed Maggie and the child. For all he knew, the Christ could come and destroy them all. However, knowing that his friend was dying, more than anything, he wanted to help him have peace before his last breath.

"I promise," he said.

"And Kinzer..." A tear rushed down Dedrus's cheek. "I don't care what you think. Ryson...it was, but it was nothing. I always loved you. That last night, before I went off, I was hoping you'd ask me...ask me to be with you...to be the one. When you didn't, I assumed you weren't ready. But I never stopped loving you." His prickly face shook violently. "I wish I would've said something before I lost my chance."

It was the most painful thing Kinzer could have heard. Had the immortal he'd loved so much really felt the same all this time? Was it true? Had it always been that simple? Had Dedrus been just as insecure as he'd been about their relationship? Had all those years of hating Dedrus really been for nothing?

Surely not. Had it turned out any different, he wouldn't have ended up with Janka. Still, Kinzer couldn't help but wonder what it would have been like had he confronted Dedrus...had he realized how much he truly loved him.

He'd always loved him. Even when he'd hated him, it was only because he believed Dedrus could never love him in return.

It didn't matter anymore. He was about to lose another love...just as he'd lost Janka.

He wrapped his arms around Dedrus.

"I love you, too," he whispered.

He pressed his lips to Dedrus's blood-filled mouth. He could feel Dedrus's breath as it caressed his face, as it steadied.

Dedrus's tremors subsided. Then, he was still.

Kinzer stayed in their embrace, because he knew it would be their last.

His mind flashed to his Janka.

*He had rocked back and forth, massaging his fingers through his lover's bloody flesh. From the corner of Janka's blue eye, staring vacantly forward, blood slid alongside the tip of his full eyebrow, across his temple.*

*Kinzer had pressed his lips to Janka's blood-smeared forehead and offered a gentle kiss.*

As Kinzer's thoughts returned to the present, he could feel himself losing control. A fire welled within him, but he wouldn't allow it to consume him. Not just yet.

He pulled his lips from Dedrus's, and turned back to the garage. His eyes filled with rage.

*Veylo, here I fucking come.*

\*\*\*

Welts formed on Kid's ass as Deter continued assaulting him with the paddle. Mika came up alongside him. Removing a bullwhip from his bag, he twisted it around Kid's throat. Kid moaned. Mika tightened the whip, restricting Kid's breath until he gagged.

"Fuck you, you bastards!" Treycore shouted.

Craetis, with an arm around Treycore's neck, pet Treycore's back like he was trying to soothe him.

"No...more! He...can't...take it," Treycore said.

Vera giggled.

"Hasn't he already?" she asked, her eyebrow arching.

"You fuck—"

Craetis tightened his chokehold.

"I'm so fucking tired of hearing you talk!" he whispered. He rubbed his free hand along Treycore's tense ass. "Mmmm...yeah, I like that."

Mika's eyes lit up as he loosened the whip just enough for Kid to catch a breath, then tensed it again.

The suffocation was unbearable. It was worse than anything Kid had experienced with Treycore. The spots were all around, but with Treycore, he trusted that he would protect him, keep him from reaching a point that was too far. With these monsters, they would take him to the depth of pain, and then he would die. And no amount of screaming or crying or desperately gasping for air was going to save him from that inevitable end...the end that he had agreed to.

***

"Leave...him...alone...you...bitch!" Treycore called out through gritted teeth, his voice straining from Craetis's chokehold as he watched his lover being destroyed. It was an agonizing sight, especially knowing that there was nothing he could do to bring Kid any relief.

Vera clicked her way over to him.

"Your mortal is pathetic," she said. "I don't imagine he can stand much more of this, do you? I remember when you would have suffered to see that happen to *me*. You would have wanted to rescue *me*. Time gives so much, so much that you can't hold on to, and promises to rip it all away from you. How many times have we been in love, Treycore? How many times have we longed for companionship only to be dissatisfied with this one or that one? How many times have we been betrayed? It's a miracle any of us can keep going on after all the sadness...all the disappointment. You think that we would have all discovered by now the futility of love. And yet, I long for it more. You think I take pleasure in the misery of others, but truly, I am the one who suffers, the one who is constantly being tortured, ravaged by my need for you. I'll admit that it gives me satisfaction to hurt him. I'll admit that it's perverse, but in some way, it lessens the pain."

Deter reached the paddle as high as he could and dropped it on Kid's ass with an intensity that left Kid convulsing.

"Enough," Vera said.

Deter stopped, a dissatisfied expression strung across his face. Mika begrudgingly loosened the whip. Kid's naked ass and legs trembled.

Vera approached him and rested her hand on his back. "How do you feel?" she asked with concern and worry.

He panted as his body forced air back into his lungs.

"Oh, you poor thing," she said. She lifted him up and slipped between him and the desk. As she rested his head on her lap, he vomited beside her.

"There, there. Shh...shh." She skimmed the back of her finger across his blood-and-vomit-stained cheek. "I know it hurts. I know. Be strong. You have to. You don't have any other choice."

Lifting his head off her lap, she slid across his vomit and set his head back down.

She stepped around the desk, opened a side drawer, and tucked her hand inside. As she retrieved it, coiled around her arm was a snake-like creature. It was thicker than a snake, and it didn't have any eyes. It was nearly twice the size of Vera's forearm, and just below its serpent-shaped head were two limbs that looked like lizard legs.

"Do you remember blaggovites, Treycore?"

"Stop!" he whimpered. "Just stop."

"You must." She twisted her arm as she stroked the blaggovite with the back of her free hand. "So much easier to control than Morarkes."

Vera lowered her arm and rubbed the blaggovite against Kid's back.

"As I recall, you were almost killed by one."

"I'm the one you want! Do it to me, you bitch!"

"I'm sorry, but I've already made a deal with Kid. And you know how I am about deals."

"Please," Treycore whined, his chin quivering, his eyes watering.

Vera's jaw clenched. She gripped her hand around the blaggovite's neck and squeezed. Its tail whipped through the air. A slit opened at the tip of its head, and a screech, like a child crying in the night, filled the room.

"Don't you see?" she said, raising her voice to combat the blaggovite's scream. "This is all I've wanted...to see you experience the pain of losing the one you love. Just like I did."

Her grip around the blaggovite's neck tightened. It screeched even louder.

She lowered it to Kid's head. It slithered off her arm and coiled around his neck.

"No!" Treycore wailed.

The immortal serpent tightened around Kid's neck, just as Mika had done with the whip.

Kid closed his eyes like he was drifting off to sleep. His face trembled and shook before he unleashed a shaky scream.

"You must know what it's like," Vera told Treycore, "the horror of being tortured by your own vicious memories...the horror of having to relive every dark moment...every fear, until you die. What horrors do you think a boy like Kid has lived that could be so cruel...so painful?"

## CHAPTER SIXTEEN

"Aaaahhh!"

The pain was too intense. Maggie couldn't bear much more. Veylo stood at the end of her bed, gazing eagerly down at her pussy, where she imagined her bloody baby's head was ripping through.

"Come on," Veylo said, "That's it. You're almost there."

Tears rushed off her crimson face. Another immortal stood by Veylo, but Maggie didn't recognize him. He was nearly as tall as Craetis, his white higherling wings stretched out beside him. Whoever he was, he sure wasn't helping her any.

"Fuck you all! Fuck you all to Hell!"

The pain inside her increased so sharply that she couldn't help but scream again.

"He's here!" Veylo announced.

*He?* she thought. *It's a boy?*

She tossed about, disoriented, her body overwhelmed, depleted.

The moment her mom had tried to prevent from happening had arrived.

Veylo held up what appeared to her to be a bloody ball of yarn, and in her delirium, she thought that was what it might have been.

"He's beautiful!" Veylo exclaimed.

She thought of the boy with the crossword puzzles.

A wailing sound filled the air.

*Is that my baby?* Maggie wondered. *Is that him?*

A thought stirred in her mind, one she was ashamed of thinking: *I want him so bad.*

*"A whore isn't fit to be a mother!"* echoed through Maggie's thoughts. But she could prove her mom wrong. If only she had the chance.

It didn't matter. They were going to take him away from her. If she didn't do something, they were going to rip him from her life forever.

*What can I do?*

She didn't have strength. She didn't have energy. She didn't have will. All she had was the pain that surged through her. The pain in her body, and the pain of knowing she was about to lose something precious...something wonderful...something that she only now understood the value of.

"There, there," Veylo cooed, rocking the bloody yarn back and forth.

*No. He's mine.*

The door behind him burst open and Kinzer ran in.

\*\*\*

Kinzer stood in the doorway, two swords gripped in his hands, fury in his eyes. Maggie was lying on the bed, her pelvis dripping with blood. But Kinzer only noticed her for a moment as his attention drew to a higherling standing beside Veylo. And in that moment, all his rage, all the hate that he had for the Raze, vanished.

"Ubba—da—ga—" He stuttered nonsense. He couldn't process a thought. "Janka?" he finally managed.

Janka stood there, silent. With wide, blue eyes, set below those all-too-familiar bushy eyebrows, he stared at Kinzer with that deep, powerful, immortal stare. Kinzer's thoughts wheeled back to that horrible day when he'd watched Veylo and the Raze beat and torture him...when he thought they'd killed him.

*How was he alive?* Unfortunately, despite all his confusion, he already knew the answer to his question.

"All this time," he said, "you've been working with the Raze?"

"Not exactly accurate," Veylo said. The baby continued throwing a fit in his arms. "He *was* a spy, like you, but the

Almighty discovered that Janka was working against Him, so He gave him an ultimatum. He could either work with us to maintain his position in Heaven, or forever be banished to Hell."

"But, I saw Craetis and Veylo—"

Veylo smirked. "A clever performance, don't you think? The Leader's Allies, you included, needed to believe that Janka was dead so they wouldn't know that he was the one delivering names to the Almighty. If anyone knew that he was the one squealing, they would've run before we had time to catch all the traitors. As long as they believed that *we'd* discovered his treachery, they'd believe it was an isolated incident...that they were safe. That's why we had time to catch Donna and Krimson."

As Veylo spoke, Kinzer's gaze remained fixed on Janka. "So you outed me and the other Leader's Allies because you were trying to maintain your position in Heaven?"

Janka's expression didn't change.

A fire stirred in Kinzer's chest. "I think you owe me some answers!"

Janka took a deep breath. Kinzer knew what he was doing. He'd seen him like that so many times before. He was massaging a most perfect response into place, unwilling to speak before he'd devised something to articulate his exact intent.

"I did what I had to do."

His response bewildered Kinzer. *That was it?*

"What you had to do?" Kinzer asked. "You were willing to sacrifice Donna and Krimson and Fie and Dedrus and Treycore...and me, rather than yourself?"

"I'm not proud!" he barked, a pink shade washing over his immortally pale flesh.

"But you still did it."

"Kinzer, I—"

The fire in Kinzer's chest exploded, as if Janka's words had just fanned its flames. "And you never thought you could come to me for help?"

"You were too committed to the cause. I couldn't trust you."

Those words were like a sword through Kinzer's heart.

"Committed to the cause?" he asked. "The only reason I was a part of the cause was because of you. Because I loved you. Because I wanted to be with you."

"I'm sorry, but—"

"I don't think you understand how many shits I don't give. How could you side with them? After all that they've done? After all that the Almighty's done?"

"Because at the end of the day," Veylo said, stroking his finger across the baby, "Janka has, and always will be, a coward who doesn't want to lose the luxurious life he has in Heaven...just like the rest of us."

A tear formed in Kinzer's eye. His mind reeled with memories of the past few days.

A horrifying realization hit him.

"It was you," he said. "You were the Tracker...you tracked me to get to Dedrus and Treycore...to get to Maggie."

The guilty look in Janka's eyes was the only confirmation Kinzer needed.

Janka reached out and touched Kinzer's shoulder. Kinzer yanked it out of his grasp.

"Don't you fucking touch me!" he shouted. "I don't know who I thought you were, but you're not the Janka I fell in love with."

"I am. I promise. I just couldn't—"

"No! The Janka I loved never could have done something like this to his friends...to me."

"Kinzer, please!"

"You watched them clip me. They took my wings. My gift. Veylo tried to make me a sex slave. Did you know that?"

Janka hesitated. He nodded.

"And you were okay with me being raped and fucked to death?"

A loud cry echoed from the hall. Kinzer knew who it was. He didn't know how he'd gotten there, but hearing him tore him up inside.

"Do you hear that?" he asked. "That's a helpless mortal. He doesn't have anything to do with this. He's never hurt anyone, and you let your sick friends terrorize him."

"I don't know what you want me to say."

The tear in Kinzer's eye rushed down his cheek. "I don't want you to say anything. I just want you to take a moment and acknowledge the terrible immortal that you really are and the horrible things that you've done."

"Don't be so hard on him," Veylo said. "I think it's safe to say that we've come around."

"What?"

"Kinzer," Janka said, "you're so much stronger than we realized. Stronger than *I* realized. Even without your wings...without your powers...you destroyed a Morarke. Do you have any idea how miraculous that is? We never imagined that you would have been able to do that by yourself, but you have. Join us, and we can restore not only your wings and gift, but also your place in Heaven."

Kinzer couldn't believe what he was hearing. After all he'd just said, how could Janka ever believe that he'd side with him?

"Are you out of your mind?" he asked. "What makes you think I'd ever want to be in Heaven?"

"Kinzer," Janka said, "I know you can't possibly forgive me right now, but give it time, and we can have all the love that we had before. Come to Heaven and be with me."

The rage that fueled Kinzer dissipated as it was steadily replaced with wild confusion.

"After all I've seen you go through," Janka continued, "after all I've seen you endure, I know now that you are the one I want to spend an eternity with."

Kinzer's eyes glazed over, as if he was trapped in Janka's spell all over again.

"Help us. With the Christ—"

"The Christ?" Kinzer asked. He was even more confused than before.

"Yes. Before we faked my death, I told Dedrus that this child was the Antichrist. I had to. The Council was too close to discovering the truth. If they believed it was the Antichrist, the Almighty would never be implicated, and the Council would come after the Leader. But I hadn't realized that Dedrus would take matters into his own hands. That's how this whole mess began. If he would have just let the Council take care of it, the Leader would have been punished, and we would have taken the Christ to a safe place to be born."

"That's the Christ?"

"Yes," Janka replied.

"*Fuuuucckkkk*," the half-conscious Maggie moaned.

"And now that he's here," Janka continued, "soon the Almighty's work will be carried out, and all that will be left is Heaven...where we can be together forever. Don't you want that?"

Kinzer looked away from Janka as he contemplated all that he was saying.

"See," Janka continued. "You're thinking about it. It means that a part of you still loves me. You still want to be with me."

Tears slid down Kinzer's face. He rushed to conceal his vulnerability with his hands.

Janka grabbed his wrist and pulled him close. Kinzer dropped Dedrus's sword, but clung desperately to his own.

"Look in these eyes, Kinzer. I love you, and I can see that you love me. You know there's only one thing you can do."

They stared into each other's eyes, as they had done so many times before. Kinzer's face twitched, his muscles spasming, reflecting the emotional war that waged within him. But the war was easily won. He knew what he had to do if he ever stood a chance at being happy.

"I'll be with you," Kinzer said, his gaze still lost in Janka's.

Janka smiled. He wrapped his arm around Kinzer and pulled him close. Their lips locked. Kinzer lost himself in their embrace. He felt his palms across Janka's rigid back, recalling many nights of pleasure and pain. He caressed his fingertips through Janka's feathers. He bathed in Janka's hot breath, delighted in how the tip of Janka's nose felt on his face. What he would have given to spend eternity in that moment...a moment where he allowed himself to forget all that Janka had done...a moment where he could pretend that he and Janka were still together and in love and that everything was just as it should be.

Kinzer relished in the fantasy...the lie. And then he let his mind and body be overtaken by what he knew he had to do.

"Ah!"

Janka pulled out of their embrace, reared his head back, and unleashed a blood-curdling cry. Blood sprayed across his feathers as Kinzer's sword slipped through the bone in his wing.

With his free hand, Kinzer snatched the wing. He shoved Janka against the wall.

Janka continued screaming out. Kinzer pressed his lips against his ear and whispered, "Go to Heaven, you evil fuck!"

He pressed an ever-so-gentle kiss on his cheek and flipped around just as Veylo was approaching him, sword-first, from behind.

Kinzer dropped Janka's wing and clashed his sword against Veylo's.

Veylo eyed the baby Christ in his arm.

"You're at quite a disadvantage," Kinzer observed.

"You haven't won," Veylo said. "Not even close."

Veylo struck Kinzer's sword with an intensity that knocked him back. As Kinzer recovered from the blow, Veylo whipped around and raced toward a wall-sized window stretched across the side of the room.

Kinzer chased behind.

Approaching the window, Veylo's wings wrapped around his body, surrounding him and the baby in a ball of feathers, as Dedrus had done for Kinzer and Maggie.

CRASH!

Shards of glass filled the air.

"Fuck!" Kinzer exclaimed, halting at the edge of the window.

Veylo's wings stretched out, glistening in the sunlight as he soared between two neighboring buildings.

Kinzer knew he couldn't get to Veylo, but he still had to deal with the now-wounded Janka. He whirled back around.

Janka was gone!

A path of blood led to the door, which was now swinging back and forth.

Kinzer rushed out. He followed a trail of blood down the hall until he heard an ear-piercing cry.

*Kid!*

\*\*\*

Treycore wiggled in Craetis's grip. He had to get free. He had to save Kid.

"Daddy, stop!" Kid screamed, his voice cracking. "Daddy, please. It hurts!"

Sweat and tears rushed down his face, which was locked in a horrified expression, one that left Treycore wondering what sort horrors from Kid's past were tormenting him, raping his soul. The blaggovite coiled its tail around Kid's arm. Drool rushed from the corner of his mouth. His tears turned red.

"Kid!" Treycore called.

Kid's scream faded. His eyelids flitted open. A film of blood laced the whites around his pupils.

*Impossible*, Treycore thought. No immortal had ever been able to retain consciousness or slip from a blaggovite's control. So surely Kid wouldn't be able to.

Mika gasped. "How is he—?"

"There must be something wrong with the blaggovite," Craetis insisted.

Kid stared into Treycore's eyes. Tears curved through Treycore's dimples. He couldn't lose him. Not like that. He wanted to spend Kid's life with him. He wanted to spend an eternity with him. And yet, time was being cruelly ripped from them by that fucking cunt.

"I love you," Treycore said.

If he was going to lose him, he at least wanted him to know how he felt.

Kid gritted his teeth, as if enduring immense pain. "I...love..."

Vera snatched the blaggovite's tail, digging her nails into its flesh. Kid's eyes sealed shut. He squealed and leapt onto the desk. His arms flailed about, like he was trying to crawl across it, but he fell face-forward, his cheek sliding across his own vomit.

The door to the office burst open. A sword sliced through Craetis's neck. Flurries of red rushed across

Treycore's back, painting the floor as Craetis's flat face went soaring through the air and landed beside Vera on the desk.

Kinzer stood in the doorway, a sword in hand. Blood streamed down his face and drenched his shirt. Deter and Mika rushed for the door. Another quick swing of Kinzer's sword and Mika's and Deter's heads dropped to Kinzer's feet, bathing the floor in red.

"It's over, bitch," Kinzer said, staring Vera down.

"So it is," she said, arching her eyebrow and taking a step toward Kid.

"Get away from him!" Treycore shouted as he scrambled to his feet, his wrists still bound behind him.

He knew what she was going to do—what she felt she had to do. And he wasn't going to lose his Kid. Not like that.

"Stop her!"

"I guess I'll just take this with me," she said, stroking the back of her palm across Kid's cheek.

"No!" Treycore charged at her.

She winked. "See you in Hell." And with that, she and Kid vanished.

Treycore froze, paralyzed by the terror of having lost the only thing in the universe that ever truly mattered to him.

\*\*\*

"Hey," Kinzer said.

Maggie started to come to. She didn't look much better than she had when he'd found her in the hospital. Her red, swollen eyes were like rubies in her shriveled skull. Her hair looked as if it'd just been pried from a garbage disposal. It'd been several hours since she'd birthed the Christ. Kinzer and Treycore had tended to her injuries, stitched her rips, and taken her to the nearest hotel. Kinzer had been waiting attentively for her to stir, and she finally had.

"Feeling better?" Kinzer asked, a pleasant smile spread across his face.

"I feel like a wolf chewed its way out of my vagina!" she barked.

Kinzer's smile widened.

"I don't know what you're fucking cheery about! I just had a baby that's gonna wipe out humanity."

"Just happy to see that you're okay."

"*Okay*?" she asked. "I may never walk again, but other than that, I guess you can call it okay."

"Anything I can get for you?"

"I don't think you immortals really get this concept, but I'll tell you exactly what you better fucking get me...right now! You ready? You need to write this down?"

Kinzer listened carefully, awaiting specific instructions.

"Pain...killers!"

He giggled.

"I don't know why you're laughing. Get the fuck out of here and don't come back without them. And I'm talking the good stuff. You bring back some Advil or Tylenol, and I'll make you wish you weren't immortal."

Kinzer grabbed his wallet and headed for the door. As he opened it, he flashed a glance back at Maggie.

Her head fell into her folded arms. Her blonde locks trembled at her shoulders as her body convulsed, as if she had a fever. Sniffles and sobs filled the room.

"*Why*?" she muttered, seemingly to a deity that Kinzer knew couldn't hear her.

He stepped through the doorway and closed the door, granting her the privacy she deserved.

Footsteps caught his attention. Treycore was coming from his room down the hall, a determined glare in his eyes.

"Where are you going?" Kinzer asked.

Treycore dashed past him, tossing a duffel bag over his shoulder and continuing to the door. "You know where I'm going!"

Kinzer slipped past him and jumped in his path.

"Get out of my fucking way." Treycore shoved Kinzer against the wall.

"Treycore, we need your help. We have to stop the Christ and keep Veylo from reaching the actual Antichrist."

The door creaked open as Treycore started out. "You are more than capable of handling this shit," he muttered.

"Treycore, please!"

Kinzer's plea stopped Treycore. He stepped back into the hall, allowing the door to close. "Right now, Kid's with that sick cunt."

"She's probably already killed him."

"If I thought that was true, I'd be relieved. But you know he's not because you know her. You know what she'll do to him. I have to get to Hell and stop—"

"You really think an angel is just going to be able to slip into Hell unnoticed?"

"I've done it before."

They stared each other down.

"Before all this," Treycore continued, "if you'd known Janka was trapped in Heaven, what would you have done?"

Kinzer reflected on Treycore's hypothetical, and try as he might to convince himself that he would've given up, he knew better. He stepped to Treycore and set his hand on his shoulder. "I understand. If you save him—"

"*When* I save him," Treycore said, "I'll bring him back and we'll take out these bastards together."

Kinzer wrapped his arms around Treycore.

"Now," Treycore said, "you get that fiery bitch well and track those motherfuckers down."

Kinzer smirked. "Yes, sir."

They walked side-by-side to the door. Kinzer let Treycore out.

"You gonna be okay?" Treycore asked.

"Of course," Kinzer said with a smile.

"Take care." Treycore's face was etched with concern.

*Funny remark*, Kinzer thought, *for the higherling who's on his way to Hell.*

"You, too."

Treycore dashed to the sidewalk, hurrying toward his new quest.

Across the street, a condemned gas station captured Kinzer's attention. An 'Open' sign slanted across the graffiti-covered entrance. Behind the gas station, kudzu draped around a wooded area. Beyond that, the sun set in a sea of red and purple.

Kinzer's eyes filled with tears. He leaned against the doorframe, sliding to his knees as his thoughts drifted back to the creatures he'd loved. He imagined Dedrus's chuckle when they'd nearly collapsed in the motel shower. It took him back to their playful years in Heaven and Hell, when they'd loved and laughed together. His thoughts shifted to Janka—to those sincere, blue eyes. He'd trusted him more than any other, yet Janka was the one who'd betrayed him the most. Musing on these creatures, who had once filled him with such joy and ecstasy, could now only bring him sadness and pain.

TO BE CONTINUED...

# DEVON McCORMACK

A good ole Southern boy, Devon McCormack grew up in the Georgia suburbs with his two younger brothers and an older sister. At a very young age, he spun tales the old fashioned way, lying to anyone and everyone he encountered. He claimed he was an orphan. He claimed to be a king from another planet. He claimed to have supernatural powers. He has since harnessed this penchant for tall tales by crafting worlds and characters that allow him to live out whatever fantasy he chooses. Devon is an out and proud gay man living with his partner in Atlanta, Georgia.

www.devonmccormack.com

Join the **Cult of Clipped** @ www.cultofclipped.com

www.ingramcontent.com/pod-product-compliance
Lightning Source LLC
LaVergne TN
LVHW021656060526
838200LV00050B/2373